WELCOME TO HANGTOWN

Jed brought his wagon to a halt. Directly in his path - in the middle of the street - was a huge hole. As his oxen pulled up to the edge of the pit a bald head popped up out of it.

"Go around! There's enough room to go around!" the bald man said. He raised a bucketful of dirt and rocks out of the hole and a short man ran over and took it from him.

"You're mining in the middle of the street?!" Jed asked.

The second man poured the contents of the bucket into a rocker at one side of the road and then indicated the ramshackle two story building next to him.

It stretched away toward the hillside, bordered by a stables and low barn.

"This is our smithy," the man said. "It's our claim."

"No troubles," Jed apologized. "We're new in town. Is this Old Dry Diggins?"

The two men laughed. "That's what it used to be called," the man in the pit said.

"Could you point me toward someplace we could stable our oxen and horses, and perhaps an inn or boarding house?" Jed asked. The two men rubbed their long unkempt beards.

"Adam's hotel has some room, don't it, Hard Head?" the man by the rocker asked.

"That's true, come to think," Hard Head, the bald man in the hole, answered. "Five Aces was shot and his partner left for San Francisco."

"Why was Five Aces shot?" Jed asked.

"Five Aces," Hard Head replied matter-of-factly.

Books from Storyteller Press

Tales of McKinleyville:
Big Doin's at the Chinese Baptist Church
by Perry Bradford-Wilson

Tales of Placerville:
Booksellers to the Savage West
by Perry Bradford-Wilson

Midnight in Never Land
by Perry Bradford-Wilson & Michael Norris

Everyday P.O.W.
by Bradford P. Wilson, Edited by Perry Bradford-Wilson

Tenaya Books from Storyteller Press

Zanita: A Tale of Yosemite
by Therese Yelverton, Edited by Perry Bradford-Wilson

http://www.storytellerpress.com

TALES OF PLACERVILLE

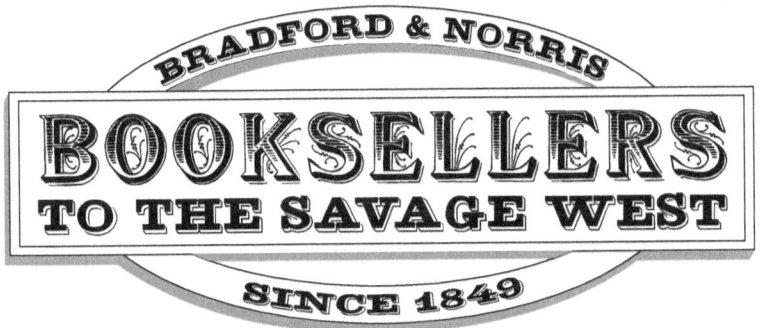

Being a series of historical fictions for your amusement

A Novel By

Perry Bradford-Wilson
author of Tales of McKinleyville: Big Doin's At The Chinese Baptist Church

STORYTELLER PRESS
Placerville, CA
Pollock Pines, CA

TALES OF PLACERVILLE:
BOOKSELLERS
TO THE SAVAGE WEST

© 2011 by Perry Bradford Wilson

Published in the United States by
Storyteller Press
P.O. Box 1978
Diamond Springs, CA 95619

http://www.storytellerpress.com

ISBN 1-880053-04-7
First Printed Edition, October 2011
First Digital Edition, October 2011

Library of Congress Cataloging-in-Publication Data is available from the publisher.
Book design & illustrations by Perry Bradford-Wilson

TABLE OF CONTENTS

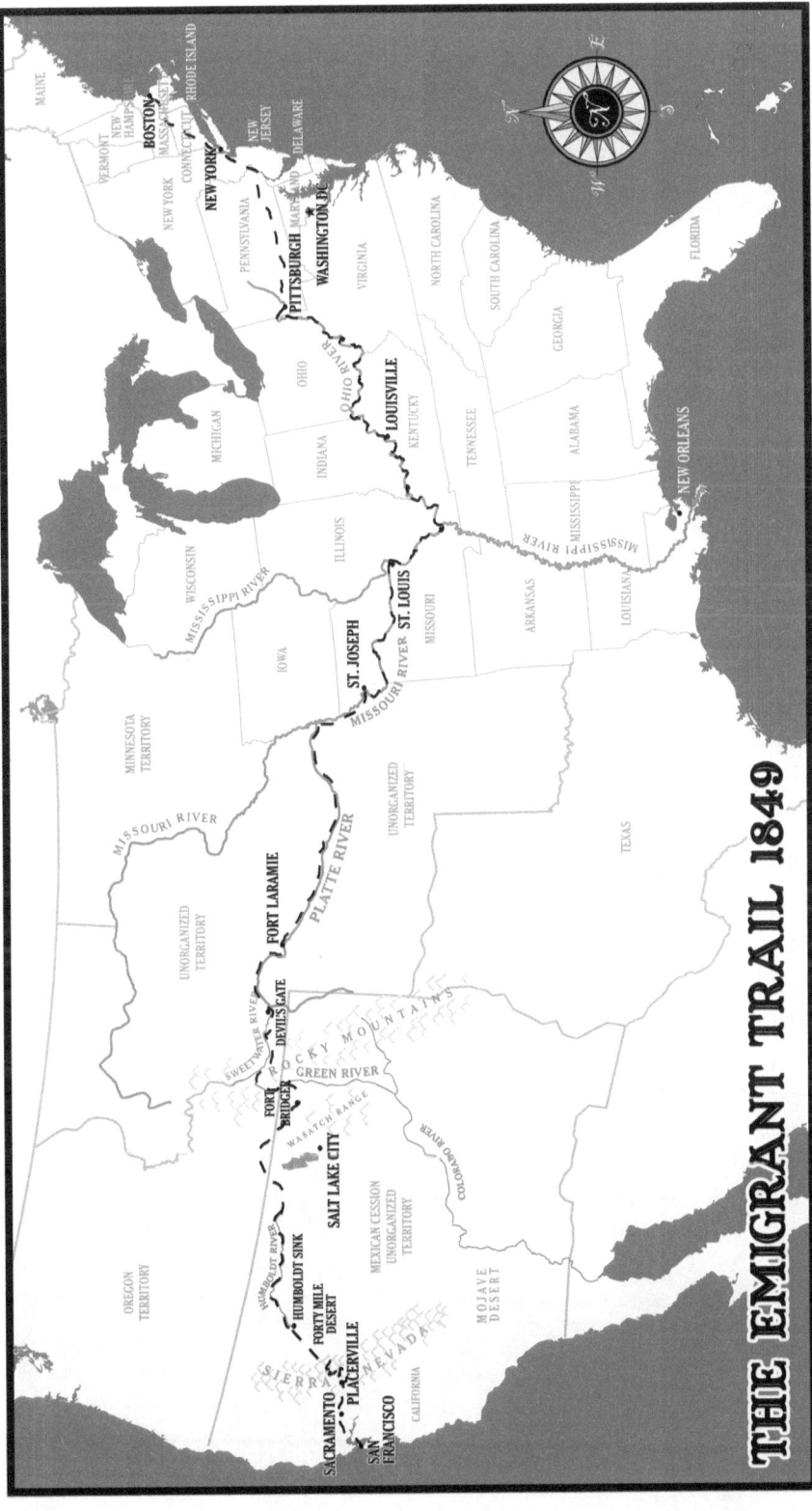

THE EMIGRANT TRAIL 1849

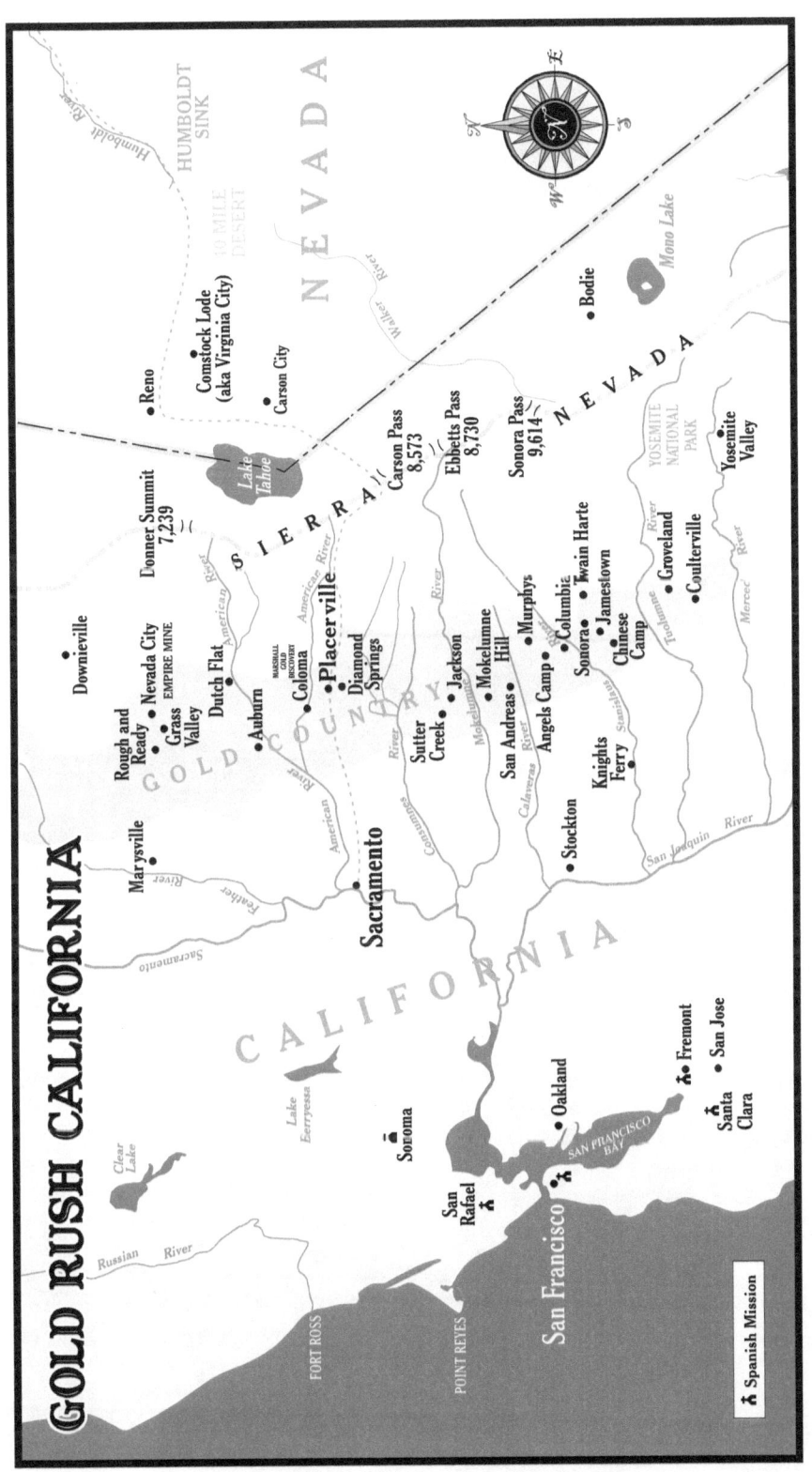

GOLD RUSH CALIFORNIA

CALIFORNIA

NEVADA

HUMBOLDT SINK

40 MILE DESERT

Humboldt River

Walker River

Reno

Comstock Lode (aka Virginia City)

Carson City

Bodie

Mono Lake

Carson Pass 8,573

Ebbetts Pass 8,730

Sonora Pass 9,614

NEVADA

YOSEMITE NATIONAL PARK

Yosemite Valley

Lake Tahoe

Donner Summit 7,239

SIERRA

American River

Coulterville

Groveland

Twain Harte

Sonora

Columbia

Jamestown

Chinese Camp

Murphys

Angels Camp

Knights Ferry

Tuolumne River

Merced River

Downieville

Rough and Ready

Nevada City

EMPIRE MINE

Grass Valley

Dutch Flat

Auburn

MARSHALL GOLD DISCOVERY

Coloma

Placerville

Diamond Springs

Mokelumne Hill

Jackson

Sutter Creek

San Andreas

GOLD COUNTRY

Marysville

Feather River

American River

Consumnes River

Cosumnes River

Mokelumne River

Calaveras River

Sacramento

Stockton

San Joaquin River

Sacramento

CALIFORNIA

Clear Lake

Lake Berryessa

Russian River

Sonoma

San Rafael

Oakland

San Francisco

SAN FRANCISCO BAY

Fremont

Santa Clara

San Jose

FORT ROSS

POINT REYES

⚲ **Spanish Mission**

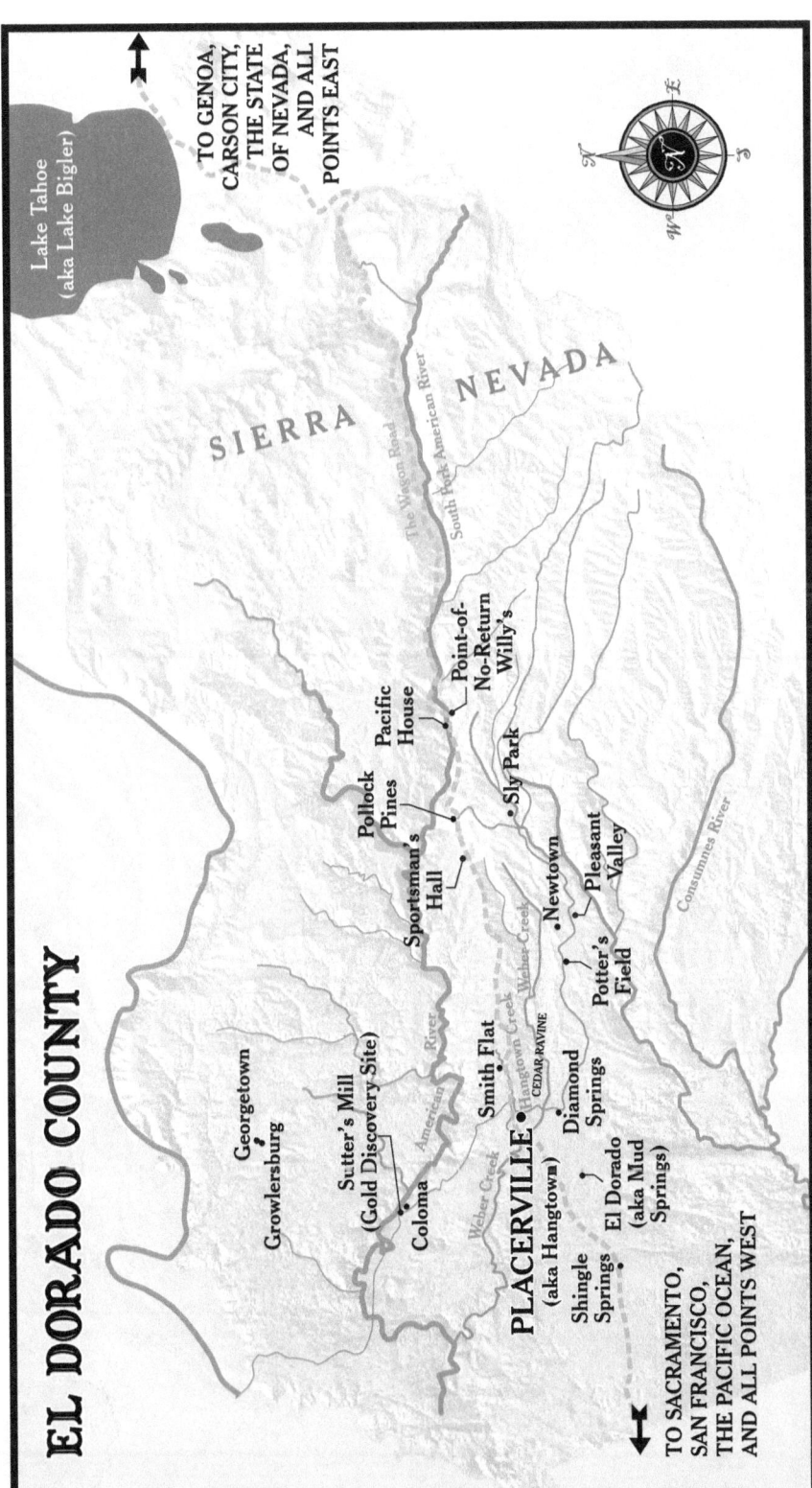

EL DORADO COUNTY

Lake Tahoe
(aka Lake Bigler)

TO GENOA,
CARSON CITY,
THE STATE
OF NEVADA,
AND ALL
POINTS EAST

SIERRA   NEVADA

The Wagon Road

South Fork American River

Consumnes River

Point-of-
No-Return
Willy's

Pacific
House

Sly Park

Pollock
Pines

Newtown

Pleasant
Valley

Sportsman's
Hall

Potter's
Field

Weber Creek

Hangtown Creek

CEDAR RAVINE

Georgetown

Growlersburg

Sutter's Mill
(Gold Discovery Site)

American River

Smith Flat

Coloma

PLACERVILLE
(aka Hangtown)

Diamond
Springs

El Dorado
(aka Mud
Springs)

Weber Creek

Shingle
Springs

TO SACRAMENTO,
SAN FRANCISCO,
THE PACIFIC OCEAN,
AND ALL POINTS WEST

PROLOGUE

1849

In which the spirit of storytelling in the Savage West is explained

In the beginning, everyone in the Sierra Nevada Mountains of California had at least three stories.

The first was the story of their life in the East, the "Old Life" they had left behind. These stories were sometimes eagerly told but were also just as likely to remain secret, because they frequently involved career failures, abandoned families, broken hearts and records of criminal conduct. The East was now a foreign place. Its clean, ordered regularity was alien in comparison to the surreality of the average California mining town. And the nature of the gold miners themselves worked against these stories; these people lived for the promise of the future, not inglorious memories of the past.

The second story was about the journey; how they made their way across the continent or, sometimes worse, by sea around Cape Horn or through the jungles of Panama. These were generally tales of hardship, but sharing these woes engendered a feeling of camaraderie among the pioneers and so they were welcomed. Eventually, however, as the difficult days and nights of mining town life came and went the travelogues faded into memory.

The third story was the story about the gold... usually the gold that got away. Nearly everyone had personally discovered the Mother Lode and had unfortunately gotten lost, had their maps burned, been driven out by snow or mudslide, or had their claim stolen by a greedy and better-armed competitor. Gold was the elusive prize which swelled California's cities every day with more and more prospective miners looking for the single strike of a shovel that would provide them with the easy life. Gold was the heartbeat that drove them. The desire for gold got them up from the hard, cold ground each morning. It planned their days from sunrise to set. And it filled their dreams each night. After a while the search for gold was the sole subject of the stories which flowed freely around their campfires, joined by laughter and prodigious amounts of hard liquor.

Jed Bradford and Jack Norris were different. They didn't come to California to mine the gold. They came to mine the stories.

I.

THE WAY WEST
or
IMPARTING MOTION TO BODIES AT REST

1849

First Story: The Old Life
In which our heroes meet, test their resolve, and find a way to go

The heart of the tales that follow is a bookstore; not a musty quiet place where ideas on paper grow yellow with age, but a place where the stories which people tell with passionate imagination and the stories that people live every day come together. The first story begins with the authors of this bookstore; two boys named Jed and Jack, who began their lives in a new country on one side of a largely unexplored continent and eventually moved to the opposite side of that continent in order to bring literature to the frontier. It is also the story of the gold rush town of Placerville, where their bookstore took root. There will be a bit of adventure, you will meet some of the strange and wonderful people who were likewise drawn to this amazing, unplanned, unpredictable community, and these folks' stories will find their way into your hands.

Now, if you're only interested in the *Tales of Placerville* advertised on the cover, then you should just skip ahead to Chapter Three. Sometimes, however, the most interesting thing about a place is how you get there, so I highly recommend sticking around and taking the journey to Placerville with Jed and Jack.

To begin with, Jedediah Bradford and Jack Norris were storytellers. They could read before they could walk. Sitting around the fire in the evening they told stories to their parents. Once they could write and draw no piece of blank paper was safe from the attack of their busy quills. They breathed plot, consumed character and expectorated theme.

Jed's mother died of influenza while he was just an infant. He was raised by his father, Aldus, who was a printer and publisher of books. This was obvious to anyone who visited their home for two reasons; first, they had hundreds of books on precarious shelves lining the walls of every room, far more than the average American could afford. Secondly, his father's fingertips were permanently stained black from the ink on the changeable type he was constantly arranging to print new editions. Jed was a smart, practical young man, although often prone to daydreaming. His daydreams were exceptional, filled with dense plotting, clever metaphor, and dynamic three dimensional characters. By some he was considered impulsive, as he might dash off someplace at any moment without warning, although this was usually because he was easily distracted by things he thought might make for a good story.

Jack's family relocated many times throughout his childhood as his father was an engineer who designed all manner of mechanical devices ranging from steam locomotives to printing presses to little steam contraptions that made grunting sounds. His homes were generally filled with technical books, schematic drawings, bits and pieces of machinery; tables of gears, springs, nuts, bolts and those little steam contraptions that made grunting sounds. Jack was every bit as smart and quick witted as Jed (although he would be the last to believe it). He was rarely considered impulsive, although this was only because he was smart enough to think things out completely before he took action (a characteristic which Jed might have benefited from).

These two unique young men met at the age of twelve while

attending the Roxbury Latin School in Boston, a stuffy school generally reserved for people of class (which, of course, the United States was not supposed to have) and of steady, rigid Puritan upbringing (which, thankfully, Jed and Jack never experienced).

In addition to their addiction to storytelling, both boys shared another common interest. They were both fascinated by what they would come to call collectively "The Savage West." They saw the great undeveloped West of the North American continent as an unformed, unorganized, undefined, undeveloped blank slate filled with possibilities. It was into this void they most often set their imaginations.

Jed liked to write stories based on the great myths with titles that did not hide this fact, such as *The Iliad in Mexico* and *The Aeneid on the Mississippi*. One his favorites, called *The Trojan Turkey*, told the story of a group of Indians laying siege to a wilderness fort manned by American explorers and trappers. The Indians built a giant wooden turkey in which they hid. The Americans rolled the giant turkey into the fort. The Indians' plan, of course, was to come out at night and take over the fort. Jed's twist on the tale was that the American explorers figured out the plan and nailed the Indians inside the turkey.

Jack wrote stories and also drew pictures - most of them images of Indians and pioneer trailblazers. He poured over books like *The Expedition of Lewis and Clark to the Western Sea* to inform his creations with facts. A big fan of Romulus and Remus (the founders of Rome who were raised by wolves), Jack's longest tale told the story of a pair of twins, Richard and Robert, who were raised by skunks.

The Boys (as we shall come to call them) also wrote books together and illustrated them. These stories were filled with pioneer explorers, wilderness men, Indian wars, killer grizzlies, frontier forts and the occasional talking duck and hat-wearing bear.

Despite being very well read and very smart, neither Jed nor Jack excelled in their classes. Their minds were so consumed by their storytelling that it subsumed every other subject. Storytellers are also dreamers, and this proclivity is sometimes their Achilles' heel. They always live in danger of losing themselves in dream, and sometimes it takes the swift kick of real life (peppered with a bit of adventure) to keep a storyteller moving.

After The Boys graduated from school Jed got a brief apprenticeship at the new *Boston Herald*, a two-sided single sheet newspaper that sold for a penny. The editor, a fellow named Bill Eaton, was just 22 years old and fancied the literary and dramatic over news (a good play was more interesting than a murder to him... he thought there were far too many murders, but never enough good plays). Jed quit after Eaton rejected four of his stories (likely because they all featured murders.)

Jack got employment doing engraving and relief prints for book illustration. Many of these were portraits of individuals dressed in Boston finery. The work was tedious, hurt his fingers, and he hated specifically engraving the folded and wrinkled cloth adorning his subjects.

"While I understand that young men need to determine their futures carefully, this period of uncertainty cannot last," Jed's father told them when they both quit their jobs. "I expect you to take action soon to build a career." What this meant to Jed was that his father wanted him to work at the print shop.

In the absence of something better to do, the boys soon began spending their afternoons loitering around the establishment of Mister John Jacob Michaels, Bookseller. Michaels' shop was a general bookstore which stocked many of the volumes Jed's father published. It was the largest such shop in Boston, with stacks that ran as far as the eye could see - or at least as far as the back wall would allow. Mr. Michaels was an older man who could generally be found hobbling down the aisles with his cane in one hand and a stack of books in the other. He took to The Boys quickly due to their encyclopedic knowledge of literature and their willingness to help alphabetize the stacks when they found them out of order. At the back corner of the store, hidden behind the biographies, there was a cozy wood stove surrounded by comfortable chairs. Here the boys sat, warming themselves by the fire each day, reading whatever captured their fancy.

"I love bookshops," Jed said one afternoon while Jack was drawing yet another picture of Daniel Boone. "I might go anywhere this afternoon; to Arabia through *One Thousand and One Nights* or to Patagonia aboard the HMS Beagle via the *Journal and Remarks*. There are so many possibilities."

"Certainly they are less depressing than the Harvard library," Jack agreed.

"Depressing? The library?"

"Yes," Jack said. "There are so many books there, many more than in the shop. Sometimes I look at them and think about how short life is. How many books I will never have the chance to read. It isn't fair. Life should be long enough that you might have an opportunity to read them all."

Before Jed could respond to this sentiment there was a loud crash to their right and they jumped up to see what had happened. Old Mr. Michaels was splayed on the floor surrounded by the more than a dozen volumes that he had been carrying. Jed and Jack hurried to help him to a chair and then collect up the books.

"Boys," Mr. Michaels said after a moment, "my back isn't what it used to be and books are heavy. As you two are already here most every day, might you be interested in helping out at the shop by working for me as clerks?"

"Bookselling!" Jed exclaimed on the way home. "Why didn't we think of it before? Part of the job itself is reading."

"I'm not sure what my father will think of that," Jack said.

"Nonsense! We'll know all of the best publishers, and what the public is buying. It's perfect!" Jed told him.

And so Jed and Jack became clerks at John Jacob Michaels, Bookseller. While Jed's father was unhappy that his son did not choose to work in the field of printing he thought that a career as a bookseller was still an honorable way to make a living. Jack's father was less enthusiastic, although reluctantly supportive.

By the spring of 1849 the Boys fell into a daily routine. Jed kept the accounting for Mr. Michaels and indexed the books; writing numbers in columns, adding and subtracting them. Jack placed orders with publishers and went down to the docks to pick up shipments from England. In between they read books and wrote stories.

Each evening, sitting snugly around the stove, they discussed the opportunities that might be found in The Savage West, despite the deadly Indian Wars and reports of lawlessness and frontier barbarism. They spoke of these as real possibilities for their own lives, but between you and me it was actually nothing more than a fantasy in which they indulged (and this made perfect sense since Fantasy was their favorite literary genre). In many variations of their *ignis fatuus* the Bookstore Boys arrived in a small town bereft of civilization bearing the world's greatest volumes of fiction, science, and history. Armed with these they used their poetry's charm to sooth the savage breast and bring civilization to the madness. The wild west in turn paid them back by providing the grist for many colorful stories which Jed believed would make them

America's answer to Alexandre Dumas. Once famous they became the toast of the town, and in most versions of the tale they were duly rewarded for their gifts to the community - in imaginative detail - by several buxom saloon girls.

The lure of the west was not limited to just Jed and Jack. Articles began to appear in the newspapers touting the discovery of gold in California. *The treasures of Aladdin are spread across the ground for all to see... it exceeds calculation!* said the Boston newspapers, and the New York papers said *It is El Dorado at last... the ground is one vast, rich mine, and the gold may be picked up in pure lumps, twenty-four carats fine!* The media frenzy, like most media events, was dismissed by some as exaggeration and believed completely by others. Then, in December, 1848, President Polk announced that it was all true and gold fever quickly infected the eastern states. Portions of New York began to depopulate as people packed up everything they had and headed west. In Boston, where the citizenry was more set in their ways, the effect was still surprising and appreciable. The excitement grew until the question was not "why" go to California, but "why not?"

Yet as often as the Bookstore Boys fantasized about the idea of going west, their discussions remained lodged firmly in the domain of wishful thinking. They convinced themselves that it wasn't the idea of daring to live in the untamed wilds that was preventing them from moving west. They told themselves - frequently - that it was the method of travel which kept them safely at home. At the time the most efficient way to reach California was by ship to Panama, slogging over the isthmus through malaria-infested jungle, and then once again sailing by ship up the coast of Mexico to San Francisco. Jed claimed that he had a pathological fear of malaria, which he believed stemmed from his mother's death due to influenza when he was only an infant. The alternative route was across the great continent by wagon train. When this course was proposed Jack confessed that he was afraid of Indian attacks.

"But all of your stories are filled with Indians!" Jed replied.

"I suppose I put so many Indians in my stories so that I might better understand them," Jack said quietly. "I had a dream once, which I have interpreted as a premonition, in which I was killed by Indians."

While these fears were real, there was a much more devastating reason that The Boys didn't seriously entertain going west. Jed and Jack had a serious lack of motivation. Their employment at the bookstore paid the rent and bought them food. Their fathers lived nearby. They knew these streets and the shops and homes along them. It was much easier to just stay in the bookshop and merely read about events in the Savage West.

They might have remained there for the rest of their lives. However, fate sometimes has other plans and by a strange confluence of unlikely (and in some cases, tragic) events, their idle daydreams became reality, and instead of just reading about adventures they finally had some of their own.

First, Jed's father installed a new steam powered press at his printing house in order to increase production. On its third day of operation he unwisely leaned into the press to fix a jammed gear. When his assistants pulled him from the machine they could legibly read several paragraphs of Dickens' *Dombey and Son* impressed across his face and apron. Aldus Bradford had been printed to death, and passed into the great afterlife where books were plentiful and fingers remained unstained by ink.

Although Jed briefly considered taking over the print shop, he decided that being there - constantly surrounded by the sounds, sights and smells of his father's trade - would be too difficult to endure. He sold his father's interest in the enterprise to the other partners and placed the proceeds in a secure account, unsure of what to do with the money but unwilling to spend it willy-nilly on inconsequential things. These funds represented his father's life work and he vowed to himself he would only spend them in a way of which his father would approve. In addition he inherited his father's vast library of nearly a thousand books. These too he was unwilling to part with, and put them safely in storage in the loft above his father's lodgings.

You might think that this life-altering event - the death of a parent - was enough to make Jed take stock in his situation. That it was the straw that broke the camel's back, the icing on the cake, the match in the powder barrel of Jed and Jack's complacency. Well, no matter how many clichéd idioms you can come up with, it wasn't. The ultimate causation which at last started Jed and Jack on their journey to The Savage West was a notice attached to a post office wall and a small advertisement in the morning's *Boston Herald*.

Jack was on his way back from mailing a letter when he saw the announcement hidden between two wanted posters and the declaration of a new tax. He would never have noticed it if it weren't for the fact that he read everything his eyes set upon. He hurried back to the store and as he walked in he heard Jed say to Mr. Michaels;
"Well, *that* would certainly make the journey easier."
Jed was reading the newspaper and might never have seen the advertisement, buried between an ad for women's clothing and the declaration of a new tax, if it weren't for the fact that he read every page.
"As easy as an Aerial Transport?" Jack asked.
Jed looked up, dumbfounded. "Exactly!" he said. The notice and the advertisement, you see, were for the very same thing. The ad and the notice alike had been placed by a gentleman named

Rufus Porter, who founded a magazine called *Scientific American* which The Boys regularly read. Jed read the copy of the advertisement aloud;

> "*R. Porter and Company are making progress in the construction of an Aerial Transport, for the express purpose of carrying passengers between New York and California. This transport will have a capacity to carry from 50 to 100 passengers, at a speed of 60 to 100 miles per hour. It is expected to put this machine in operation about the first of April, 1849. Transport is expected to make a trip to the gold region and back in seven days. The price of passage to California is fixed at $200.*"

"An *Aerial* Transport... it certainly is a fascinating idea, although I'm not positive it would be practical," Jack said.

"Aerial?!" Mr. Michaels asked.

"Yes, sir!" Jed said enthusiastically. "We could fly to California like birds! This ship uses a balloon, like the Montgolfier Brothers used. But rather than just go up and down, it will be steerable. Blanchard flew a balloon across the English Channel all the way back in 1785. I think we have a book on it here someplace..." He glanced for a moment at the towering stacks of dusty books on the shelves around them as if the tome in question would present itself. "It's scientifically possible, Jack."

"It may be possible," Jack agreed. "Although such a craft would be especially susceptible to burning, whether they're using gas or merely hot air with some sort of on-board flame. It might go down in a storm, given its profile to the wind versus its ability to propel itself. It might get blown to Canada or out to sea, for that matter. Then again it might just keep going up and up until it hits the stars. But all that aside, it's *certainly* a scientific possibility." Despite these critical comments the light in his eyes made it clear that the engineer, designer and artist in Jack were excited and the

BEST ROUTE TO CALIFORNIA.

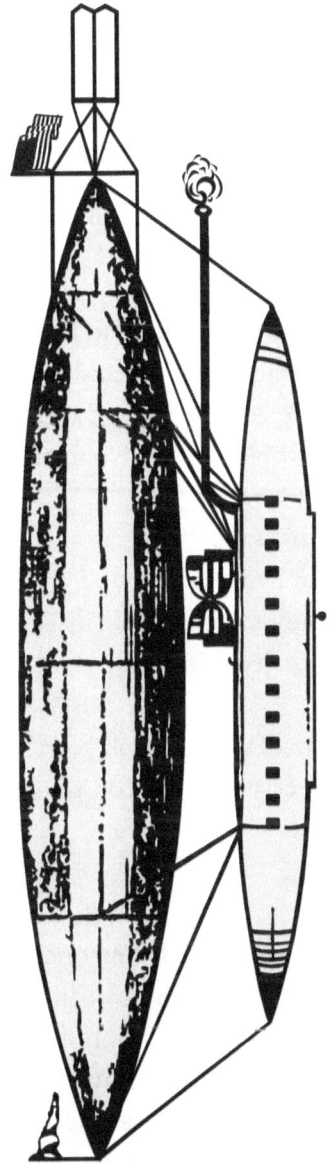

R. PORTER & CO., (office, room No. 40 in the Sun Buildings, - entrance 128 Fulton-street, New-York,) are-making active progress in the construction of an Aerial Transport, for the express purpose of carrying passengers between New York and California. This transport will have a capacity to carry from 50 to 100 passengers, at a speed of 60 to 100 miles per hour. It is expected to put this machine in operation about the 1st of April, 1849. It is proposed to carry a limited number of passengers - not exceeding 300 - for $50, including board, and the transport is expected to make a trip to the gold region and back in seven days. The price of passage to California is fixed at $200 with the exception above mentioned. Upwards of 200 passage tickets at $50 each have been engaged prior to Feb. 15. Books open for subscribers as above.

13

idea of flying captured his imagination.

"It's more than a possibility, Jack! Don't you see?" Jed asked, "Now we have no excuse for staying here! We can go west!"

Their usual conversational daydream followed, complete with books, Wild West town and generously endowed saloon girls. Today, though, it kept going after Mr. Michaels went home. It continued through dinner. It lasted late into the night and was still going at dawn.

At one point Jed turned to Jack and with all earnestness returned to his earlier point. "What if we really did it, Jack? What if we took the money and books my father left me and went west to open our own bookstore, just like we've always talked about? Really, we have no excuse anymore. No Indians. No malaria. No excuses."

Jack's eyes got big and he said, "You mean... are you serious? After all, folks *talk* about living in the west and they *read* about living in the west. But does anyone actually do it?"

Surprised by his own answer, Jed said, "Yes... yes, I think we do!"

And that afternoon Jed Bradford and Jack Norris became the proud owners of two first class tickets for the very first transcontinental air passenger flight.

Having tickets in hand is not the deed itself, however. It gave the Boys license to change the narrative of their ongoing story; now in every version they reached California in just a few days aboard the magical Aerial Transport. The decision did not seem real until March, when they received a letter from Rufus Porter saying that, although the flying machine was slightly behind schedule, all passengers should be prepared to begin their voyage at any time.

At last the Boys needed to take action, and they did so in

dramatic fashion. They spent their evenings in the loft above their lodgings, indexing the vast number of books Jed's father had left to him. To these they added their own collections and had all of them crated for a decidedly non-aerial crossing by covered wagon. (Apparently books were far too heavy to be accommodated aboard the Aerial Transport.) When they told John Jacob Michaels that they were leaving his employ even the Boys felt slightly astonished, as if saying to themselves "No, we are really going to do this?"

"What are we going to do if Porter can't get this thing into the air? Do you suppose Mister Michaels will give us our jobs back?" Jack asked Jed.

During the first week of May Jed and Jack traveled to New York for a demonstration of a 240' model of Porter's Aerial Transport, which resulted in the destruction of the airship in a "freak" tornado. This did not dissuade them much at all, as the model flew straight and true until the twister folded it up upon itself and crashed it into the ground. The next month a second 240' model sailed through the sky majestically until it was struck by lightning. The Boys' spirits flagged just briefly after this event. It wasn't as if they were in any particular rush, anyway. Yet no amount of positive thinking could maintain their morale after Independence Day.

It was a bright July morning and all of the paying customers who could make it to the field arrived early for this latest (and hopefully last before its maiden voyage) test of the full size airship. Rufus Porter came out to address the assembled passengers and press. He had a classical profile, tall and slender with a bold jaw. A Greek statue come to life, he strutted back and forth before the seven-hundred foot dirigible, proudly pointing out its advanced aero-features.

"Look at the ship's name," Jack said. Jed looked forward to the airship's nose where the word *Icarus* was painted in sweeping cursive text. "That's not encouraging."

In a few moments, however, the Boys were back in good spirits thanks to the galvanizing speech being given by Rufus Porter. With the smooth and compelling voice of an ecclesiastic he extolled the virtues of invention and acclaimed man's ability to use his genius to mold the world to his liking. He explained how the course of history itself would be changed by his amazing ship.

"God and nature challenge us," Porter said. "Obstacles are put in our way, not to make our lives harder but to allow us to improve ourselves and transcend them. In the beginning we were nothing, castaways from the Garden who cowered before the power of the storm. Yet see how far we have come from those ignominious first steps? We have tamed the wild beasts, changed the course of mighty rivers, and now... now, man has conquered the sky!" he cried enthusiastically. "A new era has come, a new age. In the classical world only the gods could fly. Through the power of science the skies are now mankind's as well!"

The audience swooned under his influence and was moved by his words. In fact, they were moved so much that they wanted to touch the airship, to feel in their own hands its distinctive modern-ness. As one they moved forward and made personal contact with this miracle of the new age, stroking its sides as if they were caressing a lover. This laying-on of hands may have been inspirational to the crowd. Unfortunately it was not as beneficial to the airship. The great gas envelope began to rip and as the hydrogen escaped into the atmosphere the huge dirigible began to collapse.

Porter yelled at the crowd to get back. Jed and Jack backed away as the dirigible sagged and fell over onto the crowd.

This was a setback, to be sure. Yet the bag might have been repaired. What happened next is a matter of some debate. Jack thought that an afternoon storm cloud moved in. Jed thought that the escaping hydrogen caused a disturbance of some kind as it mixed with the humid air above the airship. Whatever the cause, it started to rain. Buckets of water began to fall and the torn bag of the ship began taking on water. In effect, the Porter Aerial Transport sank on dry land.

Jed and Jack, soaked by this strange summer rain shower, rode home despondently.

"Some Independence Day," Jack said. "We're out $400. What are we going to do now?"

"It's worse than that," Jed said.

"How?"

"Everything we own is aboard wagons headed for California."

This was unfortunately true. Two days prior they had turned over their precious crates of books, along with several trunks of their personal belongings, and consigned them to a wagon master who was leaving for San Francisco. All they had left now were a few clothes and articles of personal hygiene that were intended to be luggage on board the airship. The two booksellers took quick stock of their situation.

"I don't suppose we have much choice," Jack said. "We'll have to have it all shipped back. Tomorrow morning we can go to Mister Michaels and beg for our jobs."

Jed sighed and stared at the gray skies to the west. Just beneath the rain clouds and barely above the horizon was a narrow slice of warm golden light. "No, Jack, it's time we tried on our own adventure, not just someone else's. *Carpe diem*, Jack. An adventure in hand is both a story to tell and an experience to remember. If we don't do it now we never will."

" *'Defer no time, delays have dangerous ends…,'* " Jack admitted.

"Are you absolutely sure, Jed? It sounds a bit rash to me. I mean, we need to think this through a bit."

"No! No thinking! I am more certain than anything I've ever felt in my life. Grant you, my resolution formed in just the last few minutes. But we have to do this now or never. This very moment. Come on, Jack. Let's go west. Right now. Right this minute."

"Don't we need to tell someone? Post a notice? Buy supplies?"

"We can do that from the road. If we are going to do this, it has to be right now," Jed said.

"What about malaria? What about Indians?" Jack asked.

"I suppose we'll deal with those as they come," Jed replied.

"It's not going to be as easy as flying above it all would have been," Jack said.

"I don't think things this important are supposed to be easy," Jed suggested.

Jack took a deep breath. The idea was both exhilarating and frightening at the same time. To find out what was going to happen next he would have to leave everything he knew and begin something new. "Alright, Jed. I can't believe I'm saying this! But *carpe viam* it is. Let us seize the road."

"Look how well it turned out for Odysseus," Jed offered. Jack made clear by his expression that this was not a good example.

And thus it was that, right there in the Independence Day rain, they wheeled their horses around and headed west. The Boys figured the wagon train carrying their belongings would make slow progress, especially through the rain and mud. It only had two days on them. Jed bet they could catch up in three.

Next: Facing demons on the journey west

18

II.

OFF TO SEE THE ELEPHANT
or
A WESTERN ODYSSEY

1849

Second Story: The Journey
In which The Boys embark on a picaresque trip through the undefined west

Jed and Jack did not catch up with the wagons carrying their belongings at all. Apparently the train master took a more devious route west than The Boys did. They camped in New York the first night and in New Jersey the second. In Pennsylvania they stopped and purchased saddle bags, blankets, and basic provisions. When they headed west from Philadelphia their mounts were laden with new clothes, food and bags of water. Each of them bought a rifle, meant for hunting and self defense, although both turned down the opportunity to carry side arms.

"I'll more likely shoot myself than an Indian," Jed said.

"I like that the long barrel of the rifle keeps the bullet further away from me," Jack agreed. "Those pistols leave them altogether too close."

Along the road from New York to Pittsburgh there were plenty of settlements where they could find food and shelter. The flood of emigrants to California created a booming industry for smart entrepreneurs. New inns and stores opened to service the hordes of people moving west. When The Boys arrived in Pittsburgh they sold their horses for slightly more than they paid for them and had all of their supplies stored aboard a steamer headed down the Ohio River. Ten dollars bought them some passable food for the journey and room on the crowded deck to lay out their bedrolls. The boat set out in the morning and carried them downriver.

"Didn't you tell me once that you get seasick?" Jed asked Jack on the second day as they stood on the boiler deck.

"This isn't the sea. This is the Ohio River. I never said I got riversick," Jack pointed out.

"Well, at least there isn't any malaria," Jed said.

"But there may be Indians," Jack reminded him with a worried look.

During the day they watched the sometimes-still-wild shores of the Louisiana Purchase drift by, lined with oak, maple, hickory, flowering dogwoods and huckleberries. One of the other travelers had a mountain dulcimer and in the evening they sat near the bow with a group of twenty or thirty like-minded individuals and sang "Oh! Susanna" and "Nelly Was a Lady" until all of the light had faded from the sky.

Further downriver the steamer took the canal and locks around the Ohio Falls and had a brief layover at Louisville, Kentucky. From there the boat made its way down to the Mississippi River and made a sharp right turn at Cairo, Illinois, to take them upriver to St. Louis, Missouri.

The Mississippi River no longer had the character of wilderness. Great timber rafts and coal barges floated south to New Orleans. Steamers loaded with goods plied their way both directions. All of the traffic on the great waterway reminded Jed and Jack of the busy Boston streets more than it did the great untamed west.

On the last day they were still half-asleep on the deck (due to a late night singing "Skip To My Lou" very loudly) when they heard the ship's bell ring three times, which meant they were coming ashore. The Boys climbed to their feet and joined other passengers at the rail. Ahead was the largest town they'd seen since Louisville;

St. Louis, Missouri. Jed and Jack knew it well from the books they'd read about the Lewis and Clark expeditions. In their minds they had pictured it as a frontier outpost instead of the huge, crowded river port city that spread out before them.

Once they came ashore they started the search for lodging and found a room at an inn run by a charming woman named Mrs. Malloy, who insisted on introducing each of her many sons (Blaine, Cedric, Cassidy, Colm, Cowan, Desmond, Devlin, Ennis, Gallagher, Killian, Riddock, Riordan, Rowan, Seamus, Sean, and Walter) to the guests before they could sit down to eat their dinner. The delay was tolerable, as the roast beef was the best food they'd eaten since Boston.

The next morning Jed and Jack spent much of their remaining travel budget at stores along the riverfront outfitting for the long ride ahead. Fresh horses, mules and better maps of the west were all available in the St. Louis markets. They carted sacks of flour, dried vegetables, beans, dried fruit, salt, sugar, rice and coffee to the small storage bin at the stables where their new pack animals and horses were boarded. Once they left Missouri behind them and headed out across the Great Plains such supplies would be hard to come by. It took them three days to gather everything they needed for the journey.

The last great gasp of civilization was at the end of another (much smaller) steamer ride, this time up the Mississippi and then Missouri River. Jed and Jack's horses and mules stood shoulder to shoulder with dozens of others, crowded onto the narrow deck. The boat reached the terminus of its journey at the docks of a community called St. Joseph. This frontier town was a quickly growing settlement on the border of Missouri and the vast unorganized wilderness territory beyond, which stretched all the way to California and Oregon. The Boys decided they would stay for a week in this pioneer outpost to get some rest before entering the great unknown.

St. Joseph was still small, and every public house and inn was filled with travelers headed west. Steamers bearing emigrants up the Missouri River docked every few hours, dumping their passengers onto the busy streets, and wagon trains poured into town by the dozens. In addition to the food and other supplies that Jed and Jack were carrying the wagons bore the signs of people headed to the gold country; shovels, picks, and gold pans. After two hours of searching the Boys finally found a room above an inn's stable which they could share with another traveler. The loft was plain - a rough wooden floor, with two bare mattresses laying directly on it. A table and basin for water sat in the corner next to the ladder. When they arrived their roommate was already snoring away on one of the mattresses. He awoke when Jack dropped wearily onto the other.

"Pardon the interruption," Jed said.

"No offense taken," the sleepy man said with a slight Scottish accent. Jack held out a hand.

"Obliged. I'm Jack Norris, this is Jed Bradford," he said.

"Thomas," the man said, without bothering to explain whether this was his first or last name. "Headed to California for the gold?"

"Not exactly," Jed said. "We're booksellers." This captured the man's attention and he sat up.

"Booksellers?!" the man asked.

"Yes, booksellers," Jack replied.

"You're educated men, then?" he asked.

"Well, we attended a proper school," Jed laughed, "although our actions rarely reflected well on our alma mater." Thomas ignored this and climbed up off of his mattress.

"Did either of you by chance study engineering?" he asked.

The Bookstore Boys gave each other a long glance. Although Jack's father was an engineer, he didn't think of himself as very mechanical. Jed's most complicated feat of engineering was his design for a giant wooden turkey.

"We both read *Scientific American* on a regular basis," Jed offered positively. This answer seemed to satisfy Thomas.

"Capital! Might you be interested in taking a look at a wee invention I've been working on? I've had some small success, although there are still some challenges to work out which you may be able to help with. We Scots are bonny inventors, though it helps on occasion to have a fresh pair of eyes."

Jed suggested that they take a look at the man's invention after they'd had a chance to eat and catch a few hours of sleep. Thomas reluctantly agreed and four hours later they went out behind the stable to take a look.

There in a fenced area sat what looked to Jack like a wagon. Jed, on the other hand, thought he was looking at a boat. After a few moments they realized it was a bit of both.

"It's me wind wagon," Thomas said proudly. "You see, it's very windy on the plains. It came to me that it might be faster to have a wagon sail across them rather than have a poor beast pull it."

"It's not supposed to fly too, is it?" Jed asked.

Of course the idea of the wind wagon - even if it was less likely to make it to California than Rufus Porter's Aerial Transport - was captivating to Jed and Jack. The possibility of cruising across the plains in a sheltered wagon was too good to pass up.

"How can we help?" Jack asked.

The next three days were spent busily analyzing the wagon and determining why the concept (to date) hadn't worked. Jed thought it was just too heavy. Jack considered the friction caused by the wheels on rough terrain. Thomas was sure there just weren't enough sails. They compromised by using all three approaches. Jed removed every unnecessary stick of wood and bolt until the wagon was as light as possible and still remained together. Jack polished new iron rims for the wheels, making them slick. And Thomas added six more sails, copying the pattern used on French frigates. By the end of the week they were ready for a new trial.

The three men gathered just after dawn on the prairie north of St. Joseph. A horse pulled the wind wagon to the starting point. Once the test began and the wind wagon started to move (hopefully) Jack would ride alongside the wagon on a horse. Jed would operate the helm - a great ship's wheel attached to the front axel - and Thomas would operate the sails.

"Looks flat enough," Jack said, staring out at the plain.

A better than average thirty mile-an-hour wind was coursing across the prairie this morning. Thomas held a flag up and watched it flap. Encouraged, he climbed into the rigging and unfurled the sails. Jed tied a bandanna to his head and smiled at Jack.

"Alright, Landlubber, prepare to raise anchor!" he bellowed.

As more and more of the sails caught wind the wagon began to roll forward slowly until it came to the end of its tether - a one inch rope tied to a stake in the ground.

"That's it!" Thomas said, and Jack pulled the end of the rope, slipping it from its knot and releasing it from the stake.

Creaking and groaning the wagon rolled forward, just barely at first and then as it gathered momentum it began to trundle along the uneven ground at a blistering fifteen miles an hour.

A few hundred yards away a black-tailed prairie dog poked its head up out of the ground to look at the strange contraption lumbering toward his hole. He had seen these things when foraging a ways to the south. Never before had he seen one here so close to the colony. He processed its shape and size through the primitive processor of his tiny squirrel brain to determine the threat level.

Was this a predator? Was it an herbivore? Even the buffalo, who weren't interested in eating members of his family, could cause damage to their dog town. He twitched his nose and sniffed the air as the object rolled closer. How far was it before it would reach the colony?

His question answered itself as the front wheel of the mammoth object collapsed into the tunnels below. The local dog town tunnels spanned about thirty acres. They were very well built, but the prairie dog engineers who fashioned them hadn't planned for them to support sailing ships. The wind wagon lurched to one side and then tipped over. The masts came crashing down and snapped as they impacted the ground.

I should note that no prairie dogs were harmed in this incident.

Jack guided his horse carefully up to the ruins of the wind wagon, concerned his mount might break a leg in the same burrows that had doomed Thomas's visionary invention.

"Are you alright?" he asked. Jed and Thomas scrambled from the broken pile.

"Still alive," Jed said, although his ego was slightly injured. "Thomas?"

Thomas was staring back at the wagon in despair.

"Bigger wheels," he said. "Aye, bigger wheels will spread the weight. The three of us will get started tomorrow."

That night Jed and Jack met behind the stables.

"We've been through this before, Jack," Jed said. "We waited for months for Porter to get his transport working and it just delayed the inevitable. Thomas isn't going anywhere. There is no easy way across a continent. We just have to go."

"Maybe we can just help him for a *few* days until he sees that it's just never going to work," Jack suggested.

"He's a Lotus Eater, Jack," Jed said. "If we don't keep moving we're going to get stuck here."

"Why do you keep going back to *The Odyssey?*" Jack asked.

"I like *The Odyssey*. Don't you like *The Odyssey?*"

"That wasn't my point. Odysseus was lost in the wilderness for ten years!"

"That wasn't my point either, of course," Jed sighed. "We can keep on looking for the easy way to get where we're going or we can just do it the hard way."

"It's tempting just to stay here, Jed. I mean, this is the frontier, too, you know. Maybe we could send for our things and open the bookstore here, in Missouri," Jack suggested. "It certainly seems busy enough to support one."

Jed pointed toward the west, where the glowing embers of the sunset still gave definition to the horizon. "That's the adventure, Jack. We have to do it, not because California is a better location for a bookstore. We're crossing a threshold. This journey is our baptism of fire. We have to do this for ourselves."

"If we survive it," Jack said. "There are plenty of things that could go wrong. Sure, you don't have to worry about malaria. But there are still going to be Indians."

"We can manage this if we just put one foot in front of the other, take one step at a time," Jed assured him. "If we run into troubles then I'll be right there with you when we meet them. And if we do run into Indians… or bears, deserts, or Mexican horse thieves… you'll be there with me. Neither of us could do this alone. Without you I'd still be back in Boston, sitting by the stove at the bookstore just talking about it."

Jack smiled. "You know, in my mind I can see the sign hanging outside our store. *Bradford and Norris… Booksellers to the Savage West.* I can imagine the colors and the brushstrokes like it's already real. Good God, Jed… I still can't believe we're really doing this!"

"Yes, we are!" Jed said, clapping him on the back.

The next day the Boys told Thomas that they couldn't work on restoring the wagon because Jed had hurt his arm in the crash and Jack had to tend to him. Jed made a sling out of an extra shirt. Thomas seemed to buy this story, even though Jed took the sling off halfway through the day and accidentally put it back on the opposite arm. Early the following morning they snuck down to the stable, packed up their horses, and rode down to the docks.

The ferry took Jed, Jack and their animals across the river. As it reached the far bank they crossed the border of Missouri. Their horses carried them along the well-traveled wagon road that led from the river bank and into the wilds of the American West.

As I have explained, the Boys never caught up with the wagon train carrying their own goods. That is not to say that they did not catch up with any wagon trains at all. Just outside of St. Joseph they joined the Oregon & California Trail, which followed the Missouri north and then turned west along the Platte River. The swath of trampled Earth would have been enough to identify this essential road to the west, but such an observation was unnecessary. A column of wagons, three and four across, stretched from the eastern horizon to the western one; covered wagons, open wagons, Conestoga wagons. Some of the wagons were common street vehicles pressed into service for the journey, while others were clearly built for long distance travel. One apparently rich emigrant had a two-story affair, complete with bunks, a wood stove, and seats on springs to cushion the bumpy ride. It took eight oxen to pull this monstrosity, which the owner called his "Pioneer Palace Wagon."

In addition to the many folks perched on the wagons and riding alongside on horseback, hundreds of men - and even a few women and children - walked among them (as the overall speed of the wagon trains was negligible). At one point Jed saw what looked like a child's disembodied head floating along the ground and only after a moment realized that the ruts worn by wagon wheels in the plains sod were so deep that only the boy's head was visible as he walked along inside one. If a wagon threw a wheel or broke an axle it brought the column to a halt until the drivers figured out a way to get past it. Then the wagons flowed like water (or molasses) around the broken vehicle. Wagons that could not be repaired were picked clean for parts and whatever could not be reclaimed (very little, actually) was left like a carcass on the prairie. There were no on-ramps or off-ramps or convenient exit-stop fast food restaurants. Only a slow moving line of beast-drawn vehicles more than a hundred miles long.

At first the Boys thought that joining this throng was a good thing; they would have company for the long road, there was safety in numbers from Indian attacks, and navigation would not be a problem as there would be always be a clear and unambiguous direction of travel. Once they joined the multitude, however, their attitude changed.

First, it was quite difficult to breathe. Imagine hundreds upon hundreds of wagons, traveling a grazed-over and rutted road, kicking up clouds of dust for miles on end. Every surface was coated with dust, including the people. Every one of the pilgrims and their animals was the same shade of brown and ocher. Whenever the wagons forded a stream a great plume of mud ran downstream. This was not so much from the river bottom being kicked up as it was from the dirt being washed off of the wagons, animals and people. Jed and Jack put their kerchiefs across their mouths in an attempt to filter out some of the dust and only succeeded in making their kerchiefs as filthy as everything else.

Looking at the bright side, Jed noted that the dust had at least one minor beneficial effect which made the journey more endurable; it covered up the smell of the emigrants themselves. The travelers, on the road for months in some cases, washed and changed their clothes only rarely. Over the summer months, traveling in the sun, the emigrants ripened to a spectacular degree. The livestock (a vast menagerie including, besides the oxen, mules and horses pulling the wagons, a variety of cattle, goats, dogs, and free roaming chickens) did not smell half as bad as the humans except in the cases of the animals who consumed tainted water and left a trail of diarrhea across the prairie. After two days riding along with the wagon trains The Boys pulled away to the south of the trail.

"I couldn't stand another moment," Jed apologized. "It was more crowded than St. Louis was. It certainly didn't feel like the wilderness to me. More like a great, stinking, never-ending dust pit."

"We would have had to leave eventually anyway," Jack pointed out. "There wasn't a single blade of grass left anywhere along that road. Our horses would have starved."

They stayed within sight of the brown, dusty skies that identified the main trail so that they wouldn't get lost. Their path took them north of the Little Blue River and south of the Platte. It was mid-summer and the South Platte was fordable when they reached it. From there they headed along the North Platte.

The terrain changed very little. Small hills at times became slightly larger hills and small prairie lands often became vast prairies. The river that meandered through this grassy wasteland was their only sure guide. Each day they rode as far as their horses could manage and told each other stories to keep themselves entertained. Once or twice they veered north to rejoin the stop-and-go traffic of the wagon trains to ask a knowledgeable wagon master how far they were from Fort Laramie, the next outpost of civilization. Within a few hours they returned to the outskirts of the trail to avoid the dust and find forage for their animals. The warm weather treated them well and they were caught in the rain just once. They replenished their water from the wide, muddy Platte or, preferably, from one of its clearer tributaries. Occasionally they shot a jackrabbit to augment their rations. At night they camped under the clear starry sky. Cooking over a buffalo chip campfire each night they talked about how they would manage things once they got to California.

"I'm exhausted tonight. I'm going to sleep like the dead," Jed told Jack one night when they were camping near a stream two or three days out from Fort Laramie. The water ran slowly here. It was green and tasted horrible. Still, it seemed clearer than the dark brown waters of the Platte. Jack filled a pot with the water and let it sit, hoping all of the green would settle to the bottom.

"Are you hungry?" Jack asked.

"No, I think I'll just turn in and get some rest," Jed answered. "If you can wait, I'll do the cooking in the morning."

"That's fine. You know, I've been thinking about the store," Jack said, "do you think we should try opening it in San Francisco?"

"Sacramento might be better," Jed opined. "Or even further into the mountains. The people will likely be where the gold is."

"You're probably right," Jack agreed. He laid back on his bedroll and examined the broad swath of the Milky Way arcing above them. "I finished the book I was reading. I've read every one we brought with us. I'm really glad we came, though I wish we'd brought more books."

"Here," Jed said, handing him a bundle of paper from his saddlebag. "You can read the one I'm writing."

"I'll be critical," Jack warned.

"I'm counting on it," Jed said. "Without you keeping me honest I'd likely be writing one of those horrible penny dreadfuls with murderous barbers, desperate highwaymen or bloodthirsty vampires."

"I'd probably still read it," Jack admitted. He poured the clearest water off of the top of the settling pot into his water bag and then a bit more into Jed's.

"That stuff tastes so terrible I think I'd rather be thirsty," Jed commented. "Though if bad tasting water is the worst we have to endure on this journey I'll be happy to drink it. Everyone told us how difficult the crossing would be, and yet we have had things pretty easy so far."

"Don't break our good luck by saying so!" Jack warned.

At that moment they heard a noise off to their left. At first Jed thought it was a night bird chirping. It repeated too evenly, though. The high-pitched squeak didn't seem natural.

"Indians?!" Jack wondered aloud. "This is it, Jed! The Indians are coming for me!"

"That doesn't sound like Indians to me," Jed reassured him. "It almost sounds mechanical."

Out of the dusky night a figure approached, illuminated by the flicker of their buffalo chip fire. He was dressed in a long brown duster and wore a high black top hat. As the man came clearly into view they saw that he was pushing a wheelbarrow. The barrow's basket was piled high with leather bags, stuffed with the man's provisions and belongings. A shovel and a pick axe rose from the middle of the bags and a blanket, stretched tightly between them at the top, provided the man shade in the daytime. The barrow's single wheel squeaked as it rolled along the ground.

"Gents," the man said as he pushed the wheelbarrow to a stop near their fire. "Mind if I stop here for the night?"

When Jed didn't answer Jack told the man, "Please, settle in."

"Obliged," the man said. "Darius Fairfax is my name,

native of Georgia."

Jack himself felt obliged to ask; "Tell me, Mister Fairfax, are you walking that wheelbarrow all the way to California?"

"Is that a man with a wheelbarrow?" Jed suddenly said, as if he were noticing the fact for the first time. Just as suddenly he stood up, perhaps too quickly, and in a swoon fell back on the bed of grass he had made for himself. Perspiration dripped off of his forehead, even though the night was cool.

"Jed, are you alright?" Jack asked.

"No... no, I don't feel too good," Jed answered. "Oh, damn! Jack, I think I've got *malaria!*" And then he closed his eyes.

Jed achieved a state of half-consciousness and became aware of a blanket wrapped tightly around him and a fire burning warmly just two feet away. He turned his head and saw Jack sitting up next to him, sleeping. Somehow he managed to roll onto his back. Above him the stars moved in blurry arcs across the sky. Suddenly the image of a man with a wheelbarrow flashed across his mind's eye. He considered this determined traveler, pushing a barrow across an entire continent. He considered his many possible fates. These fever dreams grew and interwove until the *Legend of the Wheelbarrow Man* became an epic of unparalleled length and scope. Before he passed once again into unconsciousness, Jed was able to summon a single rational thought; "I have to remember this and write it down tomorrow!" Despite this desperate edict, of course, he did not. No one, half asleep and vowing to themselves that they must remember this or that dream tomorrow, ever does. The Wheelbarrow Man was one of the few sights along this trip that Jed was never able to work into a story.

When the sun arose the next morning Jack found himself in a pickle to be sure. Jed was clearly ill and in a fever. No amount of loud noise, dousing with cold water, or shaking could wake him up. The nearest doctor, as far as he knew, was all the way back in St. Joseph, unless there was a physician traveling with one of the nearby wagon trains.

Darius Fairfax (The Wheelbarrow Man) packed up in a hurry, possibly because he feared Jed was contagious. Jack watched the man roll off to the west through the trees and then turned his attention back to Jed.

"What's the plan this time, Jed?" he asked his unconscious friend. "Do we go forward or back? What should I do?" Jack looked up at the horses, but they didn't offer any better advice than Jed did. Suddenly the wilds seemed even bigger than they were before. He reached for his rifle and sat down next to Jed's still body, placing it across his legs.

The sun was near its zenith when Jack finally stood, walked over to his horse and stowed the rifle. He tied one of the laden pack mules to his saddle and mounted the horse. "Carpe viam it is," he said, and he rode west, leaving Jed alone on the prairie, wrapped up in his blanket next to the fire.

Jed found himself, suddenly and without warning, in a small room with wooden plank walls. The room was incredibly small, more like a spacious outhouse than a room, actually. There were no windows, although Jed could see a small slit, perhaps an inch high and six inches wide, on each side, and what might be a door, although there was no handle. He put his face up against one of the tiny openings to try to see where he was. Outside he observed a number of trees, laden with apples, bowing over a still pond. The flat surface of the pool reflected back to him and image of the cage in which he was ensconced.

Jed was inside a huge wooden turkey. "Wake up, wake up," he said softly to himself and waited for the dream to end.

There was a knock at the door.

"Hello?" he called out.

"Open up," a voice said.

Jed blinked and there was a handle on the door. He reached out and turned it. The door opened inward, smacking him on the knees as it did. Outside there stood a skeletal old man, dressed in gray robes. He raised an eyebrow at Jed.

"What is this thing?" the old man asked.

"I think it's a Trojan Turkey," Jed replied.

"What are you doing in there?" the man asked.

"Waiting," Jed told him.

"Waiting for what?!"

"Well, if I stay in here long enough, eventually the soldiers will carry the giant wooden turkey into the fort. Then, at night, I am supposed to come out and take over the fort," Jed told the old man. "It's a variation on the Trojan Horse legend. Not much of a variation, actually."

The old man frowned. "What if the men from the fort never come?"

Jed hadn't thought about that. "I suppose that I would come out once I was hungry enough."

"Why don't you come out now?" the old man asked.

Jed decided that, since none of this was real anyway, there was no harm in obliging. He ducked his head and climbed out of the giant wooden turkey. As he examined the outside of it he patted himself on the back for having such a good imagination. The detail was excellent.

"Stop congratulating yourself," the old man said. "You have a long way to go, so it's best that you get moving."

"Don't tell me what to do," Jed replied. "You're nothing but a figment of my imagination. I could easily make you vanish."

"I'd like to see you try," the old man laughed.

A low rumbling sound to Jed's right made him turn. Across the prairie on the far side of the still pond he could see a wagon rolling along. It had no horses or oxen pulling it. Instead the wind provided its momentum, with several large sails billowing above it like clouds. At the same time a shadow engulfed Jed and the old man. Above them a huge dirigible floated west through the prairie *skies.*

"You'd best get started," the old man said. "Everyone else is going to beat you to California."

"Who are you?"

"I'm here to tell you something that you must remember when you wake up. It's a portent or foreshadowing or whatever you'd like to call it."

"Kind of you to admit I'm asleep," Jed said. "What is it you think I should remember?"

"You have to save the cat," the old man told him.

"I don't care for cats," Jed said.

"Don't talk back to me, boy!" the old man snapped. "It's a plot device! You'll know what it means when you see it. I know it's a bit vague and mysterious. It's not my fault... this is your imagination." Jed was at the very least impressed that even his dreams were exercises in storytelling.

"I'll try to come up with something better next time," Jed promised. "I'm working hard on improving my metaphors."

The world was shaking, rattling and bumping, when Jed opened his eyes. He realized after a moment that the world was still and *he* was moving. Clouds drifted through his field of view, along with the occasional tree limb and turkey vulture. He debated whether or not he was still in the Trojan Turkey and decided that he was not. A croaking sound came out of his mouth as he tried to call for Jack and tell him that he was awake, yet the energy to croak any louder eluded him. Finally after several minutes he gave up and returned to sleep.

Jack was frying up some bacon over a low fire when he heard a sound behind him. He hurried over to where Jed was lying on a bower of green branches and wrapped in a blanket.

"Jack? Where are we?" Jed asked. His eyes were still red and his face was pale. Still, to Jack he seemed a thousand times more hale and hearty than just twelve hours previous.

"We're camping outside Fort Laramie," Jack told him.

"Was it malaria?" Jed asked.

"No, I don't think so," Jack said. "At least the cavalry doctor here didn't think so. He believes you were infected by bad water. Maybe even cholera. They had a cholera epidemic earlier this year that killed hundreds of folks. Either way, you look a lot better today than you did yesterday." He offered Jed some water. "You've been unconscious for four days. At first I wasn't quite sure how I was going to move you. I thought about tying you to your horse, but expected you'd just fall off. I never was very good with knots."

"Then how did I get here?"

"Well, I wrapped you up, gave you water, and then left you. I rode as fast as I could until I caught up with Mister Fairfax - the Wheelbarrow Man - and traded one of our pack mules for his wheelbarrow. It took me a while to figure out how to build a rig and attach it to the wheelbarrow so that I could tow it behind my horse and also keep it from tipping over. In the end it all worked out."

"You towed me in a wheelbarrow for three days?"

"Well, the horse and the wheelbarrow did most of the work," Jack admitted. "I just made sure you stayed with them. I headed back to the wagon trail and found some other folks traveling west. They said we were almost to the fort, so I just kept on going."

"I always thought I was going to die of malaria or influenza," Jed confessed. "I guess I didn't count on you being there to save me, Jack. I owe you."

Jack turned various shades of red and waved Jed off. "It's nothing anyone else wouldn't do in the same situation. Just help me edit my novel when I finish it and we're square. You want some bacon?"

"Where did you get bacon?" Jed asked as he took a long draft from the water bag and sat up. The blood rushed from his head and he had to fight to stay upright.

"I got it from Leatherface Jackson. He's the wagon master of the group camping right over there by that big Ponderosa Pine. Traded him the wheelbarrow for a side of dried bacon, rice, beans, and a box of noiseless matches."

"So, we made it to Fort Laramie at last?"

"Yup," Jack said. "The water is safe here, so long as you get it upstream from the camp. That's what the men from the fort say."

Jed climbed unsteadily to his feet with Jack's help and surveyed the community of emigrants who were camping around them. "Well, malaria or cholera, I certainly don't recommend this as a way of avoiding the tedium of the trail."

The wagon trains traveling west all stopped at Fort Laramie for resupply, directions, and information about the local Indian tribes. Despite that fact that wagons came and went daily there was a perpetual city of more than a thousand transients camped in the hills surrounding the fort. Merchant tents selling every conceivable emigrant need were set up along the roads to the fort entrance. Occupying a grassy hill just north of the fort was a large cemetery, filled with cholera victims.

A young Cavalry lieutenant from the fort named Manteis circulated among the emigrants trying to educate them regarding the dangers of the road ahead. For those traveling the Oregon Trail there might be troubles with Indians. For those going south on the California Trail there was something much more deadly; the desert. When the officer saw Jed standing at the fire warming his hands he hurried over.

"It's good to see you up and around," the Lieutenant said. "You didn't look too good when your friend brought you in. To be honest, I didn't think you were going to make it."

"I'm feeling much better," Jed said hoarsely. "Thank you."

"Many folks haven't been so lucky."

"I appreciate that fortune has smiled on me," Jed replied. "Well, fortune and my partner over there, to whom I owe my life." Manteis surveyed their horses, pack animals and supplies.

"So, are you boys headed to California to mine for gold? Where are all the shovels and picks?"

"No, we're not miners. We're booksellers," Jack said.

"Booksellers?!" the Lieutenant said.

"Yes, booksellers," Jed answered.

"You aren't with one of the wagon trains?" Manteis asked.

"No, we're doing this on our own," Jed told him. "It's an adventure."

"It's an adventure many would rather do without," Manteis said. "If you want to survive it I suggest you stick to moving water in the future."

It was tempting to stay at Fort Laramie for a while. If you had money food and water were available for purchase from merchant tents or the fort or the other emigrants camping around it, saving all the extra work of collecting it or shooting it for yourself. Winter was coming, though, and if the Boys wanted to get to California they would need to cross the infamous Sierra Nevada before the snows hit. They decided they would leave as soon as Jed felt he had completely recovered from what he insisted on referring to as "malaria."

They were sitting around the fire the next night when an old man approached. He looked older than any individual the Boys had ever laid eyes on. The man was pale as a corpse and his blue eyes were barely visible in their dark sockets. His face bunched up when he smiled through his wrinkles.

"Mind if I share the warmth for a few minutes?" he asked. "I'm as cold as death."

"You're very welcome," Jack offered. "Please join us." The

old man lowered himself carefully to the ground and then, settling in, offered his hand.

"Thankee," the old man said.

"Have we met before?" Jed asked. "You look very, very familiar, though I can't quite remember where we met. Are you from Boston?"

"No. Don't recall seeing you boys before, though it's a long trail. I've met a lot of folk since leaving Missouri. Baker's my name. Folks call me Old Man Baker. I'm headed west to see the elephant," he said. Jed and Jack looked at one another in confusion.

"Elephant? I don't think there are elephants in California," Jack said.

"It's an expression, lad. You haven't heard it? Popular in the wagon trains. You boys must be traveling off the trail," Baker said.

"It's a better option than the smell and dust among the wagons," Jed said. "So what does it mean, 'headed west to see the elephant'?"

"Comes from a yarn they tell around the wagon train campfires to raise the spirits. You have time for a story?" Baker asked.

"We love stories," The Boys answered together. The Old Man held his hands out and warmed them above the flames.

"Well, it goes something like this; there was a farmer who heard that a circus was coming to town on market day and that this circus had an elephant. He was excited by the prospect of seeing a real living and breathing elephant, the world's largest animal, as he had only seen pictures of one before. So he loaded up his wagon with his season's harvest and headed for the market. Once he arrived in town he came across a circus parade, which was being led by the elephant. The magnificent creature was everything he had imagined and more, with its huge tree-trunk legs, great floppy ears, lethal tusks, and long trunk. As the parade passed him, the farmer's horses leapt back in terror of the great mammal. The wagon tipped over and his entire season's harvest spilled into the street and was trampled. Other spectators ran to his aide, but it was too late. 'Your harvest! What will you do?' they asked. 'I don't give a damn,' the farmer replied, 'for I have seen the elephant.'" The Old Man brought his warmed hands to his face and stared off into the dark night. "The road west is hard, and life in California will be hard too. Troubles will befall the best of us. It will be worth it, though, as long as we get the chance to see the elephant."

"So many people have invested their dreams in this land they've never seen," Jed said. "It's a good deal of pressure to put on a place."

Old Man Baker climbed with difficulty to his feet and then turned back to look at Jed and Jack. "There will be a lot to do on the road and when you get to California. Don't forget to see the elephant. Oh, and one other thing…"

"What's that?" Jack asked.

"Don't forget to save the cat."

"I don't care for cats," Jed said. Something about this exchange felt very familiar.

"Exactly," the Old Man said. With that he shuffled off into the darkness, back to his own camp.

Jack made a face, imitating the old man. "Don't forget to see the elephant. Don't forget to save the cat." He laughed. "While you're at it, don't forget to shave the rhinoceros! What do you make of that?"

"You *know* what I'm going to say," Jed replied.

"That it might make a good story!" Jack laughed.

The next morning the Wagon Train camping next to the Boys picked up stakes in order to leave. Jack helped the men load barrels of water onto their wagons and Jed helped the women store their food.

As they finished getting the wagons loaded Jack asked Leatherface Jackson, their wagon master, "Is Old Man Baker with you folks?"

The man looked confused. "I thought you boys just arrived the day before yesterday."

"We did," Jed said. Jackson now looked concerned.

"So you knew Baker from back east? I'm sorry to be the bearer of bad news, but Baker died almost a week ago. Cholera. It gets the youngest and oldest first. Damn shame, he was a sweet old man. You from Missouri?"

"No. We're talking about the same man, right? Old Man Baker? Skinny guy, looks like he is a hundred years old? Deep blue eyes?" Jack asked.

"That was him," the wagon master said. "I'm sorry for your loss. We lost fourteen in the crossing so far, and some say the worst is yet to come. May God have mercy on us all." He hurried back to his party and their wagons started moving down the hill. Jed and Jack watched them go and then headed back over to their own camp.

"Maybe we're losing our minds out here on the trail," Jack sighed, shaking his head. "We're starting to imagine things."

"Even if that is true, I find it unlikely we would share the same delusion," Jed said.

After three days the Boys left Fort Laramie with their mounts and two pack mules. Jed felt like himself again and was ready to return to the trail. They spent their last bit of cash purchasing provisions to get them through to California. All of the roads and steamers and most of the ferries were behind them now. Lieutenant Manteis gave them a hand drawn map showing the route from the fort through the mountains to Bridger's Trading Post, from there through the Granite Pass to the salt flats north of the Great Salt Lake and then onward to the Humboldt River basin.

"This is your last chance to turn back," the Lieutenant warned them. "The last thousand miles have been easy compared to what you are about to endure. There are a fair number of Indians and some pretty rough country."

"No turning back," Jed and Jack replied.

"Then you boys should stick with one of the larger groups from here on out," Manteis suggested. However Jed and Jack were now used to traveling alone, so after they caught up with Leatherface Jackson's slow moving wagon train they stayed just long enough to say hello and share a meal and then they rode on ahead. Shortly they arrived at the North Platte River crossing, where the Mormons had a crude ferry service. You could cross for free if you were a Mormon traveling to Great Salt Lake City, but all others were charged four dollars per wagon or twenty-five cents per horse and mule. Jed and Jack were down to their last coins once they got to the other side.

From here the road disappeared into a series of canyons and wound back and forth along increasingly steep grades. It was all The Boys could do to coax the mules up the hillsides. Jack commented that despite their difficulties they were lucky at least that they weren't pulling wagons. Neither of them could imagine how a master might drive an entire wagon train up some of these slopes.

When the low granite dome called Independence Rock appeared they knew they were on the right course. The rock was used as a sort of bulletin board by the passing emigrants. The sides were peppered with splashes of pitch and tar which had messages carved into them (and in some cases the messages were chiseled directly into the rock). *Potter Party here June 22, 1849. North on Oregon Trail, look out for savages* said one. Another read *Abernathy July 6, 1849 still have fifteen wagons and twelve oxen, on the lookout for savages.* Jed's favorite was *Pappy Baxter - hurry up, you're three days late, you lazy tramp! August 1, 1849.* This was also the place where the trail met the Sweetwater River. The Sweetwater, Jed assumed, was so named because it tasted so much better than the Platte.

The next landmark marked on the map Manteis had given them was called "Devil's Gate." Sure enough they soon arrived at a spot where the river narrowed and towering cliffs rose above it on either side. The Sweetwater squeezed through this slender gap and then plunged in a series of whitewater rapids into the valley beyond. Jed and Jack were forced to move south around the imposing granite domes to rejoin the river on the far side.

Seven days out from Fort Laramie they were winding through a particularly narrow canyon. The passage was so enclosed that the horses could only go two ways - forward and backward. Given this the Boys let their animals take the lead and they drifted into a state of reverie. Jack was busy daydreaming about tables of food; hot roasted turkeys, steaming baked potatoes, buttered lobster. Jed was trying desperately to remember anything about his epic *Legend of the Wheelbarrow Man.* They were rudely brought back to reality when an arrow suddenly embedded itself in the heel of Jack's left boot. He looked down in surprise. Just two inches higher and it would have split his foot.

They reigned in their horses and frantically searched the sparse trees and bushes that lined the canyon in an effort to locate the arrow's source. They were utterly alone in this wilderness canyon, easily surrounded and outgunned.

"This is why we should have stayed with one of the wagon trains," Jack whispered.

About a hundred yards behind them a group of Indians suddenly appeared on the trail.

"Let's go!" Jed cried, and he dug his spurs into his horse's sides as Jack did the same. On the positive side the horses did manage a fair trot, cantering down the trail away from the Indians. Unfortunately the mules bearing all of their supplies were still tethered to the horses and the overall combination of horses, mules, riders, and sacks of flour couldn't achieve better than a desperate lope. The Indians didn't even bother to put up a chase, which made their inadequate, slow-motion dash for freedom all the more pitiful.

They had only traveled thirty yards or so when another group of Indians rode out of the trees ahead of them. Jed and Jack pulled their horses to a halt (which didn't take much) and glanced forward and back and saw that they were surrounded. The natives in the path ahead of them formed their horses into a semi-circle, blocking the way. Two of them carried rifles which they rested casually across their saddles. Another had a bow.

"This is it, Jed! I knew this was coming, ever since I was a kid," Jack said. "That dream - it was a premonition after all. The one in the middle with the big blue feather and hat! He was there! What are we going to do?"

"Was I in your dream?" Jed asked. Jack thought for a moment.

"No."

"Well, then, it wasn't a proper premonition, was it?" Jed said. "I don't think we have much choice. There's no place to run to. Let's try some diplomacy. We might as well put our best foot forward." Jack looked down at the arrow in his left boot heel.

"At the moment that would be my *right* foot," he said. They encouraged their horses forward gently and then slowed down as they approached the Indians. Jed pulled up and held out his hand.

"Hello," he said. The Indians ignored Jed's greeting. Three of them were busy having a conversation amongst themselves. Every few seconds one would gesture toward Jed, Jack or their pack animals. "Do you speak English?" Jed asked. "We're friends. *Friends.*"

"Do you suppose they want some of our supplies?" Jack asked nervously.

"They're probably trying to decide whether we have enough goods to warrant killing us and stealing everything," Jed replied.

The Indian wearing the big blue feather and hat, apparently the leader of the group, rode forward slowly and took keen measure of both Jed and Jack. He then moved past their pack mules, lifting the flaps on the saddle bags and investigating the contents. Finally he approached Jack. Jed rode forward and placed himself and his horse between the Indian leader and his partner. Unfortunately this had the effect of making the native even more interested in Jack.

"We haven't got anything of value," Jed told him. "We're just a couple of merchants headed west. We're certainly no threat to you." One of the natives raised his rifle - not pointing it at Jed so much as reminding them that he had it.

The Indian leader slowly reached around Jed and lifted the flap of the saddle bag on Jack's mount. He seemed surprised by what he saw. Carefully he reached into the bag and pulled out a book. The Indian raised one eyebrow and then reached in and pulled out another. He stared at the covers intently.

"They're books," Jed said. "We're Booksellers. Book-sellers."

"Booksellers?" the leader with the blue feather repeated, speaking for the first time.

"Yes, Booksellers," Jack said.

Suddenly the Indian held one of the books up, showing its cover to Jack.

"*The Deerslayer*," he said in perfect English, reading the lettering on the book's spine. "I liked *The Pathfinder* quite a lot and positively loved *Last of the Mohicans*. Have you read this one yet?"

45

Jack overcame his astonishment to answer. "Yes."

"It's clear Cooper knows very little about the red man, as he calls us, though for a good tale I'm willing to allow for some poetic license," the Indian said. He glanced over at Jed. "Have you read it?"

"Yes," Jed said.

"So you no longer need it? May I have it?" the Indian asked. "I'll trade you coffee for it. I got some from a man on a wagon just yesterday."

"Sure," Jack said, his surprise written all over his face.

"My name is Wakini, and this is my hunting party," the blue-feathered Indian said. "The fellows love it when I read them books every night around the fire, but they're damned hard to find out here. So, tell me, what else have you got?"

Jack pulled the remaining four or five books out of his saddle bag while Jed brought out the ones he had packed. The Indian leader placed *The Deerslayer* reverently in a bag hanging across his horse's neck. The other natives gathered around and sorted through The Boys' books. By the time they were finished they packed up all of the books and left Jed and Jack without any.

In payment Wakini handed Jack a pouch of coffee beans, a fair amount of sugar and some dried meat. Lastly he reached down and pulled the arrow out of Jack's boot heel.

"I'm really sorry about that," he said, handing the arrow to the native who carried the bow. "Sometimes they get a bit overzealous."

"All is forgiven," Jack said.

"You know," Wakini added, "your people haven't sent booksellers out here before. Trappers, hunters, warriors, explorers, miners... but you're the first booksellers. It's definitely an improvement."

He turned to his tribesmen and said something in their own

tongue which included the identifiable words "Natty Bumppo." The other braves seemed pleased by what he said. With a nod the Indian pulled his horse around and the entire party rode off down the canyon toward the East.

As they resumed their journey Jack said, "I don't know what all the fuss is about Indians. They seem like very decent fellows."

"Good taste in books," Jed agreed.

After many difficult days winding through the mountains, including a fording of the Green River and a brief stop at a small trading post cabin that was referred to by the grandiose name "Fort Bridger," they descended a steep trail to a never-ending salt flat.

In the distant south they could see the shores of the Great Salt Lake, as uninviting and desolate a body of water as one could imagine. To the west the sight of the hot flat desert plain stretching into the distance, broken only by an occasional dusty hill, made emigrants take stock and reassess their priorities. It was hard enough hauling heavy wagons over the mountains. This desert would be even less forgiving, so travelers stopped here to adjust their loads. Piles of unnecessary items were left behind, littering the desert floor; heavy tools made of iron, furniture, and trunks of clothes. At the point where the trail vanished into the hardpan of the desert the Boys found fifty abandoned barrels of bacon.

" 'Abandon hope, ye who enter here,' " Jed said.

"Conserve water. We won't have access to any more until we reach the Humboldt," Jack suggested.

"Don't worry," Jed said confidently. "We beat malaria and we beat the Indians. We have walked through the fire and emerged unscathed! If we can get past that, we can get past anything!"

"Still, do me a favor and conserve water, *please*," Jack said.

On the sixth day of their journey across this desolate plain Jack saw what they took to be a mirage. At first it was just a dark spot on the horizon, warped by the waves of heat that rose from the hardpan. As they grew closer the rippling object grew clearer and they saw that it was a covered wagon.

A man in a black derby was standing by the wagon, staying in the shade where it was at least relatively cool. The back of the wagon was filled with barrels, boxes, and crates. A mangy golden tabby cat was curled up sleeping on the top of the highest barrel. The man twirled his mustache with one hand and watched the Boys approach. He waved to them as they grew close.

"Greetings, friends!" he called out. Jed and Jack appreciated sharing the little patch of shadow next to the wagon.

"Hello," Jed offered.

"You two boys look parched, I'd say. Tongues as tough as leather and your eyes drying out like little raisins in your skull. Lucky thing you happened by my little oasis," the man said. "Reynard is the name, Fox Reynard. I exist, I say, I am blessed to be, in order to help poor travelers like you."

"Very kind of you," Jack said, introducing himself and Jed.

"I have water, of course," Reynard smiled. "You can't get through this hellish place without plenty of water... and flour, eggs... how would you like a nice fresh egg?"

"That sounds good," Jed agreed.

"I need some slight compensation, as you might expect. It takes some resources and an iron will to come out here into the middle of nowhere and provide for my less fortunate brothers and sisters. That's fair, isn't it? Oh, what a joy it is to come to the aid of my fellows!"

Jed reached down and offered an empty water bag. "Fair enough," he said. Reynard held the bag up to the tap of a water barrel situated in the back of his wagon. The tabby cat lazily raised its head to see what was going on.

"Don't fuss, Prince Rupert," Reynard said to the cat. "Just getting some water for these fine gentlemen." He allowed about a quart to pour into the bag before he shut off the tap and held the bag out to Jed with a big smile.

"That will be one hundred dollars," Reynard said. The Boys' jaws dropped in unison.

"One hundred dollars?! For a quart of water?!" Jack exclaimed. Reynard smiled.

"It is, as you know, a matter of supply and demand," he explained politely. "I do not and never will charge any more than the market supports. Water is in scarce supply here. I am providing an invaluable public service. Isn't that right, Prince Rupert?" The cat ignored him.

Jed refused to take the bag. "Keep it, and keep the bag too. I wouldn't pay you a nickel, you charlatan!"

Reynard looked wounded. "You injure me, sir! I charge only what needs require. I am sorry that you have received an incorrect opinion of my generous nature! Please, can I make it up to you? I could offer you some flour... just two dollars a pint. Perhaps an egg for fifteen dollars? Ah, I expect you boys love your sweets! I have sugar at just six dollars a pint!"

Jed and Jack glanced at each other and then turned and remounted their horses.

"Can you tell us which way it is to the Humboldt River? Or will that cost us something too?" Jack asked.

"Well, surely you wouldn't deny an honest man a fee for consultation? Hiring a guide would cost you so much more..."

The Boys reluctantly rode out of the shade cast by Reynard's wagon and out into the hot sun. They kept their original bearings and hoped the river lay on that course. As they moved away they could hear Reynard calling after them.

"Whisky! I have whisky for thirsty lads! Fifteen dollars for a pint! I'll give you two for twenty-five!"

They made the Humboldt River by dusk. It was a narrow, slow moving channel, with brackish muddy water. Jed was slightly concerned it might be another source of cholera (or worse) though they didn't have much choice in the matter, as their bags were now completely dry. They gathered the clearest water they could find from the fastest moving channel and then watered the horses. A pitiful strip of grass grew along the stream. It was cropped short on the north side, evidence of the volume of emigrants who had traveled along its banks. Luckily the river was shallow and could be forded at frequent intervals. The terrain grew hillier and there were rocky outcroppings.

The Boys continued along this course for several days until the river grew broader and shallower, eventually flattening out into a wide salty marsh surrounded by meadows. The water settled deeper into the sandy channel until at last it was gone. A vast expanse of dry earth spread out before them.

"The Humboldt Sink," Jed muttered. "That's the end of the water. Only forty miles to go... next stop California."

"Those forty miles are also known as the Forty Mile Desert," Jack pointed out. The water here was too salty for consumption. Luckily they had filled their bags the day before with fresher water from a more quickly moving part of the muddy Humboldt River. With steady determination the Boys started out across the barren expanse. The path was easy to follow; abandoned wagons lay on their sides every quarter mile or so, amid the skulls of oxen and horses that failed to survive the trip. Jed found one with a despairing note attached; *"Bessie was a good cow. If you find her still alive and have the means to save her, please do what you can. We are out of water and out of hope."*

The wind started to pick up as the day proceeded, so much that on occasion they found it difficult to keep their balance upon the horses. Eventually they gave up and started walking.

"Maybe we should set up our canvas and get sheltered. The dust is making it hard to see anything. We might be going in the wrong direction," Jack suggested.

"It would probably blow away," Jed answered. "I don't think we have any choice but to soldier on."

Visibility dropped to only a few feet and, as Jack had feared, they lost their bearings. The gusts were at times so strong they could hardly stand. If one were to ascribe greater meaning to the random acts of nature, one might think that forces were conspiring to keep the Boys from making it to California. On the other hand, it was possible they had just had the bad luck of being in the middle of an alkali desert during a monumental wind storm.

Soon the horses, blind and confused, refused to take another step. The Boys dismounted and took the reins, leading the animals onward into the tempest. Each step forward was a battle with the wind. Left with no alternative they drove forward into the gale.

Their situation was dire when a dark shadow loomed in the swirling dust to their right. Jed figured that, whatever it was, it might provide a lee side to shelter from the wind so he moved toward it. When they arrived they saw that it was Reynard's covered wagon.

"How much do you think he's going to charge us for this?" Jack asked loudly, trying to be heard over the din. Jed mounted the wagon, then leapt down and ran around to the back. Moments later he returned to Jack, who was holding their nervous horses.

"He's not here! It's just his wagon and horses," Jed told him.

"He probably got separated from it in the dust storm," Jack said. "Let's get the wagon turned into the wind. We'll unhook the horses and get all of them behind it so that they have some protection from the dust. Then we can get inside."

Jack's plan was sound and soon the Boys were inside the wagon. The canvas cover was buffeted in the storm, the supports bending almost to the point of breaking. They lay down on the sacks of flour and blankets that Reynard had stowed there and, despite the tempest outside, slept better than they had in many nights.

When the sun rose in the morning they climbed out of the wagon. The horses were there - dusty and dirty but alive and well. Jed pulled one of the water barrels down out of the wagon and watered them. Jack stared out across the desert.

"You know, that wind wagon of Thomas's would have been halfway to China by now if it caught some of the winds we were in last night," he said. "The sun gives us a direction, at least. We know which way is west."

"Damn, the cat!" Jed suddenly said.

"What?" Jack asked, confused.

"We have to go back for Reynard," Jed said with a heavy sigh.

"Why? He wouldn't go back for us," Jack pointed out. "It's the wrong direction. We'll be going backwards. Dammit, Jed, we're *so close.*"

"I know, Jack. But do we really want to start our new lives with that on our consciences? We can't forget to save the cat. Even if we don't like cats."

Jack laughed. "Do you suppose that's what the old man meant?"

"If he didn't it's still a clever bit of foreshadowing. Whether the ghosts of the plains were giving us a message from beyond or it was just coincidence, it's still the right thing to do. We're the good guys. I suppose we have to definitively establish that at some point.

Think of it as a test."

"Yeah," Jack replied, "I know you're right. But it's so darn inconvenient."

They harnessed Reynard's horses and brought the wagon around to the east, heading back toward the Humboldt River. The last time they had seen Reynard was days away, yet the wagon and team were in good condition and the Boys hoped he had been separated from them only after the storm hit.

They found him before they reached the salty Humboldt Sink. He was sitting on the desert floor behind a low ridge which he had presumably used as shelter from the wind. His mangy orange tabby, Prince Rupert, was draped around his shoulders asleep. Jack jumped off the wagon and climbed up the ridge to the man's side. As he did, Reynard turned and looked up at him.

"Now, saints and holy men, I say, you boys are a welcome sight."

"You alright?" Jack asked.

"It was a night to be reckoned with," Reynard said. "The wind came directly from the breath of God, so powerful it was. I persevered through the might of my own indomitable will. My horses and wagon were carried off into the sky, borne aloft like birds. Only through the grace of my own wit and gumption did I survive the lethal storm and..."

"We have the horses and wagon," Jack pointed out. "Perhaps we can discuss our fee for salvaging them..."

Reynard's attitude changed abruptly. He narrowed his eyes.

"I see you boys did quite well, probably safe and sound in my very own wagon. Perhaps we can discuss the cost of renting it for the night."

Jed brought the wagon to a stop next to them and jumped down to Jack's side.

"Perhaps," he said smiling, "we can come to a fair

arrangement."

"Ah! You boys are businessmen, then?" Reynard asked suspiciously.

"You could say that," Jed said proudly. "We're booksellers."

"Booksellers?!"

"Yes, booksellers," Jack replied.

Reynard took them west to his cabin in the Big Meadows along the Truckee River. There was a small community of settlers there, about fifty strong, in addition to a variety of Paiute and Washoe Indians. These natives were quite amenable to Reynard, as the economy of the area had skyrocketed since his arrival. A number of them had learned his techniques for profitable business and had started very successful regional enterprises.

The boys camped for a few days to allow their horses (and themselves) to recuperate. Reynard gave them food and they, in turn, helped rebuild the fence around his corral and cut down four trees. Once three days passed Reynard lead them south along the foot of the Sierra Nevada to the Carson Trail. Although it was no more than a track on the earth recent use made it unmistakable.

"Thank you for your hospitality," Jack said to Reynard as they left him.

"It is my pleasure to help," Reynard said, "although I expect in general to be better recompensed. Still, you saved my life and that is a precious gift, sirs, a precious gift. Selling books, eh? I've sold a lot of things in my time, never books. I'll have to give it a try."

"That's the best thing you could have said," Jed told him. "Just don't charge your customers a year's wages in the process."

With the happy prospect that books may soon be available to enlighten the settlers of what would someday become Reno, Nevada, the Boys took their horses by the reins and lead them up the steep trail, into the mountains through the narrow Carson Pass. At some point that morning, although there were no border guards or signs to tell them so, they fearlessly marched into California, the land of dreams.

Next: Welcome to Hangtown

III.

WELCOME TO HANGTOWN
or
BRADFORD & NORRIS:
BOOKSELLERS TO THE SAVAGE WEST

1850

Third Story: The Gold
*In which we arrive in Placerville and take an involuntary trip
to the underworld*

As has been so often recounted in history classes across the United States, in 1848 a carpenter by the name of James Marshall was building a sawmill for John Sutter, who owned most of the land along the Sacramento River. The mill was located on the American River about forty miles east of Sutter's Fort. On January 24th Marshall discovered gold in the millrace. Word of the discovery got back to San Francisco and an enterprising newspaper publisher named Sam Brannan cornered the market on mining equipment (primarily shovels and picks) before telling the world that GOLD had been discovered in the mountains of California. The population of San Francisco dropped precipitously as everyone who could walk hurried to the gold fields in the hopes of becoming rich.

It may be noted here that James Marshall died destitute, John Sutter lost his land and died begging the U.S. Congress for restitution, and Sam Brannan didn't leave enough money to pay for his own funeral. Being in the right place at the right time did not work out for these three men.

However, for many others it did. The area around Sutter's Mill, where Marshall discovered gold, became the bustling community of Coloma. Every river, stream, creek and drainage ditch in the central Sierra Nevada became a target for gold seekers.

One of the resulting settlements, just a few miles from Coloma, was called Old Dry Diggins.

The town of Old Dry Diggins - if "town" could be considered an appropriate sobriquet - consisted of a single winding mud track which ran along an equally winding and muddy creek through a winding and narrow valley. Dozens of tents and roughly built log and lumber buildings lined the road. Some had whiskey barrels for chimneys and doors made of potato sacks - rushed and improvised structures built by men who would rather be out panning for gold than constructing cabins and stores. When the first miners reached Dry Diggins they could pull gold nuggets out of the cliffs with their bare hands. Gravel from the flats around the creek could be washed in nothing more complicated than a cooking pan to separate copious amounts of gold. Fortunes might be made in a day (and given the prodigious gambling in the camps squandered the very same night). Easy pickings grew scarce quickly and then the miners started digging.

The creek was diverted from its original course and now ran through a series of artificial channels so that the water could be siphoned off for mining. The exposed riverbed was converted into what looked like an immense construction project. Deep holes - dangerous for both man and beast - were hidden behind abandoned piles of rock which stood as monuments to the spots where miners had come and gone. In many areas the creek bed was still being worked, identifiable by rows of 'long toms,' the biggest placer devices the miners used to wash the gravel.

The devastation was not limited to the bottom of the ravine. The hillsides above Dry Diggins were almost completely stripped of trees. The slopes were covered with stumps that marked where huge pines once stood. The miners didn't bother to range beyond the immediate valley for wood to build with. If they needed to build a sluice or a cabin or a long tom they took their axe to whatever tree was closest at hand so that they could spend as much of their time as possible on the quest for gold.

As a result there was very little in the way of civic planning. The town was constructed haphazardly, with only the creek as a guide. Teams of miners joined together to build large barracks-style cabins or tents. These groups organized to systematically dig up the entire valley, a shovel full at a time, dump it into a sluice box, and then wash it, a bucketful of water at a time, to find any gold it held. Dressed in tattered clothes and muddy boots they worked hard from dawn until dusk searching for "pay dirt." It was a noisy, messy, dirty affair during the day and a raucous, boisterous cycle of drinking and gambling at night.

By the end of 1849 there were a number of hastily built hotels, inns, gambling houses, and several Dry Goods stores mixed in with the cabins and barracks. There was no garbage collection, so the streets around these buildings were strewn with two year's worth of castoffs; empty bottles, sardine cans, oyster tins, ham bones, worn-out boots, and broken shovels.

Along the muddy thoroughfare rode two covered wagons drawn by six oxen each. One was driven by Jedediah Bradford, so tanned and dirty from the trip from Sacramento that his face was barely distinguishable from his dark brown hat. The second wagon was driven by Jack Norris, whose face was still darker through the addition of a week's worth of beard.

Jed brought his wagon to a halt. Directly in his path - in the middle of the street - was a huge hole. As his oxen pulled up to the edge of the pit a bald head popped up out of it.

"Go around! There's enough room to go around!" the bald man said. He raised a bucket out of the hole and a short man ran over and took it from him.

Welcome to Hangtown, 1849

Britton & Rey lithograph, 1850s

"You're mining in the middle of the street?!" Jed asked.

The second man poured the contents of the bucket into a rocker at one side of the road and then indicated the ramshackle two story building next to him. It stretched away toward the hillside, bordered by a stables and low barn.

"This is *our* smithy," the man said. "It's *our* claim."

"No troubles," Jed apologized. "We're new in town. Is this Old Dry Diggins?"

The two men laughed. "That's what it used to be called," the man in the pit said.

To most of the people living in the area this town was *still* Dry Diggins. To a few of the new arrivals it had earned a different name. Earlier that year a group of thieves were apprehended by miners. As there was no proper officer of the law in Dry Diggins to oversee these criminals' disposition the mob decided to mete out justice right there and then. The big oak tree in Elstner's hay yard was used as a gallows and the thieves were promptly hung. Just a few months later no one in town could agree who the thieves were, what they had stolen, or why the administration of justice had been so swift (a void which left a great deal of room for storytelling, Jed noted). The one detail that did stay with the population was a new name for their community; Hangtown.

"What's going on?" Jack called from his wagon.

"I'm getting directions!" Jed answered. He turned to the miners. "Could you point me toward someplace we could stable our oxen and horses, and perhaps an inn or boarding house?" Jed asked. The two men rubbed their long unkempt beards.

"Adam's hotel has some room, don't it, Hard Head?" the man by the rocker asked.

"That's true, come to think," Hard Head, the bald man in

the hole, answered. "Five Aces was shot and his partner left for San Francisco."

"Why was Five Aces shot?" Jed asked.

"Five Aces," Hard Head replied matter-of-factly.

"Oh…" Jed said.

"Adam's hotel is up the street on your right. I think he put up a sign. Didn't he put up a sign, Stubby?" Hard Head asked. The man by the rocker nodded.

"Maybe."

Jed thanked them and after a few unsuccessful attempts was able to coax the oxen around Hard Head's hole and get them moving toward the hotel.

They eventually found a stable and were able to come to an accommodation to board their horses and oxen. The oxen would be sold as soon as they were sure that this was where they were staying. The wagons were stored inside a barn at the stable. From there Jed and Jack made their way to Adam's hotel.

The main room, which comprised the entire bottom floor of the building, included a sitting area, dining area, kitchen and desk where the owner conducted business. It was past the usual dinner hour and they were concerned that it would be impossible to get a decent meal. However, once the Boys showed their money they were heartily welcomed by the proprietor, a Mister Halliwell, a rotund man with a heavily waxed handlebar mustache. He hustled them to an oilcloth-covered table where several other late diners were having a meal of salt pork, sardines, potatoes, and soggy pickles. Jed and Jack were expected to supply their own cutlery, so they ate with their knives. Halliwell gave them a rich, dark brew to drink, which he claimed was fermented in his own back yard. Given how it tasted (think dark ale mixed with molasses and day-old coffee) The Boys thought that this was likely.

Mister Halliwell's cooking pot was made out of a shovel blade with a handle made from the head of a pickaxe. Bringing supplies to Old Dry Diggins cost a fair amount, so the miners reused anything that could be reclaimed from their castoffs. The strange stew-like pork and potatoes concoction inside this cobbled pot was, however, very satisfying. Jed and Jack had been on the road all day with nothing but water, dry bread and hard tack.

"Don't forget to eat the pickles!" Halliwell advised them as he returned to the kitchen.

The other men eating at the table introduced themselves - Big Mouth McMahon, Doc Hollander and Two Shovels Mitchell. Jack asked where they had earned their colorful nicknames.

"Well, I have a big mouth," McMahon explained.

"And I have two shovels," Mitchell said.

"Which he uses at the same time," McMahon added.

"And I can wash twice the gravel any other man can in the same time!" Two Shovels declared. "That's why I come up with twice the pay dirt!"

"Not as much as the Fish Brothers," Big Mouth corrected him. "Although they do work all night as well, so we aren't exactly comparing apples and apples."

"Are you a Doctor?" Jed asked the third man, Hollander. The man dramatically finished a long draught of his ale before replying.

"Not as such," he said in a slurry voice. "I am a student in the school of experience. Though I have no degree or cert-cert-certificate to hang upon a wall I have gained such ex-ex-expertise in many subjects that it has prompted my p-p-peers to hold me in such high esteem that they feel the designation is ap-propriate."

"Don't let him feel your head," Two Shovels warned the booksellers.

"Excuse me?" Jack asked.

"Phrenology, my new f-f-friend," Doc Hollander explained. "You may be unaware that the cranial bone, i.e., the skull, con-conforms to the general shape of the brain. A person skilled in the science may determine a man's entire personality simp-simply by tracing the shape of their head." Hollander held up his empty cup in order that Halliwell could refill it. "Would you care for a dem-demonstration?"

"Don't let him feel your head," Two Shovels repeated.

"Perhaps some other time," Jed suggested as he watched Hollander's empty cup sway back and forth unevenly.

"You've had quite enough now, Doc!" Halliwell said from the kitchen door. "Eat all of your sardines, boys!" he added. "They'll give you energy for tomorrow's dig!"

After they ate Halliwell escorted them to their room, which was a small affair with what looked like tables serving as beds. Still, with stuffed-hay-mattresses and a few good blankets they would be comfortable enough.

"Mister Halliwell," Jack said, "do you know a man by the name of Ashton?"

"Tom Ashton?" the portly innkeeper asked.

"I believe so."

"Hell, Tom owns the saloon and gambling place right down the hill!" Halliwell said. "The big round tent - you couldn't have missed it! Go out the back and turn left. Mind you stay clear of the Fish Brothers... last week they were working late and hit one of my lodgers with a rock. By the by, if you boys get a shave from Tom make sure you keep your mustaches!" He stroked his waxed mustache with obvious affection. "No man should be without one!"

As the Boys left the hotel they heard the clanking sound of

active picks and shovels. It was dark out now, and they could see two men hacking away at the cliff face behind the hotel by lantern light. One of the men saw Jed and Jack and paused, tipped his hat and gave a brief nod.

"Evening, gentlemen," he smiled. Jack nodded back.

"Seems like a friendly town so far," Jed commented. "Maybe too friendly. We came here for the adventure."

They carefully skirted Hard Head's hole-in-the-street, which was uncovered and a definite hazard in the dim light. Unlike the Fish Brothers, Hard Head had apparently quit digging for the night.

"Trust me," Jack said, "This place is nothing like Boston. Look at the holes everywhere! Do these men ever stop digging? Don't mines belong in a mountain or a quarry or something? These people will dig anywhere! In the middle of the street… behind a hotel…"

"They must take a break sometime. *Man shall not live on gold alone,*" Jed said as they reached the big round tent.

As if in response to his statement two men came flying out of the tent, colliding with the Boys. The four of them fell to the ground in a sprawl of arms and legs. Jed and Jack disentangled themselves, scrambled to their feet, and watched as the other two men attempted to do the same. It was clear that they were quite drunk.

"Man may, however, live on gold and *whiskey* alone," Jack said.

The tent was crowded; so many bodies blocked the lanterns that it was almost dark. Men crowded around tables playing poker and seven up, most of them perched on empty kegs and barrels instead of chairs. A makeshift bar was set up near the back and rows of whiskey bottles glowed dimly on shelves above it. Two miners were having an altercation to the right side of the tent. Their angry voices and the sounds of their scuffle were barely audible above the general din of the place until one of them brought a bottle down on the head of the other. It missed cracking the second man's skull, sliding off and dropping to the floor in a cacophony of broken glass. The other miners glanced up from their drinks and games just long enough to see that no one was dead and then resumed their prior activities.

Jed and Jack made their way to the bar where a tall and wiry fellow and a short hunched-over specimen were pouring drinks. A woman - the only female in the establishment - sat at the far end of the bar nursing a small drink and watched the Boys as they sat down at the bar. She was decidedly different than the women the Boys knew in Boston; she wore an ankle-length dark duster that draped down around the barrel she was perched on. Upon her head was a bowler hat, similar to the ones many of the men wore, although the long black hair that flowed from beneath it and around her shoulders was definitely feminine.

"Is it always this busy?" Jed asked one of the men serving drinks.

"Tomorrow's Sunday," the tall and wiry bartender said loudly, as if this explained everything. Jed just nodded as if he understood.

"Do you know where we can find Tom Ashton?" he asked.

"That would be me," the bartender answered. "T. Ashton, miner, gambler, saloon-keeper, lawyer, doctor and barber. Which hat would you like me to put on?"

"I'm Jed Bradford and this is my partner Jack Norris. Stafford Hickey sent us. We understand you have a store for sale." The doctor-lawyer-bartender nodded.

"Right, right. You're the fellas from Boston. Stafford told me to expect you. Say, Lizzie, these are the fellas from Boston who are buying my store!"

"Pleased to meet you," the raven-haired woman said. Her voice was creamy with the soft finish of a French accent. Tom Ashton took off his apron and rounded the end of the bar.

"Come on outside where we can talk," he said. He prodded the short hunched-over man with the bottle in his hand. "Hey, Hound Dog! I'm steppin' out! Keep them honest! And don't let Nebraska Joe and Old Shoes get near each other... I don't want to have to spend my night sewing up someone's head."

"Right, Tom!"

Ashton led Jed and Jack to the back flap of the tent and the three of them exited into the cool night air. Jack noticed that, just like everywhere else in Hangtown, there was a large hole in the ground just behind the Round Tent. It was surrounded by a sluice, a few picks and shovels, and a large rocking chair. An old miner with a beard as long as Moses' was smoking a cigar and rocking back and forth slowly in the chair. It wasn't clear whether he was just here to enjoy the evening or was performing guard duties on the hole.

"The store is up the street," Ashton said, pointing to a building a block or two away. "It's the one just this side of the Iowa House... a pretty big place, big as this tent. Tiny Morgan used to sell hardware there until he lost the building to me in a game of Euchre."

"Why don't you locate the saloon there?" Jack asked suspiciously.

"It's handier being able to move the saloon to where the customers are when it's necessary," Ashton said, indicating the tent. "This summer there was a big strike up in Cedar Ravine and nobody left there for almost a month. I moved the saloon up to the dig for three and a half weeks and made a bundle."

"How much do you want for the building?" Jed asked.

"Oh, I figure four hundred dollars might do the trick," Ashton said. "Five hundred if you want the yard next door where

Chinese Sam shoes horses. That's mine too." The Boys glanced at each other.

"We'll have to take a look at it, but it sounds reasonable," Jed said.

"What do you fellas plan on selling at your store?" the gambler-barber-bartender asked.

"We're booksellers," Jed said proudly.

"Booksellers?!"

"Yes, booksellers," Jack replied. Ashton thought about it for a minute.

"I suppose crazier things have been tried. New brothel, new saloon, new hotel... them I could see. New bookshop, not so much. Like I say, though, crazier things have been tried."

The voices in the Round Tent suddenly grew louder and angrier. Ashton headed back inside.

"Dammit, Hound Dog!" the lawyer-miner-doctor said. "I told you to keep Nebraska Joe and Old Shoes away from each other!"

Jed, Jack and Ashton entered the Round Tent and saw that the "disagreement" spread beyond just Nebraska Joe and Old Shoes. A general melee had broken out on the far side of the bar. More than a dozen drunken miners were engaged in a slow motion free-for-all. It was a typical late night barroom fracas. Each lazy punch thrown was followed by a moment of recovery where both the puncher and the punched recovered their balance, which was difficult considering their advanced states of inebriation. After waiting a second or two for their brains to catch up with the situation they each returned the blow, almost as an afterthought. Jed doubted that any of them was capable of inflicting any serious injury, except by accident.

Hound Dog was no longer trying to break up the skirmish. His attention was focused on protecting the Round Tent's supply of whiskey. The mass of fighting miners was getting perilously close to the shelves on which the bottles sat. Tom Ashton hurried to the bar and pulled his shotgun from a hiding place below. In one swift action he aimed it skyward and pulled the trigger, peppering the roof of the tent with shot.

The booming sound of the shotgun brought the fighters, drunk or not, to a stop. They froze in mid-punch and stared at the bar, surprised by this sudden interruption of their brawl. However, the customers of the Round Tent who were not involved in the conflict had a different reaction. Instead of freezing, the non-combatants all rushed away from the bar in order to put as much space between themselves and Tom Ashton's shotgun as possible. The crowd became denser as it ran up against the back wall of the tent. Like a terrified herd of corralled bovines they gathered, bleating and trampling each other's feet.

This might have been enough to make the evening a memorable one - and worthy of future storytelling - for the Boys. However, there was more to come.

In one improbable and startling moment the ground beneath the concentrated group of miners gave way. The dirt floor of the Round Tent rippled out from that spot, cascading into the underworld below. Miners, chairs, tables and eventually the bar and all of Tom Ashton's precious whiskey went cascading like a nightmarish waterfall into the pit. Jed and Jack felt the earth give way from under their feet and they tumbled with all the rest into the dark hole. In a last act of divine discourtesy the Round Tent itself collapsed. The great sheet of canvas settled over the opening and then covered it. To Two Shovels Mitchell, who was walking down the street when the Round Tent was consumed by the earth, it looked like the ground had sealed itself back up. The saloon and its patrons simply vanished.

Once things stopped falling there were a few moments of

silence, excepting some drunken groans.

"You okay, Jed?" Jack asked from the darkness.

"Yeah. You?" Jed asked.

"Aside from the whiskey bottle that fell on my head, I think I'm alright," Jack answered. "I landed on something soft."

"That would be me," a decidedly feminine voice said.

"Ma'am... so sorry... Miss... Lizzie..." Jack mumbled as he struggled to get himself off of her. He only succeeded in putting a foot in her back.

Jed felt the hard wood of a table next to him and pushed down on it. Hoping it was secure he scrambled onto it. Luckily he and Jack were standing in the back doorway when the Round Tent collapsed. When he held up his hand he could touch the underside of the canvas. Gathering a handful of the material he pulled and the relatively bright light of the stars shone through a small opening.

It took twenty minutes for the sober miners to crawl up out of the hole. The intoxicated ones stayed longer, partly because they were too drunk to climb out and partly because all of the whiskey was at the bottom of the hole. Amazingly, no one was seriously hurt.

"Damn that Fat Man Wiley! I told him not to dig under my saloon!" Tom Ashton fumed. Fat Man Wiley's rocking chair was empty. Apparently he knew it was not a good time to linger.

Eventually Hound Dog oversaw the recovery of the whiskey from Wiley's claim. Most of the bottles fell in soft dirt or on top of miners and were intact. Two Shovels Mitchell directed an effort to pull the unbroken chairs and tables out of the hole and Tom Ashton lead the effort to reassemble the Round Tent in the wagon yard fifty feet to the west. By midnight the saloon was back in business. Nebraska Joe and Old Shoes sat together at a table, their arms around each others' shoulders, drinking and laughing about the night the Round Tent fell into a mine. Doc Hollander wandered from table to table feeling the shape of men's heads. Knock Knees Stevenson was playing his grinding organ while Gordy McDougal did a Highland fling. Tom Ashton, cheered by the fact that his business had survived more or less intact, sat at the end of the bar and shared shots of whiskey with Fat Man Wiley (whom he had by now forgiven) and the woman named Lizzie. Jed and Jack joined them. The spirit of camaraderie seen in men (and women) forced together by difficult times was present on all fronts.

"See? I told you there was an advantage to having the saloon in a tent," Ashton said.

"You aren't hurt, are you Miss Lizzie? I'm so sorry I fell on you," Jack apologized.

"Don't worry about it, Mister Norris. I'm fine," the woman said. "Though I lost my favorite hat. I don't know why I bother to come into town on Saturday nights. Something like this always happens." She was smiling as she said it.

"It's a helluva place," Jed smiled. "I like it." Tom Ashton raised his glass.

"Welcome to Hangtown," the gambler-barber-saloon keeper said.

Most of the stores in Hangtown were general all-purpose mercantiles. The owners sold whatever they could get that they thought would sell. The F. Albertson Dry Goods store, for instance, carried a great deal of wet goods (canned food, dried meats & fruits, salted or pickled meats & vegetables and lots of liquor) and hardware (shovels, picks, hinges, nails) in addition to typical dry goods (clothing, boots, blankets). Mark Hopkins' grocery store sold mining supplies next to the food. Collis Huntington's hardware store had a healthy supply of whiskey. About the only category of merchandise that none of the stores in

Hangtown bothered to stock was books.

This was not because the miners couldn't read. Books were heavy and expensive to import from the east. Just after Jed and Jack reached San Francisco they heard of a newly arrived emigrant from New York who had sold a crate of magazines and newspapers for better than a thousand dollars. Having already collected their belongings from the freight warehouse (including the entire inventory of the store), The Boys immediately pulled all of the copies of the *Boston Herald* they had used to line their trunks and sold them for two weeks' room and board.

Tom Ashton's building was exactly what the Boys were looking for and they bought it from him. There were two rooms on the second floor which were serviceable bedrooms, so they relocated from the hotel. As soon as their wagons were unloaded they sold them (and the oxen) and used the proceeds to outfit the store properly. They purchased old lumber from Beaver Slim, who had several aged rockers he was replacing. The timbers from the disassembled rockers were turned into bookshelves. The most expensive part of the store wasn't merchandise or shelving. Jed had a cast iron wood stove brought up by wagon from San Francisco and installed at the back of the store.

After a week they were ready to open for business and gathered in front of the building to hang a sign painted by Jack. They stepped back to admire the sign as it swayed slightly in the breeze. In the center was a painting of Pegasus, the winged horse from Greek mythology, rising from the waters. Around the perimeter it read: *Bradford & Norris, Booksellers to the Savage West.*

Now, that may seem like a natural stopping point for this chapter. After all, the Boys have arrived in Hangtown (aka

Placerville in future chapters) and opened their bookstore. The stage is set and ready for further adventures. However, there is one last critical thing - critical to a bookseller, at least - which must be addressed;

Hangtown was a relatively quiet place during the week. Wagon trains passed through, coming down the Carson Trail, and they often stopped for the night. Most of the regular population was spread out across the mountains, washing dirt in the endless quest for gold. Some worked in teams and some worked alone. Their isolation came to an end each Saturday.

Late on Saturday afternoon they began to pour in from the countryside, a few at a time. The first stop for many was No Thumbs Franklin's Scale & Weights, where they had their dust and nuggets weighed. The ones with families back east posted letters. Tom Ashton put on his barber hat and cut hair. Mister Halliwell served some hot meals and made sure that everyone ate their pickles. A few smart men went to the town stores and spent some of their precious gold to buy supplies for the next week. Then, as the sun set they all settled in at one of the town's saloons to drink, gamble, and eventually lose all of the gold they had left.

A few miners went to the west end where the town's only official brothel was located. Six "ladies" lived and conducted their business there. There were only a few other women living in the greater Hangtown region and they chose a variety of ways to present themselves; the aforementioned Miss Lizzie (who, as it turned out, was half-Indian and half-French Canadian) lived out on the road to Coloma and could be found on most days wearing trousers and a duster, carrying a long rifle, out bagging venison; the Widow Rowland ran a boarding house on Sacramento Street; Miss Amy Swift was engaged to marry Mister W. H. Cooper and kept herself buttoned up in high collared blouses and long skirts that ended just below her boots; Almost Bill wore pants and generally passed for a man if you didn't look too closely (a misconception Almost Bill did not try to correct). There were also a few sundry wives, sisters, and laundresses scattered around the camps. However, by and large, this was a man's world, and women were a rare and precious commodity.

On Sunday morning the miners woke late, usually with hangovers, and those who weren't already broke drank and gambled some more. This is not to say that everyone in Hangtown was without faith. A small but dedicated group of Methodists communed for worship around ten o'clock. As the afternoon wore on the smart miners who bought their supplies on Saturday before they started drinking and gambling headed back out to their claims, loaded up with pork, beans, flour and eggs. The rest went to the stores and begged for credit. By Monday morning Hangtown was quiet again.

On the first Sunday after the opening of *Bradford & Norris, Booksellers to the Savage West,* Jed was having a brief conversation with Bad Luck Casey when the door opened and another customer entered. He did not look like the average miners who had so far visited the bookstore. He was stout and short, with long sideburns, a pale complexion, and he wore the uniform of a French military captain. Among the population of the mining country there were still some men who fancied themselves members of the American upper class or European elite, and Jean-Claude Auguste D'Autrefois de la Vieille was one of the latter. D'Autrefois believed he presented a more compelling presence in uniform than in ordinary mining clothes, and so went about dressed in this costume whenever he was in town. Unfortunately in time, and without proper laundering, it had grown worn, tattered, and dull. D'Autrefois' weary countenance lacked the assurance that might have compensated for this diminishment.

"I swear to all that's holy!" Jed was saying to Bad Luck Casey. "He was crossing the entire continent pushing a wheelbarrow. Somehow I've got to work that fellow into a story."

"*Excusé moi,*" D'Autrefois said quietly.

"Good afternoon," Jed smiled. Jack came up from the back of the store to see their new customer.

"I am Capitaine Jean-Claude Auguste D'Autrefois de la Vieille," the Frenchman said. "I understand you sell books."

"Yes, Monsieur de la Vielle," Jed said.

"D'Autrefois," the Frenchman corrected. After Jed and Jack each made an attempt at pronouncing his name, he amended it by saying, "Never mind that. Please just call me Jean-Claude. In the mines we have no titles."

The Boys appreciated his indulgence. "Very well, Jean-Claude. How can we help you?"

"I am looking for a book with the title of *La Cousine Bette.* It is written by Honoré de Balzac. Certainly you have heard of Honoré de Balzac?!"

"He's French, is that right?"

"*Mon Dieu!* Of course he is French!"

"The French Dickens," Jed said to Jack. Jean-Claude's face flushed red.

"No, sir! This Dickens is the British Balzac!"

"No insult was intended, sir," Jed smiled. He worked his way down the shelves and pulled out a book bound in red leather. "*La Cousine Bette*, although I am afraid it is the new English translation."

Jean-Claude was astonished. He took the book from Jed's hand, opened it, and gazed lovingly at its title page. "I never believed that you might actually have it! This is amazing, sirs, amazing! I must have it!"

In short order Jean-Claude paid for the book and hurried away, quite pleased with this small slice of home - even if it was a translation. When he and Bad Luck Casey had both gone Jed and Jack threw their arms around each other and jumped up and down laughing.

"He bought the book!" Jed said. "He bought the book!"

"I don't believe it!" Jack cried. Jed let go of Jack and collapsed in a chair next to the wood stove with a big smile on his face. Jack sat down next to him.

"Well, Jed," Jack said, "...that's one. That's one. But we're going to have to sell a hell of a lot more than one book in a week if we're going to make this work." He grinned. "I'll grant you it's a start!"

Next: A murder, a hanging, and an important visitor

IV.

THE CASE OF THE TERRIBLE TAXMAN
or
A MURDER IN HANGTOWN

1850

In which a murder is committed and a hanging is prevented

It was about eleven o'clock in the morning, mid-October, with the sun shining and a look of hard wet rain in the clearness of the foothills. Capitaine Jean-Claude Auguste D'Autrefois de la Vieille left the bookstore, devouring the crisp clean air and the invigorating scent of the wet earth. The clearing sky reflected from his blue uniform and his gold epaulets sparkled in the sunlight. In his hand he cradled a copy of *Tristan le Roux* by Alexandre Dumas. The Bookstore Boys, Jed & Jack, always made sure they had the most current French authors in stock for him, sometimes in the original French. When Jack told him the new book by Dumas was in stock he felt like it was his best bit of luck in a while. Life in the brand new State of California had not been kind to Jean-Claude. At the very least he could relax with a good book that reminded him of home.

Jean-Claude's last three claims turned up poor and weeks of further prospecting produced nothing resembling a decent claim. He "dropped a tool" a few times (to establish a claim to a piece of ground, all that was required was to leave it a pick or shovel that you could identify as yours) but they all turned up poor dirt. One day when he went into Hangtown for provisions Hard Head told him that someone had made a big strike out at Coon Hollow, more than fifteen hundred dollars in a single day. Jean-Claude hurried directly out to the Hollow, intending to stake off a claim in the same general area, but by the time he got there the entire hill was already staked into claims of thirty feet by thirty feet. Hundreds of men were busy to digging shafts while hundreds of latecomers like Jean-Claude were cursing that they arrived too late to make a claim.

At last Jean-Claude grew so desperate that he hired Hans Jungnickel, the diviner, to locate a decent claim. Jungnickel had a whale bone with which he dowsed for gold. The German man wandered around huffing and puffing, grasping one end of the bone in both hands saying "Kommen Sie zu mir," and mumbling about vibrations in its marrow. After a week (and $40 of Jean-Claude's dwindling resources) Jungnickel wandered across a watershed between two large granite boulders and yelled out "Ich fühle die Vibrationen!" He assured the Frenchman that there was a rich gold deposit directly under the spot. Jean-Claude took him at his word (what else could he do?) and dug for three weeks. Unfortunately he succeeded only in exposing more granite bedrock.

Just as things seemed hopeless, Jean-Claude's salvation arrived in the form of a man named Grayson Reed. Reed was renowned as a prospector. He had an amazing knack for finding gold deposits, although he seemed to have an aversion to mining itself. Reed said he enjoyed ranging the hills looking for likely claims and then, when he found one, selling them to other miners. Over the last two months this had worked out spectacularly well for him. He brought his latest discovery to Jean-Claude, knowing that the Frenchman was desperate.

"You are sure?" Jean-Claude asked. Reed's track record was good, but Jean-Claude couldn't help but think about the promises Jungnickel had made after his dowsing expeditions.

"I'll tell you what, my friend," Reed said. "I'll show you the spot and you can try it out for a couple of days. If you don't come up with pay dirt you can walk away, no harm done."

So Jean-Claude took the man's offer and Reed lead him to a spot in a flat between Newtown and Pleasant Valley. After two days of digging, rocking and washing Jean-Claude pulled about $270 in gold dust from the dig. He gladly paid Reed $1,000 for the claim and set up a permanent camp at the site.

The D'Autrefois (de la Vieille) family was, before the French Revolution, a very wealthy and titled family. Like most of the French aristocracy they were wiped out when the old order was disposed of and the new fraternatié arose. Most of Jean-Claude's cousins had retreated to modest homes, eking out enough income to pay for food and - gasp! - a single servant. Jean Claude, instead, embraced the new order. This modern world was one where old money couldn't just persist, resting on its laurels. Democracy meant that every man must make his own fortune. Jean-Claude gathered up what funds he could muster and set sail for San Francisco and the gold fields just beyond. Now the last of his precious old-world funds were in the hands of Grayson Reed in payment for this claim. Just one small and lonely coin rested in his purse. Still, Jean-Claude was confident that the next two days would bring him at least another $300 in gold, and the two days after that $300 more.

What Jean-Claude Auguste D'Autrefois de la Vieille did not know is that $300 was exactly the value of the gold dust Grayson Reed had "salted" the claim with. Reed's ability to find gold was, as most such amazing things usually are, too good to be true. His standard method-of-operation was as follows; he would find a likely (and isolated) site, stake a claim, load up his shotgun with gold dust and blast it into the ground. Hours later he led his mark to the spot and generously offered to let them mine the location before they paid him for the claim. Once the duped miner found gold at the site they were happy to pay him for the claim, generally three to four times the value of the dust he had "invested" in the site. In modern parlance he would be called a confidence man, a shady dealer, a liar and a fraud.

The next two days brought just $20 in gold dust from the claim, likely the remainder of Reed's salting. It was not as much as Jean-Claude hoped, although the continuing discovery of any gold at all kept him optimistic about his chances of striking it rich here. That Saturday afternoon he packed up his small leather sack of gold dust and his new copy of *Tristan le Roux*, hitched his mule to his rickety wagon, and headed into town.

The sun was setting behind the hills surrounding Hangtown when Jean-Claude rode in along Sacramento Street. Several men - including Dutch McGee, John Oakhurst, Grayson Reed and Two Shovels Mitchell - were gathered closely in the middle of the road, blocking his way, and he had to pull up his horse suddenly. At the center of the group was a slim stork-like man of Chinese origin. A short, fat fellow, greasy of complexion and with a signature black mustache, was prodding the Chinese man roughly in the chest.

"It's the law, Ah Moon!" the fat man said angrily to the Chinese man. "Signed into law by Governor Burnett! Twenty dollars a month. If you don't pay I'll have to report you and have Uncle Billy arrest you!"

William Rogers, the recently appointed Sheriff of El Dorado County, was known as "Uncle Billy" to the miners, for reasons which were not particularly clear. Perhaps it was because Uncle Billy understood the miners and gave them a fair amount of latitude. He realized how difficult life in the gold fields could be and that the miners sometimes needed to blow off a bit of steam. As long as they weren't stealing from each other or murdering each other he was willing to leave them alone.

"I can't afford twenty dollar a month," Ah Moon said. "I

don't mine that much anymore, anyway… I work in restaurant now! I late for work! Many men wait for dinner! Why you do this to me, Mister Matthew?" The tax collector smiled.

"It's a bonus, Ah Moon. I get paid to do away with undesirables like you. Now give me your tax or I'll have you arrested and deported back to China where you belong!"

"I don't have twenty dollar!" Ah Moon protested. Matthew pulled his six-shooter from its holster and pointed it at the Chinese man. The miners standing around to watch the altercation scattered.

"Then I get an even bigger bonus," Matthew laughed. "Let's go see Uncle Billy."

A hand came down on the tax collector's arm, suddenly and hard enough that he lost his grip on the pistol and it fell to the ground. The tax collector spun around as fast as his corpulent body would allow and faced Jean-Claude, whose tattered French military uniform, even in its current condition, gave him a certain air of authority.

"What is this?!" the taxman demanded.

"There is no need for guns, sir," Jean-Claude said. "Let us speak about this like gentlemen. This *Foreign Miner's Tax*, does this not strike you as unfair? We are *all* foreigners here, with the exception of the natives we erroneously refer to as Indians. There is no need to be cruel to this man."

"It's the law, Frenchman," Matthew sneered. The tax collector's eye remained on Jean-Claude as he picked up his gun. Once he had it in hand he looked around and saw that Ah Moon had used the distraction to run away up the street so that he wouldn't be late for work. The tax collector focused his anger on Jean-Claude. "Do you know what you have done? You've just assaulted a duly appointed officer of the state! You're interfering with official state business! I could have you jailed for that alone."

"I did not mean to assault you, Mister Matthew," Jean-Claude said, backing away. "I was merely coming to the aide of my fellow miner. You know… liberté, égalité, fraternité… it is in our Gallic blood."

"You're right that he's your 'fellow.' You foreigners are all getting in the way of honest, law-abiding Americans. You'll be next, Frenchman. You owe the twenty dollar tax the same as the Chinaman does."

"California has only been a state for a month. I hardly think it is possible at this time to determine who is American and who is not," Jean-Claude advised. "Regardless, I do not have the means to pay you any more than our friend Mister Ah Moon. Perhaps you should arrest me and we can go visit Uncle Billy together?" The tax collector was raising his gun to do just that when they were interrupted.

"Jean-Claude!"

Both men turned and saw Jed Bradford and Jack Norris standing on the boardwalk.

"We're headed to dinner, Jean-Claude," Jack said. "Care to eat with us?"

Jed smiled at the Tax Collector. "That is, if you're quite done with our friend."

"I'd be honored," Jean-Claude replied. As he gathered his horse and joined Jed and Jack the tax collector waved his pistol after them.

"This isn't over, Frenchman. I'll be coming to collect."

Jed, Jack and Jean-Claude headed over to the Iowa House. Dry Dirt Dan came by their table to take their orders and each asked for a Hangtown Fry.

A momentary culinary digression; the town's official dish was the Hangtown Fry. Essentially it is an omelet with bacon and fried oysters. Many myths have grown up about its origins. One story says that a miner, fresh off a hot strike, came into the El Dorado Hotel with a fat poke of gold dust and demanded the most expensive thing on the menu. The chef, it is said, proceeded to take the most expensive ingredients in his stores and mix them into a single dish. This story, of course, supposes that fresh eggs were difficult to come by, and that bacon and oysters were expensive. Another story said that a man placed in the Hangtown jail and destined for hanging requested the dish as his last meal, based on the expectation that the oysters would take a great deal of time to get and therefore delay his execution. The truth was much less colorful. Mule Team Fernandez, famed for his hard-hauling group of mules, also had a small ranch in El Dorado wherein he had more than three hundred chickens. F. Albertson's Dry Goods Store, famed for - as mentioned earlier - everything but dry goods, featured stacks of tinned meats brought up from Sacramento. Albertson had a personal preference for oysters, having grown up in Boston just a mile or so from where Jed and Jack once lived. The shellfish were plentiful in San Francisco Bay and popular with the miners. And bacon? Don't get me started on bacon. Quite the opposite of being rare and expensive, eggs, bacon and oysters were ubiquitous in Hangtown. It was hard to eat a decent dish that did not include them.

"...and I swear, he was crossing the entire continent with a wheelbarrow!" Jed was saying as they ate.

"Hasn't he told you that story before?" Jack wondered.

"Yes," Jean-Claude admitted, "but I figure that if he tells it enough times he will work out its problems and finally write it down." Jed turned a shade of crimson and apologized.

"So, how is that new Alexandré Dumas?" Jack asked Jean-Claude.

"Excellent," Jean-Claude answered. "Of course I wish it

were in the original French, but if wishes were horses I would be King of France."

He proceeded to tell the Bookstore Boys all about his new claim and all of the pay dirt he hit so far. They congratulated him on his good luck. "How is the bookstore faring?" he asked. Jed and Jack exchanged a glance.

"It's been a slow month," Jed admitted. "We sell every newspaper we can get our hands on, especially the ones from back east," he added brightly.

"The books are not doing as well?" Jean-Claude asked.

"We sold a copy of *Tristan le Roux*," Jack said dryly.

"That is all?!" Jean-Claude exclaimed. Jed shook his head.

"No, Jack is exaggerating. We've sold quite a few books this month."

"Seventeen," Jack elucidated.

"Eighteen," Jed corrected.

"Bad Luck Casey hasn't paid for his yet," Jack said. "And with a nickname like 'Bad Luck' I'm not making any predictions about when he's going to pay us."

"It's alright. The newspaper and magazine sales are paying most of the bills," Jed added.

"I am sure that I will make a rich strike any day," Jean-Claude said. "When it happens, my friends, I will come to your store and buy two dozen books."

"We appreciate that, Jean-Claude," Jed said.

The three of them finished their food and headed down the street to the Round Tent. Jean-Claude's dinner and the few supplies he'd ordered at Albertsons cleaned out his purse so the Boys offered to buy him drinks. They sat around a table with Tiny Morgan, Tom Ashton and Two Shovels Mitchell telling stories. This was the Boys' favorite part of the week. When the whiskey loosened their tongues the miners' stories just poured out. Jed often wished he was taking notes.

Across the tent in a dark corner Dutch McGee, John Oakhurst, Grayson Reed, and Matthew the Tax Collector sat around a table playing poker. Matthew kept an indignant eye focused on Jean-Claude throughout the evening. Jack encouraged Jean-Claude to ignore it.

"He's a little man with a little power. Put the two together and you often get a bully. Uncle Billy would never arrest you over a silly thing like failing to pay this *Foreign Miner's Tax*. He'd have to arrest half the miners in El Dorado County!"

The party broke up around midnight. Some miners, of course, would continue to drink and carouse until dawn. However, the Boys wanted to get some sleep, since Sunday was their busiest day of the week at the store. Jean-Claude was out of money. Tiny Morgan and Two Shovels had claims that were a good day's ride from Hangtown and they wanted to leave as soon as the sun rose.

The five of them exited from the back of the Round Tent into the freezing night air. As they came around the side of the tent a tall, broad figure suddenly loomed before them and blocked their way. Jack brought up his lantern to illuminate the individual's face.

The man was an Indian, with long black hair gathered in a tight braid which fell down his back from underneath a tall black hat. He was dressed in the typical attire of a miner, not in native garb, and unlike most Indians wore a short beard. His most distinguishing characteristic was his height. At more than six and a half feet he towered over Jed, Jack, and the three miners.

"*Bonsoir, D'Autrefois*," the Indian said in a low voice.

"Ah! *Bonsoir, Mon grand Shoshone*," Jean-Claude said. "*Quelle surprise!*"

The big Indian scrutinized Jed and Jack for a moment and then returned his attention to Jean-Claude. "*Venez avec moi.*"

"*Oui*, certainly," Jean-Claude said. "I must go," he told Jed and Jack. "Thank you very much for the drinks, messieurs. Good night." With that Jean-Claude and the Indian headed quickly down the street and disappeared in the darkness.

"What do you suppose that was about?" Jack asked as he and Jed returned to their rooms above the store.

"Very mysterious," Jed mused, and Jack knew from the way he said it that a tall, mysterious Indian would shortly become a character in his latest story.

The morning sun broke between the slats of a cabin wall and hit Jean-Claude squarely in the eye. Orange light filtered through his eyelids, pierced the fog blanketing his brain and he began to wake up slowly. As his conscious mind arose from sleep he noticed that it was chillier than usual. Then he became aware of a headache growing from the base of his neck and spreading across the crown of his head. Even though Jean-Claude was not in general a prodigious drinker he had experienced his share of mornings like this. It was unavoidable in the mining camps. What was unusual was that he could not remember where he was or how he got here. At last he sat up and observed his surroundings. He was lying on the dirt floor of a cabin with no blanket. Empty whiskey bottles littered the floor. As I said, none of this was completely surprising; nights in the gold country had a habit of leading to this sort of morning. The surprising thing was that he was alone. No other drunken miners lay passed out around him.

On further inspection it became clear that this was not a cabin at all. A few feet away, beyond the whisky bottles, was an anvil. As the light wedging its way through the wallboards grew brighter he saw the forge at the far end of the room, dark and quiet. Hammers and chains hung from the far wall. Although Jean-Claude was not a mechanical man he knew a smithy when he saw it.

He crawled to his feet and staggered to the door. It already hung open a few inches and the icy morning draft coming through this opening drove his headache forward and into his eyes. When he touched the door it swung open suddenly, and an object that had been resting against it fell into the building. Jean-Claude looked down at the shape blocking the doorway.

"Monsieur Matthew?" he asked.

A rattle of leaves - or perhaps the slamming of a door - woke Jed well before dawn. A cold wind was breathing in at the bedroom window. He got up, closed it and then lay in bed and listened to the wind. After an hour or two the rising sun successfully cut through the cold air and the breezes died in submission. Jed got up and washed in the old bowl on the table in the corner. He dressed in a cotton shirt and pair of denim pants and headed downstairs to the bookstore, expecting to find Jack there, preparing to open for the day. Instead he found the doors locked and the stove cold.

"Jack, Jack…," Jed shook his head. "Where have you gotten yourself to this morning?"

In either a serendipitous case of random circumstance or in direct response to his question there was a rattling at the lock and the door swung open to reveal his partner.

"Sorry I'm late," Jack said. "Stafford Hickey brought in some packages on his wagon this morning and I offered to help him deliver them." He dropped his coat behind the counter and hastily readied to open the store.

"These packages wouldn't have been for Miss Lizzie, would they?" Jed asked. Jack's face flushed ruddy with the suggestion.

"As a matter of fact they were," he admitted. "I was just helping Stafford."

"Of course you were," Jed said.

Jack opened the front door for business and Bad Luck Casey came immediately through the door. On an average day Bad Luck was an overwrought sort of fellow (an imbalance of humors, according to him), and today he seemed almost frenzied, with trembling hands and perspiration across his brow despite the cool temperature. Jed figured that he was probably going to live up to his nickname today.

"Have you heard the news?" Casey asked. "It was a busy night. Pair of murders - and with Uncle Billy out of town there's a cry for a couple of hangings!"

Although the Boys were as curious as anyone when it came to such vulgar, common, and popular affairs as hangings they weren't particularly shocked. This was Hangtown, after all. Although they believed that most of the miners intended to make an honest living digging for gold there were always a few, of course, whose weakness before temptation would invariably lead them to seek their fortune with something easier than a pick and shovel.

"What happened this time?" Jed asked with little energy.

"Well, first Irish Dick Crone - you know, the fellow who runs the monte at the El Dorado Saloon - cheated a digger from Diamond Springs and there was a fight. Dick killed the digger and now they're screaming to take him and all the gamblers in town and string 'em up at the hangin' tree."

"You chose this town, Jed, remember that," Jack said.

"And then Honest Alex arrested Jean-Claude over at Ollis and Hinds' smithy!" Bad Luck added.

Jed, who was still barely awake, looked up in surprise and said sarcastically, "What did he do, fail to pay his taxes?"

"No!" Bad Luck exclaimed. "He done gone and murdered the tax collector, that Mister Matthew! Stabbed him in the heart, they say!"

Casey's words were a cold splash of water in their faces.

Now Jed and Jack were completely awake. Jack demanded that Bad Luck give them all the sordid details. His report was concise; Matthew the Tax Collector had been found stabbed to death outside of the Ollis and Hinds' blacksmith shop. Jean-Claude Auguste D'Autrefois de la Vieille was still kneeling next to Matthew's body when several other miners arrived. The town constable was summoned and Dutch McGee quickly volunteered everything he knew about the previous night's altercation between Jean-Claude and the tax collector. In light of this clear motivation, the circumstances, and the general attitude toward quick justice in Hangtown, Jean-Claude was immediately arrested.

"It's that Dutch McGee!" Bad Luck exclaimed. "He loves a good hanging! He's always trying to get someone in trouble!"

Now, before you pass judgment on the good people of Hangtown, one might consider the following; the new state of California, just weeks old, had not yet organized its court system in 1850. The county was newly formed and the Sheriff only recently appointed. The first execution resulting from due process at an official county District Court under a judge would not occur until 1854. Hangtown had a jail, but there were no long-term accommodations available for lawbreakers in state prisons. The closest judge was in San Francisco (perhaps Sacramento). The responsibility to maintain some semblance of law and order in the gold country rested with the people, and sometimes their justice was swift.

Jed left Jack minding the store and hurried over to the jail with Bad Luck. A crowd was gathering in front of the building, many of them cursing and calling for the ne'er-do-wells inside to be immediately hung. Barely audible amidst the cries of *"Hang 'em! Justice!"* were a few voices claiming Jean-Claude wasn't capable of the act of murder and demanding his release. (No one, I might add, was making any similar pleas on the behalf of Irish Dick. Most of the assembled miners had suspected him of waxing the cards for quite some time.) The town constables, Honest Alex Hunter and Johnny Clark, were doing their best to keep some order and prevent the angry mob from lynching their prisoners. It took Jed a few minutes to get Hunter's attention.

"Alex, where is Uncle Billy?" he asked.

"Billy got an order from Governor Burnett to muster two hundred men for a militia to fight Indians up near Auburn and Illinoistown," Hunter said with a worried expression. "He won't be back to Coloma till tomorrow night."

Cursing this turn of events, Jed turned around to find Tom Ashton, Hangtown's resident miner, gambler, saloon-keeper, lawyer, doctor and barber, standing at his elbow. Today, if asked, he would likely have left "gambler" out of his title thanks to the nefarious deeds of Irish Dick.

"Shall I put on my lawyering hat?" Ashton asked. "Sounds like Jean-Claude is going to need some representation quick."

"That's a good idea," Jed agreed. "Maybe you can get in to see him and find out what happened."

While Tom appealed to Honest Alex and Johnny for the opportunity to speak to his "client," Jed searched the crowd for any individuals who were prone to believe Jean-Claude was innocent. The Fisher Brothers liked Jean-Claude and were disposed to supporting him, as were Two Shovels Mitchell and Point-of-No-Return Willy. Doc Hollander offered that he had felt Jean-Claude's head on several occasions and according to his detailed study of phrenology he could attest to the fact that the Frenchman was a decent, stand-up individual. Eventually Jed had a small group gathered on the north side of the street opposite the jail.

"We need to make sure the crowd doesn't get out of hand," Jed told them. "Give them some time and they'll calm down."

"That's going to be hard, considering how mad the diggers

are about Irish Dick," Two Shovels said. "The miners have been robbed one too many times by these professional gamblers. This sort of fight was bound to happen eventually, and the diggers are calling for blood."

Tom Ashton joined them. "Alex and Johnny won't let me see Jean-Claude until Uncle Billy gets back tomorrow, or maybe the day after that."

"They'll have him tried, sentenced and hung by that time," Jed said. "We have to do something."

When Jed returned to the bookstore Jack was busy pouring through the pages of a thick leather-bound volume. Jed was perplexed that his partner would be reading while their best customer and friend was in danger of immediate death until Jack made clear his method.

"*The Murders in the Rue Morgue* by Edgar Allan Poe," Jack said, indicating the book. "Featuring the brilliant rationalist C. Auguste Dupin." He held up another volume for Jed to take. "This one includes Poe's other two Dupin stories, *The Mystery of Marie Rogêt* and *The Purloined Letter.*"

"How is reading Poe going to help us free Jean-Claude?" Jed asked, taking the book.

"Elementary, my dear Jed," Jack said. "The only way we are going to free Jean-Claude is to prove his innocence. We must use Poe's *ratiocination* - rational deduction based on information obtained - to discover the true murderer and show that Jean-Claude didn't commit the crime. Just as Dupin's clever mind proved the innocence of Adolphe Le Bon on the Rue Morgue."

"Seems like a sound idea," Jed agreed. "It's better than just waiting here for the crowd to lynch Jean-Claude. Where do we begin?" Jack scanned the text of *The Murders in the Rue Morgue* for a moment.

"Dupin started at the scene of the crime," he said. "I suppose we should start there too. Get depositions from the witnesses, that sort of thing."

The Boys locked up the store, leaving a sign on the door which said they were temporarily closed and would return the next morning, and hurried down the street to Ollis and Hinds' blacksmith shop.

The smithy was operating in a business-as-usual manner with no outward evidence that a murder took place there that very morning. The forge was so hot that even twenty feet away on a cool October morning the Bookstore Boys could feel the radiant heat. The smith's owners were busy working, one shoeing horses and the other at his anvil repairing mining equipment. In the wagon yard young Johnny Studebaker was attaching a metal rim to a wagon wheel. Just as it was for everyone else in Hangtown, Sunday was a busy day for Ollis and Hinds. Their customers wanted to get back to their claims.

"Johnny," Jed called out, addressing the teenager in the wagon yard. The boy looked up for just a moment.

"Hello, Mister Bradford, Mister Norris," he said politely as he wrestled with the metal rim which was refusing to settle onto the wagon wheel without a fight. "Is there something I can help you with?"

"We're enquiring regarding the murder that took place this morning," Jack said. "Attempting to gather depositions and what-not."

Johnny Studebaker gave up with a heavy sigh and let the uncooperative rim drop to the ground. "I told everything I know to Honest Alex Hunter this morning," he said. "I wasn't here when they found that dead Mister Matthew and Jean-Claude. I was still asleep over there in the haystack." He leaned in and quietly added, "Enjoyed a good bottle of sloe gin last night and neither heaven nor earth was going to wake me early this morning."

Jed glanced around the smithy yard. "Johnny, do you have any idea why Jean-Claude and Mister Matthew were here in the first place? Doesn't seem a likely place to be on a Sunday morning."

The boy shrugged. "I can't say I know why either of them was here this morning, because I don't. I suppose Jean-Claude was here for the same reason I was here. Too much sloe gin." The Boys gave each other a surprised glance.

"Jean-Claude was drinking here last night?"

"Sure," Johnny said. "He and the Indian stopped by with the gin. The Indian wanted his wagon fixed and offered me a few drinks in exchange for the repairs." The boy rubbed the back of his head. "More than just a few drinks."

"When did they leave?" Jack asked.

"I don't know," Johnny replied. "I finished fixing the wagon and fell asleep in the hay loft in order to stay warm. When I woke up this morning the Indian was gone and Honest Alex was arresting Jean-Claude for killing Mister Matthew."

"Do you know the Indian's name?" Jed pressed. Johnny Studebaker thought for a moment.

"No, I don't think so. I mean, they might have said it, but how is a body to know? Those two are always speaking French."

"Always? You've seen the Indian before?"

"A few times, always with Jean-Claude. I don't think he lives around here, though. His wagon has been repaired before by Tongs Logan, the carpenter over in Coloma. I'd recognize Logan's work anywhere." Johnny reached into his pocket and pulled out a kerchief. "He left this here last night. I was going to keep it for the pretty picture, but I suppose if it will help find him its better that you had it."

Jed and Jack inspected the cloth, which appeared to be silk - much finer and more delicate than the average fabric found in frontier California. A coat of arms was embroidered on the kerchief in splendid colored threads; a shield illustrated with several rows of deer antlers capped with a hunting horn. Out of the horn's mouthpiece sprouted three feathers in red, white, and blue. Below was a stylized "W."

"An Indian with a family crest?" Jed asked.

"This looks familiar," Jack said. "I think I've seen it somewhere before."

"Maybe it's Jean-Claude's. He comes from some sort of old blood," Jed suggested.

The Boys thanked Johnny for his help and headed back down the street toward the jail. It seemed clear to them now; The Indian had killed the tax collector and left Jean-Claude passed out at the smithy to collect the blame. The general attitude of the miners concerning Indians was hardly any better than their attitude concerning gamblers, so the prospect of placing the blame for Matthew's death on the Indian in order to exonerate Jean-Claude was good. They hurried back to the jail.

"What Indian?" Dutch McGee asked after the Boys had presented their case to Honest Alex, Johnny Clark, and the gathered miners. "What's his name? Did anyone see him around the tax collector? Why did he want to kill Matthew? Sounds like a trick to get the Frenchman out of the noose!" The crowd grumbled in agreement.

"Sorry," Honest Alex said to Jed and Jack. "You boys will have to do better than that. Just wait until Uncle Billy gets back, he'll sort it all out." Still, the proposal that a rogue Indian committed the crime rather than one of their own sat well with some of the miners and others were less forceful in their calls for Jean-Claude's death. (I might add here that the calls for Irish Dick to be executed were as forceful as ever.) Even though Jed and Jack's new scenario was not universally accepted it had at the very least reduced the chance that

Jean-Claude would be lynched before Uncle Billy returned. This state of affairs would not last, however. Jed could see Dry Dirt Dan thinking hard about the situation. Thinking hard was a bother to most of these miners, and taking the easy route and just calling for Jean-Claude's death would eventually win the day.

"This rational deduction thing is not going to be as easy as we'd hoped," Jack said. "What are we going to do now?"

"We have to find that Indian!" Jed exclaimed.

They split up and began asking around to see if anyone else knew the Indian. Of course Tiny Morgan and Two Shovels Mitchell had seen him when they left the Round Tent along with Jed and Jack, but didn't know any more than The Boys did. Tom Ashton, still wearing his lawyer hat, had the only helpful suggestion.

"Johnny Studebaker said that the Indian's wagon had been repaired by Tongs Logan over in Coloma. Maybe Tongs knows who he is."

"That's a day's ride. By the time we get back Jean-Claude might be dead," Jack worried.

"Well, even if we don't learn anything new, at least we might meet Uncle Billy halfway and tell him what's happened," Jed offered. "Let's stop by the store and get some things."

Jack packed some food, water, and blankets in their saddle bags for the trip to Coloma. When he came searching for Jed he found his partner sitting in one of the bookshop aisles pouring over a dusty tome.

"More Poe?" Jack asked.

"No, take a look at this," Jed said. He pointed to the kerchief that they had gotten from Johnny Studebaker and then turned the book around so that Jack could see it. The illustration on the page matched the embroidery exactly. "It's the coat of arms of the Dukes of Württemberg, one of those German states near Bavaria."

"I swear I have seen that crest somewhere before. What would an Indian be doing with a silk kerchief belonging to a royal family from Württemberg?" Jack wondered. "This just gets stranger and stranger." Jed picked up a different book from the floor next to him.

"Do you recall that Jean-Claude referred to the Indian fellow as '*Mon grand Shoshone*'? If you recall your Lewis and Clark, the Shoshone are from the Missouri River valley and north along the Montana territory. All of the Indians around here are from the Mi-Wok, Maidu and Mono tribes."

"So the man we are looking for is Shoshone, many hundreds of miles from home, speaks French and knows European royalty," Jack concluded.

"Well, that should make him easier to find," Jed offered.

They hurried down to Elstner's Yard where their horses were boarded and saddled them for the ride to Coloma. The road took them out through Log Cabin Ravine and up to the Coloma Road. Hangtown was now far below them in the canyon formed by Hangtown Creek, although the view of the town was obscured by the smattering of oak trees that remained on the hillside. The road continued along the ridge until it dropped precipitously in a series of switchbacks into the American River canyon. Not long after they achieved the heights and were descending toward Coloma they passed a small cabin almost hidden from view in a thicket of oak trees to their left. Jack stared at it longingly; the way a thirsty man might yearningly gaze at cold, clear well as he passed it without drinking.

"Jack, isn't that where Lizette, lives? The woman you keep finding excuses to visit?" Jed asked.

"Yes," Jack answered. "That's Lizzie's place." Jack's horse complained as he suddenly reined it to a stop. "That crest! The coat of arms of the Dukes of Württemberg!" he said. "I think I remember why it seemed so familiar. It was on a silver tea pot I saw in Lizette's cabin!"

Several revelations came to Jed all at once. "Jack, isn't Lizette half-Indian? And wouldn't you consider Lizette a French name?" he asked.

Jed wheeled his horse around. "I think that ratiocination requires that we pursue this."

The Boys left the road and followed a narrow track through the dry grass to the pile of friendly lumber in the middle of the clearing. It was no more than twelve by twelve feet in size, made of rough hewn timbers and shaded by a huge oak tree. The uneven roof was hidden under a thick coat of bright green moss. Both Jed and Jack dismounted and Jed knocked at the door. Lizzie answered, her hands covered in flour, and leaned over to pick up a fallen spoon. Even bent over she seemed tall. Her milk and coffee skin was radiant and her long dark brown hair hung enchantingly about her shoulders. With eyes that smiled before her mouth did, she looked up at Jack. The Boys were instantly charmed.

"Hello, Mister Norris," she said. "Back so soon?"

"Yes, maam," Jack replied.

"Miss Lizette," Jed said. "Thaddeus and I would like to talk to you if you have a moment." Jack frowned at the use of his formal name.

"Jack," he said. He smiled at Lizette. "Everyone calls me Jack."

"Certainly. What may I do for you?"

Jack stood at hand, speechless for the moment, so Jed took up their purpose.

"We're looking for a man, an Indian. He has long hair that he wears in a braid, tall black hat, and has a short beard. Very tall fellow."

Lizette turned away from them to wash in a bucket of water that was sitting on the porch. It clouded white as she rinsed the flour from her hands. "Excuse me," she said, "I have been making breads and am quite a mess." She reached back into the cabin for a towel, dried her hands and wiped her face (beautiful face, Jack thought.)

"Very tall? Black hat?" Jed asked. "He carried this." Jed held up the kerchief with the coat of arms.

"No, no..." Lizette apologized quickly. "I don't believe I do. I am not from these parts and do not know many of the natives."

Jack indicated the kerchief. "It's strange, Lizette... Miss Charbonneau... yet I might have sworn that I saw that same crest on a tea pot in your cabin when I helped bring in your supplies from Sacramento."

"No, no," she said, her hands trembling (although not as much as Bad Luck Casey's). "You must be mistaken. I have never seen such a crest."

Jack tipped his hat to her. "I'm sure you're right. We didn't mean to upset you. Thank you very much for your time." He started to take his horse's reins (still looking at Lizette) when Jed spoke up again.

"*Mon grand Shoshone*," he said. Lizette looked up in surprise and then turned back to the milky white water in the bucket. It was too late. Her startled expression had already given her away. "So, you *do* know him," Jed said.

When Lizette turned back to face them her eyes were pleading instead of smiling. "Messieurs," she said, "please leave him alone. He has done nothing. He likes his privacy, and who can blame him? He is a good man who merely wishes to be left alone."

"We don't want any trouble," Jack said. "We need his help. Our friend, Jean-Claude, has been arrested for murder and this

Indian man may be the only person who can clear his name."

"Jean-Claude?! D'Autrefois? Arrested?! *Mon Dieu!* Please, come inside!" she said. She brought them into the tiny cabin and offered them seats on a short wooden bench. Jack, hopelessly smitten, watched her move gracefully about the room and until Jed began to speak almost forgot the mission that had tasked them to this place.

"This man… are you close?" Jed asked. This idea (at least the way Jed presented it) had not occurred to Jack and he froze waiting for Lizette's answer. Luckily for Jack relief was quick in coming.

"The man you ask about is my brother, Jean-Baptiste," she said. "He lives near Growlersburg on the divide. That kerchief was given to him by the Duke of Württemberg, Paul Wilhelm, a good friend. Jean-Baptiste was here this morning. He arrived just after you delivered my packages from Mister Hickey. You might have passed him on the road. How is it that he can help Jean-Claude?"

Jed and Jack told Lizette the entire story; how Jean-Claude argued with the tax collector the night before, how he left them at the Round Tent in the company of her brother, how he was seen drinking with her brother at the Ollis and Hinds smithy, and how he was found kneeling over the body of the tax collector the next morning. As she listened, furrows of resolve formed around Lizette's smiling eyes and then she leapt to action.

"Jean-Baptiste left here no more than an hour ago," she said. "His wagon is not in the best of repair, so he will travel slowly. We should be able to catch him on horseback."

"We had best hurry," Jed said.

"I should come with you," Lizette said. "My brother, as I said, is a bit of a recluse. He will speak to you more freely if I am there."

They hurried out of the cabin, Jack lifted Lizette to his horse and then swung into the saddle in front of her. She put her arms around his waist as he spurred the horse and it galloped forward following Jed, who was already riding fast toward the road. Despite the urgent and desperate mission they were on, Jack thought it was the most enjoyable ride of his life.

The oaks, pines and firs flew past the riders as they took a breakneck pace down the winding trail. More than once innocent riders, taking their leisure for a Sunday ride, were overtaken by the two fleet-footed steeds and collisions were narrowly avoided. In less than an hour the trio of riders reached the bottom of the canyon and the road widened. Just a few miles short of Coloma they came upon a slow moving wagon and Lizette called out that it was her brother.

Jean-Baptiste Charbonneau stood up on his wagon and watched in surprise as his sister approached. She did not wait for the Boys to introduce themselves before relating to her brother the entire story of Jean-Claude Auguste D'Autrefois de la Vieille and the Tax Collector. The Indian was completely silent as Lizette told the tale. When she finished his response was brief and to the point.

"Thank you, my friends," Charbonneau said as he unharnessed his horse from the wagon and mounted it bareback. "I will return with you to seek Jean-Claude's release." Their tired horses turned around and with some trepidation started back up the winding road toward Hangtown.

"This ratiocination process doesn't seem all that difficult," Jed said smugly.

"Especially when it is helped along by dumb luck," Jack replied.

In the absence of the Bookstore Boys things in Hangtown did not remain fixed. Dutch McGee, still angling for a decent hanging, circulated through the crowd doing his best to breed resentment and anger. Eventually the tide of rage grew until two members of the mob, Dudders Humphrey and Biscuit Foot Wallace, were appointed Justices of the Peace by acclamation. In little more than five minutes they reviewed the facts at hand (most of them completely inaccurate, as the tales of the crimes had become embellished as they were passed around, as always happens with such hearsay and gossip) and they declared both men guilty as charged. Upon this pronouncement the miners at last moved on the jail. Honest Alex Hunter and Johnny Clark considered their situation judiciously and made a tactical retreat. The miners broke down the door to the jail and emerged carrying Irish Dick and Jean-Claude. Jean-Claude's supporters - and there were many now - called for his release, yet they were drowned out by the miners calling for blood. Amid cries of *"Hang 'em! Hang 'em!"* the mob carried the two to the hanging tree in Elstner's hay yard.

Irish Dick kept a stiff upper lip. As a gambler he was used to presenting a good poker face. Jean-Claude likewise showed little emotion because he had to do his family and his nation proud. He straightened and dusted off his uniform as best he could so that he could die looking like the *Capitaine* he used to be.

Dutch McGee, of course, was the man who tossed the rope over the monstrous limb, almost as big around as the trunk of the terrible oak. The end of the line was already twisted into the noose through which Jean-Claude's life would soon pass.

The two prisoners were mounted on horses. On occasion the folks of El Dorado County built a gallows in order to conduct a proper hanging, but in Hangtown the citizens had a particularly warm spot in their hearts for the tree in Elstner's Hay Yard. Several men laid out picnic lunches on an abandoned pile of rocks and dirt. They were not necessarily any more cold-blooded than the average fellow. In a land that, at least until recently, was without law, the pursuit of justice was reassuring and satisfying. In addition to the solace offered by the rule of law, in this particular case one of the men about to take the tumble was a professional gambler, and the miners *really* hated the gamblers.

Johnny Clark, resigned to serving out the people's will, brought his horse up alongside Jean-Claude's and lead it up to the noose. He slipped the dreaded rope around the Frenchman's head. Holding Jean-Claude's horse tightly he said, "Any last words?" A hush spread throughout the mob from its center.

Jean-Claude said a brief prayer, which no one else understood, of course, because it was in French.

"Wait! Stop!" a voice cried out.

Three exhausted horses came thundering through the crowd, and the hundreds of assembled miners dashed from their path to avoid being trampled. Jed Bradford stood high in the saddle of the first, Jean-Baptiste Charbonneau rode bareback on the second, and Jack Norris was on the third with Lizette Charbonneau clinging to him. Jack pulled up his mount directly in front of the horse on which Jean-Claude sat so that it couldn't move. Jed addressed Honest Alex Hunter and Johnny Clark and at the same time spoke loudly enough to be heard by a fair number of the miners gathered around them.

"We have a witness who can testify on Jean-Claude's behalf!" he cried. A rolling murmur of curiosity, disbelief, and common gossip spread across the hay yard. "This is Jean-Baptiste Charbonneau, who was with Jean-Claude last night. Jack Norris and I, Tom Ashton, Tiny Morgan and Two Shovels Mitchell can all attest to the fact. Please give him a chance to speak!"

The tall Indian remained on his horse so that he could look at his friend's accusers directly. "My friends, I am not, I fear, the most social of men. I apologize for being at times less than friendly with all of you. Many of you have, I am sure, seen me with Jean-

Claude D'Autrefois from time to time, that he is *mon amie*. I was with him last night, drinking while my wagon was repaired at Ollis and Hinds. I left him, very early in the morning, passed out near the forge. I am certain that he was in no condition to kill anyone."

Now, truth be told, most of the assembled mob was there to celebrate the hanging of Irish Dick. A few of them had genuine affection for *The Capitaine* and were actively campaigning for his release. The rest did not know Jean-Claude personally and had no stake in his continued survival. Neither did they have any specific desire to see him hung. His death was, at best, merely an opening act to the execution of Irish Dick. In fact, quite a few would have been willing to let Jean-Claude go right there and then if it would let the show proceed directly to its main event. A general consensus reflecting this attitude began to circulate.

Unfortunately Dutch McGee had other plans. His personal opinion was that if one hanging was good, then two were sensational. "Hold on just a damn minute!" Dutch exclaimed. "That doesn't mean anything! Are you sayin' that the Frenchman couldn't have killed the Tax Collector because he was drunk?!" He turned to the mob for support. "Nobody has ever killed a man when he was drunk, have they, boys?" A fair number of the miners laughed.

"Listen!" Jed shouted. "A lot of you are friends with Jean-Claude. Do you really think he is capable of such a thing?"

The tide turned again. Miners who knew Jean-Claude nodded and across the mob they told their neighbors stories about the Frenchman's goodwill and kind spirit. Dutch McGee grew visibly frustrated and took up a shovel and gold pan, banging them together.

"The tax collector was going to have him arrested! We know it!" he yelled. "And who is this 'witness'? An Injun! Are you going to take the word of an Injun over your common sense?"

"We don't listen to no Injuns!" a miner yelled from the crowd. "Hang the Frenchman!" The passions of the assembled men again changed, growing more angry and insistent. Jed looked at Jack, Jack at Jean-Baptiste Charbonneau, and none of them could think of another thing to say.

"That man is no Injun!" a strong baritone voice called out. "He is my brother!" The assembled citizens turned as one to watch a tall man riding a proud black stallion force his way through the crowd. He wore a uniform which was recognized by a number of the miners; that of a major in the Missouri battalion. The buttons on his jacket shone, a perfect pile of lustrous hair cascaded luxuriantly from his head. His lantern jaw and cleft chin framed a perfect face with brilliant eyes. His flawless smile radiated across the hay yard as he waved to Jean-Baptiste Charbonneau. Like a great marble statue, revealed from natural stone by the imagination of a great renaissance sculptor, he paused gloriously in the middle of the mob.

"Clark!" Charbonneau called out. *"Mon frère!"*

"We are trying to have a hanging here!" Dutch McGee howled. "Who the hell are you?!" The dashing figure on the horse took off his hat and waved it to the crowd.

"I am Meriwether Lewis Clark, late of the war with Mexico, son of William Clark - best known for the expedition which bore his name - on my way back home to Missouri, come to see my dear brother in spirit and heart, Jean-Baptiste Charbonneau, son of the Indian squaw Sacagawea, who was instrumental in the success of my father's mission!"

A cheer went up through the crowd. No man here, especially those who had made the long journey across the North American continent by land, was unfamiliar with Major Clark's nationally famous father. The miners standing closest to Meriwether Lewis Clark reached out to shake his hand. Those who could not quite reach him merely touched his horse. It is possible that a few of the men swooned in a faint. The great black stallion pranced forward until it stopped between Jean-Baptiste Charbonneau's horse and the mount Jean-Claude D'Autrefois sat precariously upon. A fair amount of the glory emanating from Clark's splendid uniform transferred to the worn, yet proud uniform which Jean-Claude wore. Next to Meriwether Lewis Clark, Jean-Claude D'Autrefois resembled a brave and noble war hero, recently returned from battle. The lionhearted Clark put his hand on Jean-Claude's shoulder.

"If my brother testifies to this man's character, then I tell you that he is an innocent man!"

A cheer went up from the gathered citizens, including cries of "let him go!" Jed took the sudden reversal as an opportunity to reach out and remove the noose from Jean-Claude's neck. Honest Alex Hunter did nothing to stop him.

"Now, hold on a damned minute!" Dutch McGee shrieked. "Nothing has changed, just because this man says so! I say, no matter how agreeable the Frenchman is on an average day, he got drunk and when the tax collector came to collect, he killed him! He was found bending over the body! If you folk are so positive that the Frenchman didn't do it, then I ask you this; who did it?!"

The miners fell quiet and then began to talk amongst themselves. This time Tom Ashton, miner, gambler, saloon-keeper, lawyer, doctor and barber, spoke up, presumably wearing his lawyer hat.

"He committed suicide," Tom suggested.

"What?!" Dutch McGee cried.

"It was suicide," Tom Ashton said, more reassured. "He came to the smithy to collect Jean-Claude's taxes, but then, in a moment of despair, threw himself on a knife."

"Sounds right to me!" Major Meriwether Lewis Clark

declared, and the mob cheered. Honest Alex Hunter threw up his hands and signaled that Jed could go ahead and release Jean-Claude. Jed grabbed the reins of the Frenchman's horse and they worked their way through the crowd to Jack and Lizette Charbonneau's side. Jean-Baptiste joined them and with Tom Ashton they all headed over to the Round Tent for drinks. Major Clark joined them about two hours later, having been surrounded by miners begging for his autograph.

"You're absolutely right, Mister Clark!" they said. "He was completely innocent!"

"No friend of yours could possibly have killed a government official!" others said, asking for stories about Major Clark's illustrious father.

And thus it went, establishing the exoneration of Jean-Claude Auguste D'Autrefois de la Vieille as the first in a great tradition of celebrity justice in the state of California.

After Major Clark retired to the Round Tent the crowd of miners, comforted by their act of charity toward Jean-Claude, proceeded with the other matter at hand. After all, this was Hangtown. Irish Dick was hung. (I will not type that sentence again, so if you are a reader of prurient mind you may go back and read it again yourself.) With both their consciences salved and their thirst for blood quenched, the mob dispersed. As a result of the hanging most of the professional gamblers in town left for gold camps with less acrimony toward their profession. For the next several weeks (at least) the miners were able to lose all of their money fairly in games that weren't fixed.

The next day Jed Bradford went by the smithy and thanked Johnny Studebaker for his help. While there he told Johnny the non-story of the Wheelbarrow Man. Johnny wasn't really interested in Jed's tale, but it gave him an idea; instead of repairing wagons for Ollis and Hinds he decided to start his own business making wheelbarrows. This turned out to be highly lucrative and a couple of years later "Wheelbarrow Johnny" returned to Indiana to join the family wagon manufacturing firm. By the turn of the century he was building "horseless carriages" under the Studebaker name, including a 1902 model (beloved by Thomas Edison) which was one of the world's first electric cars.

By the end of the week things calmed down a bit in Hangtown, on account of the fact that Major Meriwether Lewis Clark left for Missouri. Jean-Baptiste Charbonneau, a recluse still at heart, returned to his cabin in the mountains beyond Growlersburg. The miners finally got back to their claims and the fevered hunt for gold became once more the topic of life in the camps of El Dorado.

Over the following month Jack Norris began leaving work early and taking Saturdays off, riding up the Coloma Road to visit Lizette Charbonneau. Over dinner he drew pictures for her and soon the inside of her tiny cabin was wallpapered with sketches of gold country life. Many of the drawings featured portraits of Lizzie herself.

That leaves, I suppose, just one loose end to this story. Just who did kill Mr. Matthew, the tax collector? Was it really suicide? History does not provide an answer. However, several days after the tax collector's death, a disagreement broke out down on Weber Creek over a particular claim. The miner, who had purchased the site from Mr. Grayson Reed, felt the quality of the location and the quantity of gold therein was not what Reed had promised and accused the latter of "salting" the claim. In the ensuing argument punches were thrown, guns were fired, and Grayson Reed wound up as dead as Irish Dick. Curiously, a leather poke which was identified as belonging to Mr. Matthew was found amongst Reed's belongings.

Jean-Claude Auguste D'Autrefois de la Vieille would not have had cause for such a disagreement with Reed. In the weeks following his release he struck a rich deposit of gold at the claim that Grayson Reed had sold him. It was not enough to send him home to France in triumph, but that was just as well. California was now his home and the citizens of this town - despite the fact that they almost hung him - were now his family. The only money he would ever require was just enough that he could join his friends for drinks and a Hangtown Fry.

Next: The Power of Books changes Placerville

V.

THE GREAT FIRE OF 1856
or
THE MODERN PROMETHEUS

1856

*In Which the Play's The Thing, Nugget Buys a Book,
and the Spirit of Men, Women & Players is tested by the fiery holocaust*

The story of The Great Fire of 1856, a cataclysm whose aftereffects still inform the character of El Dorado County a century and a half later, begins with a digression of sorts. It starts one morning before the sun even had a chance to show its pretty face, at the Big Secret Diggin's Mine.

The Big Secret Diggin's Mine was, as the name might suggest, the worst kept secret in California. In the early days of the Gold Rush there was a lot of claim jumping, and during 1849 Patrick "Big Mouth" McMahon twice lost a choice spot of pay dirt to better armed men. So when McMahon discovered a large quartz vein that seemed to accompany a great deal of gold he filed his claim and then clammed up. McMahon never discussed the location of his mine. Every time he headed back out after buying supplies in Placerville (as the new, more genteel Hangtown had come to be called) he took a different route. He drank alone, because he was afraid that if he drank with others he might let the mine's location slip in a moment of inebriation. People started to call him "Close Cards" McMahon, and it wasn't because he played poker well.

Eventually his success made it difficult to maintain the secrecy. As the mine grew he had to hire men to help him dig into the hillside following the veins of gold-bearing quartz. He hired still more men to build a flume which could carry water to the mine site. The operation kept getting larger and larger until McMahon and his team were conducting daily blasting in order to burrow further into the heavy slate mountainside. Then he built a stamp mill to crush the ore into powder and wash it with water and quicksilver to separate the gold. By that time the secret was definitely out, since you could hear the stamp mill in operation more than a mile away.

In the summer of 1851 McMahon's paranoia proved well-founded. Just before breakfast, about a quarter hour after sunrise, one of his new men pulled out a shotgun and tried to steal the week's take. Unfortunately for the gunman McMahon had secretly hired a group of Irish mercenaries for just such an eventuality. Fortunately for the robber most of the Irish mercenaries decided to switch sides and join him in the robbery. Unfortunately for all of these traitors and turncoats McMahon had also hired a group of German mercenaries to keep watch on the Irish mercenaries. The German mercenaries stayed loyal to McMahon, tied up the gunman and back-stabbing Irish, and hauled them all off to meet justice in Placerville. This faithfulness was lucky for the Germans, because McMahon had also employed a group of Chinese mercenaries to keep watch on them.

Despite all of these men coming and going from the mine they still referred to the operation as the Big Secret Diggin's Mine. Some folks called it the No Big Secret Diggin's Mine. Virtually everyone knew about it. That wasn't so bad in itself, because the worst days of gunmen and claim jumping were just about over. What was really bad for Close Cards McMahon was that the mine was starting to play itself out. To make matters worse there was a fire in the stamp mill, and all mining was on hold until the damage could be repaired. McMahon and the twelve men he employed spent the last week rebuilding the stamp mill at no small expense.

Among these five men (who actually got paid on occasion) was a seven-foot 380-pound giant named David "Nugget" Dravot.

Dravot was the most reserved, close-mouthed, taciturn, and tight-lipped fellow that McMahon had ever met. It wasn't a bother to McMahon… he didn't mind that the big man didn't talk much. He figured Dravot had always worked solo, mining his own claims or working the rivers, and he wasn't used to having people around with whom he might socialize. It wasn't 1849 anymore, though, and all of the big lodes that were easily accessible had been grabbed by the mining companies that were quickly taking over the business. To make a good living working alone you had to keep moving farther and farther into the wilderness. That didn't work for Nugget Dravot, because he had a strange addiction that kept him close to civilization.

Close Cards McMahon couldn't remember a time he'd seen Nugget without a book in his possession. It seemed as if the huge man only put down a book to get his pick or shovel, and then put down the pick and shovel only to get a book. McMahon didn't really care what the big man did in his leisure time - what little of it there was - but found it disturbing that Dravot never played cards, never drank, and never visited any of the very popular houses of prostitution in Placerville. It wasn't natural.

Back when Nugget first started working for him this unusual habit aroused McMahon's paranoid suspicions and, in consideration of the man's immense size, he added two more Germans to the payroll. These days he couldn't afford mercenaries, but he'd come to realize that Nugget was harmless. A strange, book-obsessed man, but harmless.

To be fair, McMahon didn't feel like he could sit in judgment, since books weren't really his bailiwick. He hadn't read one since Mrs. Johnston forced him to finish *Mr. Frog Visits a King* during his childhood in Philadelphia. Oh, he read newspapers and magazines sometimes, and had a battered copy of *The Miner's Commandments* in his tool locker, but books were too expensive, too long, and used too many big words. None of these seemed to be deterrents to Nugget, though.

Today was Saturday, and the men were all headed into Placerville for supplies. Close Cards decided to stay in camp instead of joining them.

"There was a time when going into *Hangtown* meant sellin' your dust, playin' some cards, drinkin' some damn fine whisky - or what goes for damn fine whisky in these parts - and maybe buyin' an hour or two with one of Missie's girls over at the Stone House," McMahon complained. "Not anymore! Nowadays we go into *Placerville*, and all of them lawyers and mayors and county supervisors are circulatin' petitions and politickin', and the Reverend Platt is walkin' up and down the street grabbin' good miners and tellin' us to go to church. The whisky tastes like vinegar and the card games are all rigged - not that they weren't before, but at least then you knew who was doin' the rigging."

"You can still visit the Stone House," Dry Dirt Dan suggested.

"Naw, even that ain't any fun no more. I'm gonna stay here and work on the mill."

McMahon wandered by himself along the flume that brought water to the mine and then up through the ruins of the stamp mill. About half of the mill was made of bright new timbers which still smelled of sap. The other half was burned beams, chunks of charcoal and ash. No one was sure how the fire started - the men were all asleep in their shacks at the time. Sometimes the quartz sparked as it was crushed in the stamp mill. Perhaps the fire had smoldered for half a day in the grass next to the mill before spreading. Or perhaps a lantern had accidentally been left alight. McMahon's paranoia did not run so deep that he considered it anything other than an accident. Still, it brought the mine's work to a halt and his profits along with it.

Dry Dirt Dan called out to McMahon as he rode away to say that he would be back by sundown on Sunday. Close Cards watched as Nugget swung up onto his horse (which seemed small under the huge man) without a single word and started down the trail to Placerville. The giant glanced back once, his face more bleak and cheerless than usual. "Probably going to buy more books at that damned bookstore," McMahon thought.

By 1856 the fabled lawless gold rush community of Hangtown had refashioned itself from a hard-drinking, hard-gambling, hell-raising mining camp into an actual town where people lived, worked, bought and sold, prayed, and raised families instead of hell. Miners were a transient bunch, always going to where the gold was (or was rumored to be.) After just a few years there was enough turnover in the population that Jed and Jack were considered "old time" residents. Gambling had all but vanished. There were plenty of hotels now; The Placer Hotel & Bar, The Philadelphia Hotel, The Union Hotel, The What Cheer House, The Iowa House. A rather prudish woman named Mrs. McKenstry bought the Eagle Hotel on Main Street and renamed it The Temperance House. Unfortunately for Mrs. McKenstry it was surrounded on both sides and across the street from the town's most popular saloons. As the non-mining population of wives, children, priests, and genteel folk increased there was pressure to relinquish such crude nomenclature as "Old Dry Diggin's" and "Hangtown" and adopt a proper name for the growing community. The name Hangtown was especially opposed by Mrs. McKenstry's Temperance League and a number of the churches. There was a Catholic Church down on Sacramento Street where Father Ingoldsby (a good name for a gold mining town) gave his sermons.

At some point around 1854 the name "Placerville" was settled upon and adopted.

The bestselling category at *Bradford & Norris: Booksellers to the Savage West* was, as always, newspapers. The Boys even gave a moment's thought to starting their own newspaper, then decided to avoid the risky endeavor altogether. Many local newspapers had come and gone during the last few years; *The Miner's Advocate* and *The Placerville Appeal* were out of business by 1853, as was *The Placerville Herald.* The *Empire County Argus* ceased by 1855, T*he Placerville American* and *Georgetown Herald* gave up the ghost early in 1856. The *Times & Transcript* and *Squatter's Journal* vanished in a matter of weeks. Only Dan Gelwicks' *Mountain Democrat* (formerly the *El Dorado News* and *El Dorado Republican*), which started in 1854, would survive. Sometimes in a pinch Jed helped Dan out at the *Democrat* by setting type. Jed expected his father would appreciate that he had finally taken up, at least part time and on rare occasion, the family business.

The earliest editorials were often on a common theme; the muddy winter streets and dusty summer streets. Civic improvements to these streets required funds, and an act to incorporate Placerville as an honest-to-God city passed in 1854. Honest Alex Hunter was elected as the first mayor.

Along Main Street there were several exchanges where miners could cash in their dust and nuggets; The Adams' and Co. Exchange, The Wells Fargo Company, and The Alex Hunter & Company Exchange.

A local militia was organized to aid the Sheriff and serve the governor in times of trouble, and they met weekly in the back of the law offices directly across the street from the bookstore. Jack volunteered (although he never saw action) and took his orders from Billy Jones (the First Lieutenant) and the Captain, Alex

Hunter.

Tom Ashton (miner, gambler, saloon-keeper, lawyer, doctor and barber) became rich by running the sawdust on the floor of his saloon through a sluice each night. In a matter of months he collected more gold dust in this manner than any miner in El Dorado County. Ashton decided to take his riches and move to San Francisco, so he sold The Round Tent to a fine woman named Caroline Tannenwald, who turned the old saloon into a dry goods store. She had shirts for $20 and stockings for $3 a pair. It still cost a lot to haul merchandise to the gold country, so unless you were prepared to make the trip to Sacramento yourself you paid the going rate and didn't complain. Ashton's other hats were filled by new barbers, saloon-keepers, and doctors, some of whom actually had medical degrees. The most prominent attorney in town was a fellow by the name of Alex Hunter.

The South Fork Canal was started in 1853 to bring water to the miners even in the dry summer months. By the summer of 1854 it was complete and The Placerville Water Company announced that water for domestic use would be available for just $1.50 a week. The President of the Water Company's board was a lawyer named Alex Hunter.

The water supply had unforeseen consequences for the miners of El Dorado County. Once available, large mining concerns began buying up the water rights and organized huge operations which specialized in hydraulic mining. Whereas in 1849 most of the miners had worked for themselves, panning and placer mining for gold, now most of them were employees working for these big companies.

The availability of year-round water did have some other benefits. Plumbing was installed in Placerville and a fireplug was placed at the corner of Main and Coloma Streets. The Neptune Hose Company formed to fight local fires. So successful were they at putting out the minor fires that frequently erupted in Placerville that they were celebrated and the team presented their foreman with a silver trumpet. Their foreman was Alex Hunter.

It was a small town. What can I say?

The primary political subject was the location of the El Dorado county seat. The citizens of Placerville repeatedly circulated petitions to have the county seat moved to their town from Coloma. After all, Placerville was the third largest town in the state of California (following San Francisco at #1 and Sacramento at #2.) Coloma, it was argued, was far too small to represent El Dorado County. Coloma wasn't even as big as Diamond Springs (#6) or Georgetown (#13.) Heck, Coloma wasn't even as big as that desert town Los Angeles (#15) way down south.

The 20 Largest Cities in California in 1854
(by number of registered voters)

1. San Francisco	
2. Sacramento	
3. Placerville (aka Hangtown)*	EL DORADO COUNTY
4. Marysville*	YUBA COUNTY
5. Nevada City*	NEVADA COUNTY
6. Diamond Springs*	EL DORADO COUNTY
7. San Jose	
8. Stockton	
9. Grass Valley*	NEVADA COUNTY
10. Columbia*	TUOLUMNE COUNTY
11. Mokelumne Hill*	CALAVERAS COUNTY
12. Iowa Hill*	PLACER COUNTY
13. Georgetown*	EL DORADO COUNTY
14. Sonora*	TUOLUMNE COUNTY
15. Los Angeles	
16. Weaverville*	TRINITY COUNTY
17. Downieville*	SIERRA COUNTY
18. Santa Clara	
19. Coloma*	EL DORADO COUNTY
20. Auburn*	PLACER COUNTY

*Gold Rush town
Not even on the list: San Diego, Oakland, Fresno

115

Still, Placerville lost the 1855 vote to claim the county seat. The vote was split due to the fact that Diamond Springs and Mud Springs got themselves on the ballot as well. Dutch McGee, a well known supporter of Placerville, spread the rumor that the Springs (Diamond and Mud) had bought off voters and that the election was fixed. Just days after the election the Diamond Springs Hotel had a mysterious fire and within hours a similar blaze broke out at a stable in Mud Springs. Although no one could prove that he had anything to do with them, Dutch McGee was seen in both towns just before the fires started. There were accusations of arson, and things only got worse when Honest Alex Hunter saw to it that the issue was once again placed on the ballot (due in May), this time without all those Springs in the mix to mess things up.

It was still dark on the ravine floor when Jed Bradford pulled his leather boots on, snapped his suspenders over his shoulders, and hurried downstairs and out the door.

He was in much more of a hurry than was his usual habit. This promised to be more than just another day selling newspapers to poor, dirty and tired miners who didn't really care what was happening outside Placerville except for the current price of gold. This wasn't going to be just another day picking the penny dreadfuls out of the book stock so that he could avoid a reprimand from Reverend Platt. Today's highlight was going to be more exciting than his daily trip to the Iowa House to see if any lemons or oranges had come in on the morning stage for Constance Flannery (although he was still heading over there to find out). Today was going to be more eventful than any day in the last year. Today was the day of the *Big Show*.

A fair number of theatre troupes traveled up and down the gold country offering entertainment (in a variety of forms) to the

116

overworked and bored miners, but most of them were amateurish. The main reason the Placerville Theatre filled its seats was nostalgia. Miners who had left their wives and families far away to hit it rich in California enjoyed some small solace from the plays, which frequently took place in New York or Chicago or St. Louis or some other city that was similar to the home they had left. It was pleasant to be back in the east for a few minutes, even if the buildings and walls were pasteboard and the women were men in wigs as often as not.

But today's show was going to be different. Today Placerville was hosting a celebrity, an actual actor, the renowned Shakespearean McKean Buchanan. Buchanan was famous in the States (as Jed still insisted on calling them, regardless of California's status as a state itself.) He had debuted at the St. Charles Theatre in New Orleans and played Hamlet at The Broadway in New York. According to Mr. Cary up at the Placer Hotel, McKean Buchanan had even won an award of some kind in Boston. Not just anyplace, mind. In The Boys' "home town" of Boston.

A week ago Jed went to Sacramento to buy stock and at that time he picked up thirty playbills for the show from Mr. Greenlaw. He spent the next few days putting them up all over town (in between Alex Hunter's campaign posters calling for Placerville to be the new county seat.) Jack Norris went door-to-door spreading the news about the big show (taking the opportunity to simultaneously hand out sales notices that listed all of the new titles received at the store.) George McDonald went all the way to Marysville to see Buchanan's show so that he could have his review published on the front page of the *Mountain Democrat* the day before the first Placerville performance. It was just that important. And *today* was the Big Day.

When Constance Flannery, proprietor of the Iowa House,

first came to Placerville she saw a makeshift structure with a canvas roof calling itself the Dry Creek Hotel, which offered hot meals for a dollar. The tables overflowed with miners and the owner was making his own mint. The entire enterprise inspired her to start her own modest food tent. The very first night of business she was baking biscuits and a miner arrived before they had finished baking. When she told him that the sweet smelling biscuits weren't ready he offered her five dollars for a biscuit, apparently believing that she was holding out on him for more money. Constance wasn't quite sure what to say to this extravagance, and when she took a moment to answer the miner doubled his offer to ten. After that she never looked back, and soon was selling plenty of her biscuits (for reasonable market rates).

Jed walked into the lobby of the Iowa House and did a quick scan of the room looking for Constance. Doc Hollander was waiting by the counter. Standing at the foot of the staircase were Dutch McGee and Boom Boom Abernathy, a miner from Diamond Springs who was famous for his boxing skills. The two were having a heated discussion which grew louder with each statement. Jed really didn't want to get involved in a dispute, especially on the day of the Big Show, so he turned his back and whistled a bit while he waited for Constance to return. The argument between the two men finally came to an end as Dutch pulled his hat tightly around his ears and headed toward the door, saying very loudly as he did; "I'd see Diamond Springs burn before I let it become the county seat!"

Boom Boom shook his fist at the retreating McGee and offered back, "That's just fine! I'd be happy to return the favor and put the torch to Placerville! There's plenty of men in Coloma who feel the same way! Just you wait, Dutch McGee!"

Abernathy stormed up the stairs to the second floor while Dutch slammed the front door behind him and stomped his way down the porch.

"That man has a bad head," Doc said. Jed wasn't sure which of the arguing men Hollander was referring to, though he agreed the statement could like be applied to either one.

"What was that all about?" Constance asked as she came through the kitchen door.

"I have no idea," Jed lied. Like Close Cards McMahon he was fed up with the constant bickering about the county seat issue. "So, are you ready for the Big Show?" he asked instead. The perpetually happy matron beamed.

"Oh, Jed, I can hardly wait! Donald has laid out his best waistcoat and Stafford Hickey brought me the most beautiful dress from Sacramento. I expect I'll be the belle of the ball."

"Any oranges today?" Jed changed the subject again.

"No," she replied, feigning unhappiness. The act couldn't hold and she held up a sack of bright red apples. "How about one of these instead?"

"Constance, you're a goddess!"

Jed was strolling down Main Street toward the bookstore, munching on the apple, when he stepped into sudden shadow and the temperature dropped by several degrees. Two steps later he was stopped in his tracks by the shadow's source. There, ankle deep in the muddy street, towering over him, stood all seven feet and 380 pounds of Nugget Dravot. The giant didn't move, but he didn't say anything either. He just stood there, his massive and strangely flattened cranium weighing heavily on his thick neck.

"Hey, Nug, where are you headed this morning?" Jed asked politely, but he was slightly taken aback by Nugget's appearance. The big man was clearly out of sorts, oily perspiration pouring down his face, fists clenched, at the very least mightily unhappy. "Hey... are you alright, Nug?"

Nugget wasn't a popular man in the area. Perhaps it was because men were intimidated by his immense size, but Jed thought it was because Nugget rarely spoke - especially about himself. He was a mystery and people hated or feared a mystery. Jed and Jack were among the small number of men who could say they knew anything at all about Nugget. He often bought books in their store. But even then he rarely spoke to them, so most of their knowledge of the man came from his choices in reading material.

His selections since coming to Placerville were eclectic ones, especially for a forty-niner. First he went through all of Jane Austen (he said he preferred *Sense and Sensibility* over *Pride and Prejudice* because he tried to be neither proud nor prejudiced). Next he bought some Nathaniel Hawthorne, a few collections of Wordsworth, and then ordered *Moby-Dick* by Melville. After that he ran through the entire available Charles Dickens catalogue. Last week he purchased Frankenstein by Mary Shelley and ordered a new book Jed wasn't familiar with called *Leaves of Grass* by some fellow named Whitman. Not even the school teachers went through as many books as Nugget did.

"Never, Mister Bradford," Nugget suddenly said. Jed forgot what he had asked him.

"Excuse me, Nug. Never what?"

"Never alright. I'm afraid I'll be havin' to come see you later today, Mister Bradford," the giant said almost tearfully. With that the big man lumbered down the street toward Cedar Ravine. Jed almost expected to see a dark cloud hovering over the man's head as he walked away.

"It's really not that bad, Nug! We'll be glad to see you!" Jed offered. He couldn't imagine what about a trip to the bookstore would make Nugget so glum. Then again, it was hard to understand any of Nugget's moods. Mercurial was the way Jed thought of him.

The whole affair practically snuffed out Jed's joyous anticipation of the play, which had ignited his happy temperament all morning. He tried to get himself back into that more invigorating state of mind by stopping at the Post Office to pick up the previous day's *San Francisco Daily Evening Bulletin* and *Daily Alta California*. The distribution of his favorite San Francisco paper, the *Evening News & Picayune*, had become irregular and Jed resigned himself to the fact that the periodical was probably close to its demise. Today's *Mountain Democrat* had a fair number of short stories, poems, and editorials, but not much news (other than coverage of the Big Show.) It wasn't the paper's fault, Jed figured. Nowadays not much happened in Placerville. In fact, some days Jed wished that something - anything - out of the ordinary might happen to break up the monotony and provide an idea for a new story. He was sure that tonight's Big Show was finally going to do that.

When he got to the bookstore Jack had already thrown open the doors and set two tables of old newspapers and battered books out on the boardwalk to entice the passers-by. They would have to close the doors by noon to keep the dust out, but in the morning most of it stayed in the street where it belonged.

"Sold a copy of *The Miner's Commandments* already this morning," Jack said as Jed entered.

"The fewer miners there are the more copies of that we sell. Is that thing ever going to get old?"

"I think they just buy it to laugh. 'Thou shalt not remember what thy friends do at home on the Sabbath Day.' That's funny!" Jack pounded his fist on the counter and engaged in some mock laughter.

"I think they buy it to keep their resolve," Jed disagreed. "'Thou shalt not grow discouraged, nor think of going home before thou hast made thy pile.'" Upon this Jack laughed in earnest.

"Too bad most of the copies out there are bootlegs. Hutchings would be a rich man if he'd gotten paid for every copy of that thing that's been sold."

Jed placed the day-old newspapers on the counter next to the spot where Jack was sitting. "Jack, did you see Nugget out there this morning?"

"No, can't say as I did."

"He was acting like his momma had died or something, and then he told me he'd be in to see us later. What do you suppose is wrong with him?"

"Maybe his momma died," Jack suggested.

"Did you finish doing your rounds telling folks about the Big Show last night?" Jed asked, changing the subject.

"Well, yes, in town," Jack said. "I wasn't going to go all the way up to Smith Flat. Tiny Morgan said he would take some show bills out to Diamond and Two Shovels Mitchell took some out to Coloma day before yesterday."

That satisfied Jed. The Bookstore Boys had done more than could be rightfully asked of them, considering the fact that they didn't stand to make so much as a penny from the performances. Civic pride and their desire to improve the cultural amenities of their fine town were their only motivating factors in promoting the play.

The morning was passing slowly for Jed, who was of course anxious for it to pass quickly so that the hour of the Great Show would arrive. As the well-known adage about the boiling pot makes clear, this only made the day pass slower. The store was uncharacteristically empty today, probably because people were getting ready for the Show. Usually the busiest days of the week were Saturday and Sunday (although the Reverend Platt was trying to get a Sunday Law passed that would force all of the stores to close on the Sabbath). Constance Flannery stopped by to offer Jack an

apple (equal time for the Bookstore Boys) and Jed told her the story
of the Wheelbarrow Man for the tenth time. Just before noon Jack
was pulling in the book table to close the doors (because of the dust)
when a ruckus started in the Plaza. The Boys stepped out onto the
boardwalk to see what was happening. In the middle of a gathering
crowd they saw a familiar wagon. A row of barrels were set up
along its side with boards laid across them to form a low staging
area. A man in a long coat and black derby strode back and forth
across these boards gesticulating to his audience. For a moment Jed
thought that the magnificent McKean Buchanan had decided to put
on an early street show.

Jack closed the front door of the store and the two
booksellers walked down the street to hear what the man was saying.

"I, say, my young man… you there, lurking about the back.
You look out of sorts. Perhaps your humors are not in balance. No
need to hide there among your fellows! Come forward!" the man
said. Two Shovels Mitchell shrugged and approached the man in
the black derby.

"I have just the thing for you!" the man said. "The brilliant
Doctor L.J. Czapkey has devised a physic which can cure a man's
aversion to society, timidity, desire for solitude, self distrust, as well
as pimples on the face and sexual infirmities!"

Jack shook his head. "Fox Reynard," he said to Jed. "I'm
surprised it took him this long to find his way to Placerville."

Reynard, who looked a little older and, if possible, even
craftier than the man they had saved from thirst and starvation in
the forty mile desert, strode boldly up and down his makeshift
platform, waving a bottle of dark brown liquid.

"How do I know it works?" Two Shovels asked.

"Well, I see we have a Doubting Thomas in the crowd. You,
sir, are exactly the sort, I say, the specific variety of ailing and ill-bred
man who requires this amazing tonic! Now then, if you're ailing

from matters which are less of the spirit and more of the body, may I direct your attention, my fine gentlemen, to Dr. Jacob Webber's Invigorating Cordial? It has been found to cure dyspepsia, indigestion, languor, nervousness, trembling, loss of appetite, rheumatic and all other pains, improve a man's memory, and remove his longing for the taste of liquor."

"How exactly does that work?" Doctor Ober asked as he stepped out of the crowd. "I am a physician and know something about these matters." Reynard frowned for just a split second and then smiled broadly.

"Of course you do, my friend! Then it should be no surprise, no news to you at all, that during sleep it provides for a cleansing and natural perspiration, during which the humors find their proper equilibrium. I have seen it raise men from their death bed and put them back to work with the vigor of a sixteen-year-old!"

"I figure my sense of humor is just fine," Bad Luck Casey said. "People is always saying, 'Bad Luck Casey, you are the funniest man I done ever met!'"

"I see," Reynard said, and he dropped the brown bottle into a box and pulled out a pair of tall leather boots. "Perhaps you folk are interested in items which are not, I say, not of a medicinal sort. I have for sale an entire crate of brand new boots, with reinforced leather soles, imported from the finest shoemakers in Europe! These are triple-pegged, sewn with the finest craftsmanship, made from waterproof cowhide! Mister Casey - may I call you Bad Luck? My, what an unfortunate monicker - I think this pair would fit your road-smashers exactly!"

Bad Luck took the boots from Reynard and held them up to his feet, which were barely covered in a pair of battered shoes held on by a series of thongs. Eagerly he took off the torn and tattered shoes and pulled on the shiny new boots.

124

"Now them's boots!" Casey exclaimed.

"Amazing! Aren't they just the most comfortable Wellies you've ever had the privilege of wearing? I can tell they were made, no, born unto this world, to be worn on your mud-splashers and your mud-splashers alone! And for three and a half ounces you can keep them!!"

Reynard had finally found a product the assembled citizens wanted at a price they deemed reasonable. They descended on his wagon and as his assistant Chesley weighed their dust or took their coins he handed out boots. It should be noted that a fair number of them also bought Dr. Czapkey's Physic and Dr. Jacob Webber's Invigorating Cordial, including Doctor Ober. Jed and Jack, who were not in the market for boots, physics or cordials, waited at the back until everyone had a chance to make a purchase.

"Carrying books yet, Fox?" Jack asked at last. Reynard looked up from his earnings and his patented smile illuminated the Plaza. He walked over and slapped them each on the back.

"Boys! It is so good to see you!" Reynard bellowed. "Many is the time I have wondered whatever became of the two lonely booksellers I saved from certain death in the desert! Yes sir, I have added books to my inventory, though only in my own stores at home. They are quite heavy, yes, far too heavy to pull over these mountains in a wagon. Have you set up business in these parts?"

"Yes, we have a store down the street," Jack told him.

"Quite a few customers in town today," Reynard said. "More than I expected." The Boys told him about the Big Show.

"That's why everyone is here," Jed said. "They wouldn't miss this show for the world!" Reynard was lost for a moment in contemplation, greed and avarice weaving their plots and plans behind his glassed-over eyes. Then he smiled again.

"Perhaps they'll let me set up my wagon outside the theater!" he said.

The boys bid Reynard farewell and returned to the bookstore. Time slowed again to a crawl and later that afternoon, when the temperature soared to unseasonable heights and the flies became a particular annoyance, Nugget came in the front door.

The big man was calmer than he was during their morning encounter, but he was still clearly unhappy. He wrung his hat slowly in his fists, which were as big as hams, as he approached the counter.

"Mister Bradford, sir ..." Nug began.

"Please, for a hundredth time, Nug, call me Jed. It saves you three whole syllables."

"Of course, Mister Bradford." He nodded to Jack. "Mister Norris."

"What can we do for you, Nug?" Jack prodded.

"Well, you know that book you got for me last week, the one by Missus Shelley about the scientist in Europe?"

"Sure. *Frankenstein*. What about it?" Jed asked.

"Do you have another copy?" Nug asked, starting to tear his hat as he twisted it around tighter and tighter.

"I think so," Jack smiled, and he rolled the shop ladder halfway down the west wall and climbed it to search among a selection of large volumes. While he looked Jed tried to lighten the mood by striking up a conversation.

"I'm sure we do, Nug, it's no problem. So, you're up at Big Secret Diggin's these days, right?" Jed asked, trying to rope the giant into some small talk. Even though it was like pulling teeth to get a word out of him, Jed was always up to the challenge. "That place isn't as much of a big secret as Close Cards McMahon would like. Especially after that fire that took out McMahon's stamp mills last week. I guess anybody who didn't know where the Big Secret is knows about it now... you could see the smoke in Georgetown!"

The huge man went bright red in the face and began to rock

back and forth from foot to foot.

"Close Cards brought in a fair amount of pay rock the week before the fire, especially for these days, so I guess you guys are anxious to be back up and running, eh?" Jed prodded.

Nugget nodded slightly and looked the other way. Rivulets of muddy sweat trailed along his brow.

"So, Frankenstein," Jed said, changing the subject since the first was clearly unsuccessful. "Are you enjoying the book? What happened to the first copy?"

"I lost it, Mister Bradford! I swear, I lost it in the creek!" the giant erupted. His loud voice carried out onto the street and Bad Luck Casey slowed down as he passed to peek in and see what all the fuss was about.

"That's alright, Nug!" Jed said, holding up his hands. "It was your book, you paid for it. It's no skin off my nose if you dropped it in the creek. We'll be happy to sell you another copy. Heck, we'll make more money by selling you the same book twice!"

Nugget calmed himself once more and Jack walked up with a book.

"*Frankenstein!* I knew we had another copy I was hiding in the back from Reverend Platt. He seems to think this book is an affront to God or some such nonsense. I mean, after all, it is just a novel." Jack smiled. "It's not as if some crazy German inventor will really raise the dead to life and send them tottering down Main Street to break up the Reverend's congregation!"

"Still," Jed said, "I think one's time would be better spent with the Dickens. This is pretty much boogeyman stuff." He remembered that the customer who was buying the book was still standing directly in front of him. "But *good* boogeyman stuff."

"Are you going to the play tonight or heading back out to the mine?" Jack asked Nugget. Dravot didn't like to talk about himself, but he was usually polite to a fault.

127

"I'm reading my book tonight. In my room at the Iowa," he said.

"Well it's going to be a great play, Nug. It would be great to see you there," Jed suggested.

"I still owe you for that Walt Whitman book, don't I, Mister Bradford?" Nugget asked, changing the subject. Generally the Boys required customers to pay in advance for orders, since procuring a book from back east and getting it shipped to California could cost a fair amount of upfront cash. Those rules were sometimes set aside for the very best clients.

"You can pay for it when it comes in, Nug," Jed said. He wasn't sure he would be able to get it anyway.

"Thank you, Mister Bradford," Nugget said, placing the price of *Frankenstein* on the counter, taking his book and leaving. He had to step around the inquisitive Bad Luck Casey to get out into the street.

"That's a good one," Jack chided Jed after Nugget was out of earshot. "Insult the customer's choice of books why don't you?" Jed ignored him and checked his pocket watch.

"Is Lizette coming to the big show?" he asked.

"She's supposed to meet us there," Jack replied.

"What do you say we close up a little early today so that we can get a couple of beers and some food before the Big Show?" Jack had to admit that this sounded like a very good plan and they locked up the store and headed down the street in the general direction of the Placerville Theatre. There were a number of places they could stop for beer between the store and the theatre. The closer they were to the theatre the longer they could eat and drink before show time and still get a decent seat.

While the Bookstore Boys ordered their beer and chicken and Fox Reynard assembled his platform next to the theatre, Nugget Dravot climbed the stairs to his second-floor room at the

Iowa House. He pushed the door open as far as it could go - it was stopped by the stacks of books behind the door - and squeezed his massive frame through the narrow gap. He climbed over still more books to open the window and let in some fresh air. The frame creaked as he lowered himself onto the bed, his new book in hand. And as most of the residents of Placerville converged on the Theatre to see the amazing thespian McKean Buchanan, Nugget fell into the words of Mary Woolstonecraft Shelley.

The curtain went up at the Placerville Theatre and the assembled audience, which included at least a third of the county population, rose and gave a standing ovation. The play hadn't even started yet, but that didn't matter. McKean Buchanan was going to be on stage. Culture and refinement had finally arrived in El Dorado County, even if it was only on the stage and would last just a few precious hours. The miners, hoteliers, traders, blacksmiths, doctors, lawyers, and even the two bookstore owners in the front row had gotten used to making the long trip to Sacramento to experience modern civilization, and sometimes they made the even longer trip to San Francisco. But everything was finally changing. It was unusual for Jed and Jack to see all of their Placerville peers dressed to the nines at the same time. Jean-Claude D'Autrefois sat two rows behind them, his Capitaine's uniform newly cleaned and pressed. It still looked worn and a bit faded, yet the buttons shone more brightly than they had in years. Bad Luck Casey was wearing a tie. Perhaps most surprising of all, Almost Bill was wearing a floor-length dress; the first time anyone in town had ever seen her in such feminine attire.

There were a fair number of other women in the audience as well, in huge skirts supported by hoops or crinolines, with overlaying flounces and covered about the shoulders by capes in the fashion of Indian shawls. There were so many, in fact, that as Jed looked out across the theater it occurred to him that the time might have finally arrived to consider marriage prospects (Jack, of course, was already involved in an undefined, yet indisputable relationship with Lizette Charbonneau).

At the same time that McKean Buchanan was walking out onto the stage to the second standing ovation of the evening, David Dravot, stretched out on the bed in his room at the Iowa House, proceeded into the fifth chapter of his "current book." Nugget tended to think of the book he was in the midst of as his "current book," and the books he had already finished as his "former books." There were lots of his former books in the room, stacked in great teetering piles around the bed and behind the door. He frequently promised himself that he would take some of them over to Jed and Jack's bookstore and trade them in for new books, but he couldn't bear to part with any of them. Once he had read a book it became a part of his life, almost like a child, and the idea of selling them felt like abandonment. Besides, if he liked a former book enough he might read it another time, and then it would become a current book again. Nugget was positive that any book he traded in at *Bradford & Norris - Booksellers to the Savage West* would be the very book he would want to read the next day.

His "current book" tonight was a frighteningly good read, full of mad scientists (were there another kind?) giant creatures and arctic wildernesses. Reading in this light was difficult for Nugget. He didn't use candles anymore. Instead he had a very robust lantern with a glass enclosure which he placed on a stack of books several feet away from the bed where there was no risk that he might bump it while tossing about in his sleep. He kept the lantern barely half full of oil so that it would burn out quickly if he dozed off. Possibly due to this the lantern tended to flicker, and it cast the shadows of the towering book stacks onto the walls where they shifted back and forth like monsters, adding to the cold terror in the book's pages. *Frankenstein* wasn't the kind of book Nugget usually found himself interested in - he preferred Austen and Dickens - but he needed something escapist at the moment. And being a social outcast and a rather tall man himself, he identified in some not-so-small ways with the pathetic creature in the novel.

Things were just getting exciting when Nugget felt his eyelids grow heavy and the sentences started to vanish from his conscious mind almost before he had finished reading them. This always happened after an hour or so. He'd hoped that a more exciting book would keep him awake longer, because he always felt cheated when he awoke in the morning and realized that he had slept his reading time away. Mornings were the hardest for Nugget - knowing that there were another twelve or fourteen hours of hard labor in the mine before he would be able to open his book again. Sometimes in the mine during the day, while working a vein of quartz with nothing but a pick and shovel, he would start to think about his "current book" and imagine the many directions the characters might take the story next. On long days when he was alone he might imagine their whole lives, from the point at which he stopped reading until their deaths many years later. He imagined families for them, new loves, new babies, new careers, new travels to exotic new countries. There would of course be new obstacles, but he imagined how the stalwart characters would deal with them as well. Part of his excitement about getting back to his book each night was to see how closely the written events would mirror his own imagination. These characters had lives much richer than he did. There was a time when he imagined that his life could be as fascinating as a fictional character's life could be. Those days were now ash.

In the novel the "monster" came to Geneva and met a young boy in the woods. Nugget tried to keep reading but the words came to him slower and slower, as if the book were a train approaching a station.

This happened to him regularly. As much as he loved his books, he had to work for a living and always came together with them at the end of a long day. Only a few pages in he would start to fall asleep. Tonight he fought to stay awake, fought to spend five more precious minutes with his book. The paragraphs began to shimmer like oases in the desert and Nugget had to reread the last over and over again.

"Not again," Nugget said, shaking his head. Finally he was overcome. The book, still open, slid from his chest to the sheet, and Nugget began to snore.

In the room directly below Nugget's a clandestine gathering of sorts was taking place. Dutch McGee and his cohorts were meeting to discuss the county seat issue. It was the perfect night for their rendezvous since the Sheriff, Honest Alex Hunter, and anyone else in town who might give them any grief was busy at the theater attending the performance of the unsurpassable McKean Buchanan. The Iowa House was, as far as they knew, completely abandoned, with the exception of Mrs. Rockwell who had stayed home with her two-year-old son.

"We can stuff a ballot box as good as those idiots in Diamond and Coloma," McGee told his followers. "We can give as good as we can take. Those losers are just watering holes in the wild compared to Hangtown. You know that they're plotting against us right now, and we have to be ready! We're going to make sure this next election goes down right! There will be justice!"

"Damn right, Dutch!" Gum Eyes Johnston declared. Dutch's rousing speech excited Johnston and the other conspirators to the point where they started to stomp and clap and chanted "Hangtown! Hangtown! Hangtown!" (which was still the preferred name for the community amongst Dutch McGee's circle of friends). The windows began to rattle and dust fell from the ceiling boards.

"Hush up!" Dutch said. "That no-good woman down the hall will be poking her nose in here if we wake her damn baby!"

Mrs. Rockwell's child did not wake, luckily for Dutch and his gang. His admonition was too late to prevent a different consequence, however. Upstairs a pile of books swayed due to the vibrations caused by Dutch's acolytes. The lantern perched on top of them slid to their edge. For a moment it hung, suspended over the spine of the uppermost book, before it dropped to the floor. Its glass chimney shattered, oil splashed across the floor, and the burning wick ignited the oil. Several feet away Nugget Dravot snored.

Down the street at the Placerville Theatre the play began. The audience was held in thrall by the amazing McKean Buchanan as he displayed his prodigious thespian talents. Unlike the average road show theatricals which traveled the gold country everything in this play seemed incredibly genuine. The pasteboard sets were as real to Jed and Jack as they would if they had been actual castle parapets and forest glades. The actors, while as melodramatic as one could rightfully expect from a decent amusement, performed with a sincerity that allowed complete and total suspension of disbelief.

"Look at the costumes!" Lizette said very quietly to Jack at one point - she didn't want to be stoned by her fellow citizens for speaking so loudly that they missed a single word uttered by the incredible McKean Buchanan. "I've never seen such fine clothes! And for nothing but a play!" Jed knew that this night's entertainment would be the subject of conversation for many days to come.

The second act was drawing to a triumphant close when

133

Jack sniffed the air. "Smells like something's on fire," he whispered. Jed motioned for him to hush.

"It's just the lamps or the torch-bearers on stage. The scent is probably part of the illusion of reality," Jed said. But Jack felt differently.

"No, that's a wood fire. Smoky..." he craned his head and looked around the house to see if he could spot the source. The mystery was cleared up just moments later.

"FIRE!" a voice came, a yell from the back of the theatre, up near the lobby entrance. The audience didn't respond at first, perhaps because they thought the cry was a part of the play. But then the cry was made again with even greater urgency.

"FIRE! Fire at the Iowa House!"

On stage, the incomparable McKean Buchanan stopped speaking midway through a line and peered out into the house. There was a half second - no more but no less - of complete silence, and then all hell broke loose.

Men leapt from their seats, dashing for the exits with their hats in their hands. The doors on all sides of the theatre were thrown open and the population of El Dorado County spilled out onto the streets of Placerville, heading up Sacramento Street toward the Iowa House. Jed and Jack took a moment to look at each other in surprise and then they ran out too, Lizette trailing Jack as he pulled her along. They headed for the storehouse owned by Four-Fingers Ironwood where the fire buckets were kept. Alex Hunter and Joe Fisher headed up Main Street to the recently acquired home of the Neptune Hose Company No. 1 in order to fetch the hose and carriage. They almost seemed pleased with the situation and chanted "We're ready! We're ready!" (which was the Neptunes' motto) as they ran up the street.

Things were worse than expected when Jed and Jack reached the Iowa House - or what was left of it. The structure was engulfed in flames that towered high into the black sky, and the fire had already spread to Dr. Rankin's office, Sacramento Street Dry Goods, and the Orleans Hotel. The Round Tent was smoldering. Old Man Stevens was trying his best to put out every glowing ember that landed on the grounds of his brand new livery stable. The wind was against him and in several areas the flames took hold.

"Oh, my goodness!" Constance Flannery declared and she burst into tears. Her husband Donald put his arm around her and said nothing as they watched the building burn.

"It's those villains in Diamond!" Dutch McGee shouted. "Or that damn Coloma! They'd rather see our town burn than become the county seat!"

Honest Alex Hunter's cry of "Shut up and help with the buckets!" was the only response McGee received.

The Neptunes arrived and unloaded the hose from the carriage. A bucket brigade formed to transport water from the horse troughs along the street. The entire county community, in town late for the play, gathered into a fire fighting force that seemed formidable. Unfortunately the fire seemed more so.

A strange-looking middle aged man whom Jed did not recognize took up a place in the bucket line next to him. He took more than a dozen buckets from the man before he realized that it was the indefatigable McKean Buchanan himself, still in makeup and costume, hauling water to save a town that wasn't even his. In fact Jed noticed that many members of the theatre company were helping the injured leave the area or shoveling dirt onto burning timbers that had fallen into the street. It made Jed proud of the efforts he and Jack had made - at no profit to themselves - to promote the evening's performance. For here these talented thespians were, working beyond all call.

The night might have gone better if not for the Great Fireplug Malfunction. The Neptune Hose Company screwed their hose to the plug and turned the valve. The fireplug, so proudly boasted about by the Placerville Water Company, did nothing. The Neptunes shouted back and forth, yet all of this shouting did little to coax water from the useless fireplug. All of this took place, unfortunately, just as the bucket brigade ran out of water.

"We need water!" Tiny Morgan shouted. A voice rang out from the direction of the theater.

"These barrels are full!" Chinese Sam yelled. The bucket brigade members hurried to his side and Chinese Sam and Ah Moon pulled the lids off of the barrels. In moments a new line of buckets was traveling to the fire. This time, however, the "water" they were passing along was brown and smelled funny.

"My physic!! My cordial!" Fox Reynard screamed. "Stop! I say, stop and put those buckets down! That is not water, it is medicine!" The folks with the buckets ignored Reynard, which was fine because the physic and cordial was just as good as water for putting out the fire. In fact, Jed and Jack surmised that the concoction actually was primarily water (otherwise the alcohol that they could smell in it would have made the fire worse.) A few of the older citizens who suffered aches and pains due to the physical labor of lifting bucket after bucket merely took a few sips from them as they went by and soon were feeling fine. Doc Hollander took more than a few sips.

Desperate for water to fill their namesake hose, the Neptune Hose Company disconnected from the malfunctioning fireplug and instead jerry rigged the hose to some plumbing inside of the Soda Works. With water at last pouring from their hose they joined the bucket brigade and attacked the fire.

Despite their efforts, the Iowa House was clearly doomed. The Neptunes finally decided to give it up and direct their efforts toward other structures that had a chance of being saved. Just as they trained their hose on the building next door a cry went up. It was so filled with agony that Jed thought someone had lost a family member to a fiery death. In the street in front of Stevens' Livery an injured woman who was being tended by one of the actresses from the play crawled to her feet. Before the girl could stop her the woman ran screaming toward the burning building. Jed recognized her as Mrs. Rockwell, a resident of the House, and despite the searing heat of the flames a chill ran through him as he realized what she was saying - her youngest child was asleep inside.

All of the others present suffered from the same chill and after a mere moment of inaction a number of men came running forward. There was no shortage of heroes to be found here. The first to respond was Jackie Ober, Dr. Ober's son. He was a member of the Hose Company, no more than thirteen or fourteen years old, but bright for his age and utterly fearless. He threw his coat over his head and pushed headfirst into the main entrance, even though it was completely in flames. Joe Fisher dumped a bucket of water on a horse blanket and wrapped it over his shoulders, going into the burning building through a gap that had once been part of the south wall. The fire was less intense here, but the real danger now was the collapse of what was left of the building. And at the back, near the rear entrance, Jed saw a third man enter the inferno. A towering figure pushed through the burning back door and vanished into the smoke. There was no doubt in his mind that this last man entering the fiery wreckage of the Iowa House was Nugget Dravot.

The firefighters grew quiet, continuing to work silently as they waited to see which, if any, of the would-be rescuers would emerge from the burning building. Only the roar of the fire and the sobs of Mrs. Rockwell broke that eerie silence. The longer they waited, everyone knew, the less likely that any of the men would live.

Suddenly a cheer went up from the Neptunes closest to the building. A silhouette appeared in the burning entrance, lit from behind by the golden flames. Coughing from the great amounts of smoke he had inhaled, Jackie Ober stumbled out into the street. The tiny child - still peacefully asleep - was curled up in his arms. Mrs. Rockwell ran forward through the crowd (which had now, by and large, surrendered in its attempts to fight the fire.) Jackie gently placed the sleeping child in its sobbing mother's arms and his fellow Neptunes caught him before he fell into the street. His arm was burned, his eyes red and watering, and he could barely breathe in the smoky air, but they were glad to discover that he was otherwise healthy.

And then, no more than a minute after young Master Ober brought the child out of the inferno, there was a loud cracking sound, like the sound the ice makes when it begins to break up in the spring. The remains of the front wall fell outward into the street, and the interior walls of the Iowa House began to collapse in on themselves. The ruin of the roof finally fell in on the second floor, which in turn crashed to the ground. Great clouds of sparks flew up into the air and smoke billowed out in a ring. The firefighters and assembled citizens ran backward to escape being trapped by the falling timbers.

At the same time the incredible McKean Buchanan raised his arm and pointed. "Look!" he bellowed in great stentorian tones worthy of performing only the best of The Bard. "There!" Revealed by the collapsing building were Joe Fisher and Nugget Dravot, each with his arm around the other's shoulder (which was only possible because Joe was well over six feet and could actually reach Nugget's shoulder). The two men coughed as they stumbled out in to the street and, even though in the same deplorable condition as Jackie Ober, they hurried over to Mrs. Rockwell to check on the welfare of her child. Nugget was so concerned over the child's well being that Bad Luck Casey had to put out a fire on the taller man's back. After Casey beat at the flames repeatedly with the wet horse blanket taken from Joe Fisher's shoulders, Nugget finally

138

noticed what was happening and removed his burning coat.

The Neptunes shortly gave up on the Placer Hotel, watching the flames consume it without opposition. The Orleans Hotel collapsed shortly after. Tom Ashton, wearing his barber's hat, helped Doctor Keene and Caroline Tannenwald bandage the wounded and salve the burned in the ashen lot where The Round Tent had been. Providing medical help kept Dr. Keene's mind off the distressing fact that his precious Masonic Lodge Hall had just burned to the ground. Henry Hooker picked through the remains of his store, now reduced to ashes, looking for any merchandise he might be able to salvage.

Jed and Jack nervously made their way down Main Street to see what was left of the bookstore. Upon arrival they found it unharmed (so far). The two-story stone edifice of the Soda Works next door was blocking the fire's advance. They agreed to a new and inviolable rule; always open your bookstore next to a Soda Works.

The only thing that saved the entire town from being razed was that the wind finally shifted just before midnight and the flames moved away from the rest of Main Street. As the fire ebbed The Neptunes finally wrapped up their hoses, yet found they had nowhere to go, as the Fire House had burned down. Luckily the rest of Placerville was spared (at least for now). But there would be no play tonight.

"Are you all right, Nug?" Jed asked the huge man as they stood looking at the burning pile of rubble that remained where the Iowa House belonged. Nugget did not respond.

"Guess you're going to need another copy of *Frankenstein*," Jack said.

Nugget looked at him sharply, then moved off down the street and started the long, dark hike through the forest and deep into the mountains to his little shack near the Big Secret Diggin's

Mine.

The population of Placerville remained in the street surveying the ruins of their town far past midnight. Some of them were merely aghast at what had happened and could not imagine sleeping. Others had nowhere to go, since their homes or hotels were destroyed.

Fox Reynard sat in the street crying over the charred remains of his wagon. His empty physic and cordial barrels escaped the fire's wrath, although with the wagon burned he had no way to return them home. "Does anybody, I say, is there a man here," he called out, "who has a good stiff drink?"

The Boys stood next to Alex Hunter and Dutch McGee and stared at the smoldering foundation of the Placer Hotel.

"I tell you, those desperados from Diamond Springs did this," Dutch said. "They were mad we kept 'em off the next ballot. Boom Boom Abernathy said as much."

"I doubt that," Jed said, although he remembered hearing Abernathy make just such a threat that very morning.

"You may be right," Dutch agreed. "Boom Boom hasn't got the smarts to pull this off. I have a notion it might have been them dogs from Coloma. They were sore that we keep trying to take the county seat from 'em, so they burned our town down."

"That's not what I meant," Jed said.

"It may require an investigation at the very least," Honest Alex Hunter said. "I'll talk to the sheriff."

"You gotta fight fire with fire," McGee argued. "Mark my words, this will happen again. Coloma and Diamond would burn just as easy." Alex Hunter took McGee's arm and looked at him sternly over the tops of his wire-rim glasses.

"We both know you've already been down that path, Dutch, and if Coloma or Diamond had anything to do with this its likely blood on your hands. Now, don't you go do anything stupid. I will talk to the sheriff." McGee's eyes widened and he held up his hands.

"Not me, Alex! I wouldn't do anything stupid!" It was clear that Alex Hunter was not convinced, and Jed and Jack were similarly doubtful. Doing stupid things was second nature to Dutch McGee.

The next morning Close Cards McMahon awoke to a number of loud sounds coming from the cabin... no, shack... lean-to, maybe... that Nugget Dravot kept in camp. The towering man, his forehead glistening with sweat, bent down as he came out the door carrying a large leather travel case, a soft-sided duffel bag, and three saddle bags. It appeared to be everything he owned.

"What are you making all the noise for, Dravot?" Close Cards asked, at the same time running his hand over his face and deciding he could go at least one more day without shaving before the whiskers drove him mad.

"I'm quittin', Mister McMahon," Nugget replied. "I'm sorry it's such short notice, but I have to move on from here."

Nugget's resignation caught McMahon by surprise. "Why, for cryin' out loud? We just hit new dirt this week!"

"I'm so sorry, Mister McMahon," Nugget repeated. Replacing a worker as hard working and trustworthy as Nugget would be difficult, but Close Cards found a silver lining.

"Gosh, Dravot, I don't have the cash to pay you, and this week's ore hasn't been run through the stamp mill since we're still rebuilding from the fire. I owe you - what - a month's pay?"

"That's okay, Mister McMahon. I have to move on," Nugget said. Close Cards could hardly restrain himself from celebrating the idea of a free month's labor when Dravot added, "When you get the chance you can leave my pay in the care of Mister Bradford or Mister Norris at the bookstore in town. They'll get it to me."

"Oh," McMahon said, more than slightly disappointed.

"I'm real sorry about the stamp mill, Mister McMahon," Nugget added.

"Yeah, sure Nugget," Close Cards said. "Well, it's not your fault, and those things happen. We've almost got it rebuilt. We'll sure miss your arms and back when we're finishing it." The tall man gave his employer a nod and, hoisting his belongings onto his back he headed toward Placerville.

The Bookstore Boys were no happier than Close Cards was to hear about Nugget's departure from Placerville. He was one of the store's steadiest customers.

"Gosh, Nug, I wish there was something we could do to change your mind," Jed said.

"Well, Mister Bradford," Nugget replied, "I'm afraid there isn't. Can I ask you a favor, though, if it isn't too presumptive of me?"

"You name it," Jack said.

"I was wondering if once I find a new place I could send you my new address and you could get my mail from Mister Theodore and forward it to me. I'll send you money for the postage, of course."

Jed smiled and patted Nugget on the arm, as close to the shoulder as he could reach. "That's not a problem, Nug. We would be happy to. And if you can't find a book you're looking for - wherever it is you end up living - you let us know and we'll forward that too."

"I appreciate that Mister Bradford, Mister Norris." The big man paused, examining the rows of bookshelves and the hundreds of books they supported. "You know, sometimes you keep looking for a new story that you can love. Hard thing is, sometimes the old stories keep following you around and won't let you be." And with that David Dravot left, bending low to get out the door. His hulking frame got smaller as it shuffled down the street and disappeared behind the blackened timbers that had once been the Placer Hotel.

Within a few days Jed and Jack forgot about Nugget Dravot. The business of running the store, coupled with the rebuilding of half of Placerville after the fire, provided plenty of fodder for thought. At first the townspeople started rebuilding in wood. That changed when, in July, the portion of Placerville that had escaped the first fire burned in a second. But I'm getting ahead of myself.

You see, the election for county seat was finally held in May. Honest Alex Hunter was stunned when the returns showed Coloma winning, 7,413 to Placerville's 5,895. Dan Gelwicks, the publisher of the *Mountain Democrat,* had an apoplectic fit in print, declaring the election a farce and accusing Coloma of ballot box stuffing. "Through the rascality of the agents of Coloma, the will of the people has been thwarted," he wrote. "A few men, in whose leprous hearts honesty never found even a temporary resting place, are the guilty parties."

Alex Hunter presided over a "Meeting of Indignation" in Placerville where the ballots were investigated and recounted. Curiously, 872 votes for Coloma came from a precinct called "Dry Creek," which didn't actually exist. Equally strange was the fact that Coloma's voting population had mysteriously doubled in the last year, even though a number of mines in the area had closed. The meeting became a rally and the rally became a riot. The Sheriff was forced to break up a fight that broke out between a gang of Coloma supporters and a group of Placerville advocates who blamed them for both the fraudulent election and the fire that burned Placerville. This latter group was lead by Dutch McGee.

Five Coloma men were eventually indicted for ballot stuffing and election fraud, but that didn't stop the bad blood.

A week later Boom Boom Abernathy's cabin and the largest

stables in Diamond Springs burned to the ground. Abernathy blamed Dutch McGee, who swore on his mother's grave that he was innocent (Dutch had hated his mother). The miners from Diamond demanded justice.

So, come July, Placerville found itself on fire again. The new fire ran down the opposite side of the street and extended further than the first fire. Both the Placer and Empire Theatres were consumed. The bookstore survived once again due to the Soda Works barrier (God bless that fizzy edifice.) Interestingly, Georgetown and Greenwood - both contenders for the county seat honors - suffered from fires on the exact same day. Three weeks later Diamond Springs was gutted by a fire. The only town in the running for county seat that escaped the inferno was Coloma, possibly because the Sheriff took Dutch McGee into custody right after the Diamond blaze. In the end, four towns burned; partly over a spat concerning the county seat honors and partly in retribution for a fire that, unbeknownst to all of the feuding participants, was an accident.

By August construction in Placerville resumed. By October a new, larger and better theatre stood at the location of the former Empire. Virtually every lot along Main Street was built upon, even those that had been vacant before the fires. Most of the buildings were raised in hard fireproof stone this time. Elstner's Hay Yard wisely became Elstner's Brick Yard. Some of the resulting changes to the town were difficult for the Boys to accept. Caroline Tannenwald rebuilt The Round Tent as a square brick building but kept the name. Although the designation and the architecture seemed incompatible to Jed ("The Square Brick" made more sense to him), most of the people in town enjoyed keeping the more comfortable and familiar title.

Although Dutch McGee only spent a few months in jail that

was enough to resolve the general situation. In January, 1857, the California State Legislature decided the entire issue of the El Dorado County seat needed to be settled once and for all. They bypassed the voters, and moved the county seat to Placerville by decree. Dan Gelwicks wrote in the *Mountain Democrat* that "the intelligence of the passage of the bill through the Senate was received in Placerville with the liveliest gratification. Our citizens seemed drunk with joy." In most cases the citizens were actually drunk, though Dan may be excused this slight deviation from the truth. The celebrations, organized by the Placerville Chapter of the miners' benevolent society *E Clampus Vitus*, were so infectious that the Masons and Oddfellows forgot that they didn't like the Clampers and joined in. The party lasted several days and by its conclusion there was a severe whiskey shortage in Placerville.

Passions in the county cooled and with Dutch McGee in jail the fires ceased. After his release Dutch decided to give up mining and took a job building the Carson Valley Wagon Road. After several months of work he fomented a workers rebellion because he felt that he and the other laborers were being underpaid. In protest McGee and the workers piled all of the contractor's construction equipment on top of a few barrels of gunpowder and blew them into the river. Unfortunately he didn't get clear of the explosion in time, and the "Great Carson Valley Wagon Road Rebellion" was the last anyone ever saw (at least in whole) of Dutch McGee.

In Placerville, out of the ashes, a new community arose. With each new building it seemed less like the gold camp of old. "Our community is reborn," Reverend Platt said one Sunday, while Jed sat in the back pew reading a copy of *Frankenstein* that had just come in to the store.

And that's the story of the Great Fire of 1856.

Oh, I suppose you are wondering whatever happened to Nugget Dravot, why he was so unhappy and why he left Placerville. Alright, I'll tell you.

Another year passed before Dravot reentered the Bookstore Boys' lives. One afternoon a letter showed up in the mail, addressed to David Dravot in care of the bookstore. Jed wasn't quite sure what to do with the missive, since he had never received a forwarding address from Nugget. He let the letter sit on his desk gathering dust for the first few weeks and then had a conversation with Jack about it.

"What if this is important?" he asked Jack. "Maybe we should open it up and see what it is."

"Jed, you can't go around opening other people's mail," Jack scolded.

"There's no return address. We can't send it back."

"Winkin' Theodore down at the Post Office can open it then," Jack suggested. "He's a duly appointed officer of the Postmaster. Let him do it."

"Maybe," Jed said. He didn't take the letter to Winkin' Theodore, though, and when a second letter showed up a few weeks later, also without a return address, he put the tea pot onto the wood stove and got it up to a boil. By the time Jack walked in he had already steamed open the first letter and was busy steaming the second.

"Jed! There are laws!" Jack cried. Jed pulled open the second letter and started reading.

"Don't worry, I can seal 'em again. They're both from Nugget's wife. Bet you never guessed that ten-foot tombstone was ever married!" Jed smiled. "There's a note in here. Both letters were originally sent to the navy base in San Francisco where Nug used to serve back in 1850. Imagine that, not only was the boy married, he was in the navy!"

146

"Nug sure is full of surprises," Jack agreed.

"They got wind he was working for a shipping company in Sacramento and forwarded the letters to a foreman there. Apparently Nug unloaded timber there around 1852. Eventually the foreman tracked down a dry goods store in Mormon Flat where Nugget worked delivering supplies to miners. The manager there had the bookstore address and forwarded them to us."

"Nice of all those people to make the effort," Jack said. "What do the letters say?"

By this time Jed had set aside the note from the dry goods store manager which detailed the complex journey these missives had taken. He had in hand the letters proper, written in the beautifully graceful handwriting of one Madeleine Dravot.

"Well?" Jack asked.

"She...uh...," Jed paused. "She says she doesn't blame him. She says it wasn't his fault."

"What wasn't his fault?"

His face as white as good expensive bookstock, Jed dropped the letters on the counter and dashed for the back room. Jack walked over and picked up the first epistle, so short it hardly qualified as more than a note. *I don't blame you… It wasn't your fault…* and then just a dozen more words.

A few minutes later Jed returned with two stacks of yellowed newspapers. There were copies of both the *Californian* and the *Alta California*, dated 1850 and 1852.

"Here," Jed said. He held up a copy of the *Alta California* from September of 1850. A fire had raged through the city, claiming multiple blocks. It started in a hotel popular with navy personnel. Next he pulled out a copy of the *Californian* from 1852. It detailed a fire which claimed a good section of the area around the south pier. It was believed to have started in a rooming house in the dock district.

"Now, doesn't that just frost your whiskers?!" Jack said.

Five years later, in the fall of 1862, Jack Norris found new evidence of Nugget Dravot's whereabouts. A newspaper article reported a fire in the city of Troy, New York, which consumed more than five hundred buildings. Deep in the final paragraphs of the article was a mention of several heroic men who braved burning buildings to save people trapped by the inferno; Walter Fraser, Ross Asbridge, and David Dravot. Fire Engine Company No. 1 blamed sparks from a locomotive igniting a covered bridge as the source of the blaze, but eyewitnesses claimed it began in a nearby neighborhood bookstore.

It was finally in the spring of 1871, fifteen years after they had last seen him that the Bookstore Boys at last heard directly from David "Nugget" Dravot. Jed got back to the store after picking up his kids from home and taking them out to their uncle's house in the long wagon to play with their cousins. (The existence of and the circumstances leading to these and others will be detailed in tales to come). Jack and his wife Lizette were at the store, sitting on the divan in front of the wood stove. Jack held up a letter.

"Guess who we got a letter from?" Jack asked.

"Johnny? Two Sheds Bishop?" Jed guessed.

"Nope. David Dravot."

"Who?" Jed asked. Jack handed him the envelope.

"Nugget."

"Nugget Dravot! Oh, good lord!" Jed's mouth hung open. "I don't believe it!"

"At least the old boy hasn't set himself afire!" Jack smiled.

And then he read the letter.

Dear Mister Bradford and Mister Norris,

I am so sorry for not writing to you earlier. I was remiss and I offer my humblest apologies. You were good friends during my time in the gold country.

It was with great surprise that I received the two letters which, I was to learn, found me only through your good offices. A similarly honest and steadfast friend who is a bookseller in Columbus, Ohio, forwarded them to me. He, in turn, received them from individuals in Maine whom I understand were sought out by you.

Although these letters have taken a score of years to reach me their content has brought me some small measure of peace, and I can never repay you for your faithful efforts to put them in my hands. I am forever indebted to you. Perhaps this unwelcome story which has dogged me for so many years can at last be put to rest with a simple "The End."

Enclosed please find three dollars, payment for the copy of Leaves of Grass by Walt Whitman which I ordered those many years ago. My hope is that the volume arrived and has been enjoyed by many readers since. Please accept this small token of my appreciation.

Nothing would make me happier than to hear from you. Please write and tell me how life in Placerville has changed in these last years. Do not spare any details. You know how much I love to read.

You may post your letters to the boarding house where I reside; David Dravot, in care of Catherine O'Leary, 137 DeKoven Street, Chicago, Illinois.

I must go now - Mrs. O'Leary's cow wants to be milked, and I have a book that is waiting patiently for me.

All the best and my eternal thanks, yours perpetually,
David Dravot

And that's what happened to Nugget.

Next:
An amazing race, villainy is afoot, and a path to the future takes
a definitive course

VI

THE AMAZING RACE
or
AROUND THE WORLD IN 21 HOURS

1864

In which an amazing race by water, rail, stage and foot determines the fate of an entire community

Jack Norris, as he had in Boston, enjoyed sketching and painting when he had the chance (although oil paints and watercolors were dear to come by in gold rush California). He did most of his work in charcoal or pencil on whatever paper he could find and then hung his best work on the wall in the bookstore. On occasion a customer offered to purchase one and Jack was always happy to accommodate them. His sketches became highly sought after. Every Sunday miners lined up to have their portraits drawn, mostly because the portraits resembled much more handsome specimens than the genuine articles. "Pretty me up," the miners said as they posed for him. Jack took to ordering what the miners called "fancy paper" from a store in Sacramento. It cost two dollars and fifty cents a sheet, but the miners were happy to pay for it. For a while Jack made more money drawing than he did selling books. Unfortunately, as with everything in Placerville, his business began to dry up when the miners left for more promising fields. By 1864 Jack sold a portrait a month and no more.

The problem was that the gold fields were picked clean. Some enterprising miners joined together into larger operations and ran flumes from high mountain rivers down to the alluvial deposits that contained the gold. They used the resulting massive jets of high pressure water to wash whole mountainsides at a time. Other miners concentrated on deep digs, burrowing into the ground following veins of gold-bearing quartz. Neither of these methods realized the sheer volume of gold the old 49ers had collected. A fair number of Placerville's miners picked up stakes and headed east due to the lure of Nevada Silver. But since the best road to Nevada went through Placerville the town survived as it became the main conduit for equipment and individuals headed east to Virginia City and the Comstock Lode. That wagon road was sufficient to keep the economy afloat for the present, but it wouldn't last. The future was railroads.

This is the story of *two* railroads, actually. The first California railroad was organized in 1852 and named the *Sacramento Valley Railroad Co.*. An eager young man named Theodore Judah was retained by the owners to survey routes from Sacramento to the most popular gold country destinations. Ted Judah was a man after Jed Bradford and Jack Norris's hearts; he liked to dream, and dream big. He was a railroad engineer and his personal vision went far beyond local branch lines. Jed and Jack first noticed Ted Judah in 1857 when he published a pamphlet titled *"A Practical Plan for Building the Pacific Railroad."* It described building a railroad over the Sierra Nevada and across the Great Plains, a two-thousand mile transcontinental rail line that would connect California with "the states" back east, providing an ease of cross-country travel Rufus Porter and Wind Wagon Thomas could never have offered. Unfortunately, as most big dreams are, it was prohibitively expensive. Judah spent more time looking for investors than he did investigating routes for his ambitious road. After four years the Sacramento Valley Railroad had laid just twenty miles of track.

The Bookstore Boys didn't sell any copies of Judah's tract, but that didn't stop them from talking about it to anyone who would listen.

"This is the future!" Jack told people. "The wagon road has saved Placerville for now. But if we want to survive in the long term, we need the railroad. The towns that get the railroad will get the business, and the rest will just wither away."

Jack's evangelizing on the railroad topic eventually had an effect. The El Dorado County Supervisors petitioned the Sacramento Valley Railroad to extend its line to Placerville. A deal was made for El Dorado County and the City of Placerville to help finance the construction of the line, and the combined *Placerville & Sacramento Valley Railroad Company* (P&SVRR) was incorporated on June 12, 1862 to build it.

People in California weren't the only ones who wanted a nationwide railroad. On July 1st President Abraham Lincoln signed into law the generously titled *Pacific Railroad Act of 1862: An Act to aid in the construction of a railroad and telegraph line from the Missouri river to the Pacific Ocean, and to secure to the government the use of the same for postal, military, and other purposes.* This Act, with its ridiculously long title, promised free land and large quantities of money per mile to any company willing to take on the immense challenge of building the transcontinental railroad. However, the southerners wanted it to go through the southern states and the northerners wanted it to go through the northern states, so nothing happened at all, as is often the case in Washington. Once the southern states succeeded from the Union it became clear that the northern route would win out. However, then there was no money for anything besides the war effort, so again nothing happened.

The turning point in this stalemate took place when, in Sacramento, Ted Judah met with a new group of potential investors that included; grocer Mark Hopkins, hardware merchant C.P. Huntington, Governor of California Leland Stanford, and ironmonger Charles Crocker. These businessmen looked at the fat sums President Lincoln was offering to anyone crazy enough to build a railroad and the shovel-ready plan that Judah was presenting to them - and they imagined a huge empire they could build on a complete transportation monopoly. Within days the four men, known to history as the "Big Four," incorporated the second of the two railroads around which our story revolves, the *Central Pacific Railroad Company.*

At first this was good news to Jed, Jack and the citizens of Placerville. In fact, Honest Alex Hunter threw a party. The Placerville & Sacramento Valley Railroad was already building toward Placerville. Now a second railroad was starting up, and two of the Central Pacific's main investors - Mark Hopkins and Collis Huntington - were former merchants of Placerville. In fact, when Jed and Jack opened their store in 1850 they bought the nails and brackets used to construct their bookshelves at Huntington's store. The local citizens felt this ensured a certain amount of loyalty and that *any* railroad route would now end up going through Placerville. Their good mood didn't last very long. The Central Pacific Railroad soon started building its line - but not toward Placerville. Instead it took a new route much further north, through undeveloped land over Dutch Flat and through Donner Pass (near the site where the infamous Donner Party met its grisly end).

So, the competition between these two railroads was on. Both applied for federal money under the Railroad Act and intended to penetrate the impenetrable Sierra Nevada. You might think that the winner would be determined by who did a better job or got through the mountains first. That's certainly what the people of Placerville thought. The truth is that railroads aren't really constructed on level playing fields.

Central Pacific owner Leland Stanford, as Governor of California, pressured the legislature to invest millions of dollars in his railroad in exchange for transporting (someday, when the railroad was completed) state employees, state militia, convicts, and people bound for asylums. He then coerced Sacramento and Placer Counties and the City of San Francisco to purchase stock in the railroad. At the same time Collis Huntington headed to Washington, DC, to wine and dine the U.S. Congress.

Next, the Big Four created a railroad construction firm and, as the directors of the Central Pacific, awarded themselves the contract to build the railroad. That way, even if the Central Pacific went bankrupt and couldn't pay back its investors, they could keep all of the profits in their construction company. They also incorporated the *Dutch Flat and Donner Lake Wagon Road Company* to build a wagon road along the railway route and set up toll booths on this new road to make side money on wagon traffic.

Their sleight of hand didn't stop there. Since the Railroad Act paid more per mile for construction in mountainous terrain than it did in flat territory, the Big Four also decided to move the Sierra Nevada fifteen miles further west, which would earn the Central Pacific almost a quarter million dollars more. This proves that if you're single minded and greedy enough you can move mountains.

Ted Judah felt betrayed. He confronted the Big Four and demanded to be treated as an equal. They suggested that if he wanted a larger share of the railroad so badly he should buy them out. This was sarcasm, of course, since the Big Four would never sell their cash cow, but Judah took the offer seriously. He bought passage on the next ship to Panama, headed to New York to meet with investors like Cornelius Vanderbilt who had the means to buy the Central Pacific. During the land crossing in Panama Judah caught a tropical fever. Just a few days after his ship arrived in New York he was dead.

Ironically, the first four locomotives purchased by the

Central Pacific arrived in San Francisco by steamship just a few days later. They were named the *Governor Stanford*, the *Pacific*, the *C. P. Huntington*, and… the *T. D. Judah*.

"The Big Four are crooks!" Lester Robinson told Jack Norris one day when they ran into each other in the train station at Folsom. Robinson was one of the owners of the Placerville & Sacramento Valley Railroad and he was bitterly opposed to anything involving the Big Four and the Central Pacific.

"It seems like dirty politics, bribes, and lies are how big business is conducted these days," Jack admitted. "Why aren't the newspapers exposing their tricks? I think our side needs better press."

Unfortunately the newspapers were all in the pocket of the Central Pacific. The Big Four "contributed" two thousand dollars in company stock to the editor of the *Sacramento Union*, and many reporters got similar "gifts". To counter the "biased media," the Placerville & Sacramento Valley Railroad self-published their own pamphlet titled *The Great Dutch Flat Swindle*, which charged that the Big Four had no intention of building the railroad any further than Dutch Flat, and that the plan was to end the railroad line there and make millions from the wagon road.

By the summer of 1864 bad blood between the two companies was boiling, and in Placerville the citizens began to fear that they were going to be cheated out of their railroad and that the community was doomed.

The conflict came to a head one evening in August, 1864, in Sacramento, just a few blocks from California's half-constructed capitol building, which was being constructed in a flood plain and spent much of the time underwater (some folks called it "The Swamp"). Two men walked along a quiet street and approached a large, ornately decorated Victorian edifice. There was no sign indicating the nature of the building's resident, only a large brass knocker with a lion's head at its center situated on a dark red door. One of the men reached up and knocked twice, paused, knocked twice again and then followed with a solitary knock. In answer to this clandestine pattern the door opened and a butler admitted them.

This was the Sacramento chapter of the *Society of Merchant Adventurers for the Mystery and Discovery of Regions, Dominions, Islands, and Places Unknown,* a secretive group originally founded in 1551 in order to discover the Northwest Passage. Now it was the most elite of social clubs, and only the richest and most powerful of men had an opportunity of even knowing that it existed. The members didn't do anything as grand as world exploration anymore. These days they mostly drank brandy, played whist, and plotted together on how to steal other people's money.

"Misters Robinson," the butler said in addressing the men.

The Brothers Robinson went directly to the library to enjoy their after dinner drinks. The good humor they entered with vanished when they saw Leland Stanford, their nemesis, sitting with his partners Crocker and Hopkins. The three-quarters of the Big Four grew quiet when they saw the Robinsons walk in.

"So, Stanford, busy figuring out new ways to fleece the public?" Lester Robinson asked the portly Governor.

"You are a delightfully funny man, Robinson. It is a wonder you aren't on the stage performing the *comédie en vaudeville,* " Stanford said with a snort.

"We all know that the Central Pacific is nothing but a beard for the Wagon Road," Lester seethed.

"The wagon road was necessary to get supplies to our workers beyond the end of the line," Crocker said, as if his matter-of-fact response would solve the issue.

"And it's just a coincidence that you're making better than a million dollars a year on the wagon road tolls?" Lester asked. "At the expense of the Placerville road, I might add."

"It's business, Robinson, and you're an idiot," Stanford said, no longer trying to be politic. "You seem to enjoy losing money. The rest of us are in business to make money."

"You don't intend to make a penny off the railroad," Lester said accusingly. "In fact, I expect you mean to bankrupt it. Once you have all the money, the railroad declares bankruptcy and the investors are left holding the bag. You walk away with all of the construction profits and collect tolls on your wagon road. Quite brilliant, except for one thing."

"What's that?" Crocker asked.

"*We're* actually going to *build* our railroad. Our route is the superior one, and you know it. The Placerville & Sacramento Valley will get over the summit to Nevada first. Then *we'll* receive all the government money and your wagon road will be empty. We're faster, we're better, and your pitiful bridges and trestles will collapse the first time there's a good rain."

"Listen, Robinson," Crocker said, "your little toy railroad is already a sorry sight. Even as it stands right now, the Central Pacific and our wagon road are superior to the pathetic line you've cobbled together. Freight taking our route could be in Omaha before you got to Virginia City. The whole state knows it."

"Prove it," Lester Robinson fumed. "Perhaps we should put a wager on it. A race, our line against yours, to get a parcel from Freeport to Virginia City. Come, now, Crocker, are you willing to put your stolen money where your mouth is?"

"I am," Leland Stanford spoke up. "And I won't even ask you to put up a sum, since we both know how broke you are, Robinson. If you win, I'll pay you twenty-thousand dollars. If we win, you must retract that deplorable and libelous pamphlet you've been circulating, recant your accusations in the press, and admit before the public and God the results of the challenge."

"Lester, let's just go have our brandy and let this be," Lester's brother John said. "Any agreement you make with these men, even this one, is nothing but a deal with the devil." John's advice fell on deaf ears.

"You accept my challenge, and I accept your wager," Lester said. Stanford smiled.

"Alright, Lester, is next Monday good for you? That should give us enough time to plan the particulars," he said. "Perhaps a week will give you enough time to lay a few more inches of rail."

"That will be fine," Lester said, ignoring the insult, and he grabbed his brother by the shoulder. "Let's go, John. I find the Club atmosphere deficient tonight."

Two days later, in Placerville, Jack Norris hired a part time clerk.

Ah Moon was born in rural China on a family farm and spent his youth helping his father plant potatoes, rice, beans, and yams. Lots and lots of yams. This simple life was completely at odds with what he was told in school, that the Chinese Emperors ruled with the wisdom of gods and had illuminated the world with civilization, art, and literature. Planting yams was definitely not the work of civilized, illuminated beings - at least to Ah Moon. Convinced he was meant for more than just farming, he traveled to Hong Kong and sailed for the land of opportunity: California. At first, living in San Francisco, he got a job in the Chinese quarter that paid $3 a week. That was barely more than he made in China, so he moved to Placerville to try his hand at mining. He disliked mining more than he disliked yams, so he quit and took a job working at the Iowa House serving meals. Serving food was not his cup of tea either, so he gained employment at Lee Chew's laundry, hoping to

158

Booksellers To The Savage West

work his way up through the organization and into management. A dalliance with Chew's daughter killed those dreams, and he became a freight handler for the stage line, a groomer at the Pacific Street Stables, and most recently a day laborer building a bridge near Riverton. After fifteen years in Placerville he found himself going door to door looking for any job that would pay for his food and shelter. And that is how he ended up at *Bradford & Norris: Booksellers to the Savage West*.

"You're sure you can do this job, Ah Moon?" Jack asked. "You're certainly a jack-of-all-trades, I'll give you that. However, the job requires a very thorough knowledge of English."

"A-B-C-D, E-F-G..." Ah Moon started singing. Jack cut him off.

"I know you know the alphabet," Jack said. "How often do you read?"

"The Chinese invented literature," Ah Moon replied. Although he was skeptical of this statement, Jack gave the Chinese man the benefit of the doubt.

"What do you think, Jed?" he asked his partner. Jed was busy writing and just waved.

"This is your call," Jed said. Ah Moon looked at Jack with such pleading eyes that he couldn't say no.

"Alright, but I expect every effort!" Jack said. Ah Moon smiled and jumped up and down like a little boy.

"You bet, Mister Jack! I'll show you what I can do!"

They were interrupted by Dot-Dash Adams, the clerk at Alta Telegraph, who threw the front door of the store open. Jed's papers went flying due to the resulting rush of air and he scrambled to recover them.

"Sorry, Jed," Adams said. "I have a telegram for Jack!"

"Who is spending money to send me a telegram?!" Jack wondered. He took the envelope from Adams and tore it open.

159

"Well?" Jed asked.

"It's from Lester Robinson," Jack said. "He's taking the train to Latrobe and then the stage to Shingle Springs and wants me to meet him there tonight. He says it's important."

"What's important?" Jed asked.

"I don't know, he didn't say. They charge by the word, you know!" Jack checked his watch and then grabbed his hat. "I'll have to leave right now if I'm going to make it in time."

Jed pointed to Ah Moon, who was still standing in front of the newspaper racks. "Don't you dare leave him with me! You hired him, you're going to train him!" Jack thought for a moment and then took Ah Moon by the arm.

"Come with me," he said. "You can help with the horses."

Ah Moon rigged up the horses so quickly that Jack was already impressed with his new employee. They hopped aboard and their wagon rambled off down Main Street and out the west end of town toward Shingle Springs, several miles distant.

Lester Robinson was waiting at the General Store in Shingle Springs when they arrived. The westbound stage would be there soon and he was going to take it back to Latrobe and catch the same train back to Sacramento. He'd made the entire journey just to make some arrangements and to meet with Jack.

"What's so important?" Jack asked, flattered.

"Jack, you've been one of this railroad's best friends from the beginning," Robinson said. "Without any sort of compensation you've argued our case wherever necessary and I thank you immensely. Now, I have to ask for your help again. We have been challenged, and I need you to protect our honor." He proceeded with the details.

The Challenge, as determined by both railroads, was simple; the steamer Chrysopolis would bring two bundles of San Francisco newspapers to the railroad ports. Once the papers were brought ashore the race began and the winner would be the group that delivered them to the Silver House Hotel in Virginia City first. The Placerville & Sacramento Valley Railroad left from Freeport and terminated in Latrobe, where their stage partner, the Pioneer Stage Company, would collect the papers and continue up the Placerville road hellbent for Nevada. The Central Pacific would bring its bundle ashore in Sacramento, take them to the end of its line east of Newcastle, and then consign them to the California Stage Company (which, of course, they had a financial interest in) for the trip over the wagon road to Virginia City.

"In each case, the bundle of papers will be entered into the care of a third party," Lester explained, "who is not in any way associated with either railroad or stage line, and who must be approved by both myself and The Big Four. They've chosen a surveyor from the Sacramento Assay Office named Sam Hamilton, and I can't find any evidence that he is compromised by Stanford and his bunch, so I've approved him. For our carrier, I've named you."

"Me?!" Jack said. "Why me? I'm a bookseller, writer and artist. I don't know the first thing about railroads, races, and whatnot."

"That's exactly why you're perfect for the job, Jack. You've always been a staunch defender and proponent of this railroad, and I know you're an honest and reliable man. You have my complete trust. All you have to do is stay with the papers, take a ride on the train and then the stage, and within the bounds of the rules set forth in The Challenge get them to Virginia City before those scoundrels at the Central Pacific do."

Well, of course Jack accepted, and Lester hopped aboard the westbound Pioneer Stage. Ah Moon already had the wagon ready to depart for Placerville.

"This all sounds very exciting," Ah Moon told Jack.

"That's good," Jack replied, "because I think I'm going to have you come along with me."

When Jack returned to the store he told Jed everything he could recall about the race while Ah Moon took the horses and wagon back to the stables.

"I think Lester is playing with fire here, Jack," Jed warned. "I don't expect Crocker and Stanford have ever played by the rules in their lives. And who was that surveyor that Lester said they picked as their carrier? Sam Hamilton? Why does that name seem vaguely familiar?"

"How hard can it be?" Jack said. "I have a nice little train excursion, a bumpy stage ride. There's not much I can do to influence the outcome."

"Do you want me to come along?" Jed asked. "You know, tt sounds like it could become an adventure!"

"No! No adventures!" Jack protested. "It's just a little vacation, that's all. I'll take Ah Moon along for company," Jack said. "Besides, someone has to mind the store."

Jed was clearly disappointed, but he saw Jack's point. "I guess that's alright. I'm busy trying to get this Wheelbarrow Man story figured out, anyway. Just remember to write down anything interesting that happens."

Word about the race spread fast throughout the region, from Placerville to Sacramento to Auburn. It was the headline of every newspaper and the subject of every dinner conversation. In Placerville there were plans to have a big party to celebrate the passage of the stagecoach as it headed east. Bill Cary considered illuminating his hotel for the event, and then decided against it. Back in 1858, when the first Overland Mail Stage was scheduled to arrive in Placerville, Cary rigged lights across the front of his hotel and set up a receiving platform for the stage. The entire town turned out to see if they had any mail (although, of course, most of them didn't). Bad Luck Casey, who was dabbling in the brewing arts, cooked up a big batch of his molasses ale and gave it away free to the partiers. Almost Bill roasted up a batch of turkeys, paid for by Henry Hooker, and Reverend Platt served the white meat while Jim Halliwell served the dark meat and soggy pickles. When the sun started to set and the stage still hadn't arrived, the citizens started to lose some of their enthusiasm. By nine o'clock the population of Placerville headed home to bed, full of turkey and ale. When the stage finally rode into town a little after ten, the driver took in the empty street and said, "Damn, I expected more of a reception than this!" Rumor had it, already, that the Great Race's stage would be arriving fairly late. Cary decided that this time he'd skip the illumination and just concentrate on the turkey and ale.

So, the following Monday, August twenty-second, Jack Norris and Ah Moon arrived on the afternoon train at the docks in Freeport. The location got its name from its origins; the railroad built the port facility on the river a few miles from Sacramento to avoid heavy duties and fees the city was charging the Placerville & Sacramento Valley Railroad on its freight.

Lester Robinson met Jack at the railway's ticket office and told him that the bundles of newspapers - both theirs and the Central Pacific's - would be coming in aboard the Chrysopolis, which was due any moment. He pointed out a group of men on the far side of the platform.

"Those are the fellows from the Central Pacific. The original rules were that they had to wait for the ship to arrive at their port station in Sacramento before taking their bundle ashore," Robinson said. "But they complained that due to the schedule the

Chrysopolis would have to wait for a higher tide to get to their dock and that wasn't fair. So they're going to take it by horseback from here to Sacramento. They're *already* cheating!"

"You agreed to it, right?" Jack asked.

"Yes, but it's still cheating!" Lester complained.

The *Chrysopolis* ("Golden City") was an elegant floating palace. It was a Victorian masterpiece buoyed upon the water, reminiscent of the great riverboats of the Mississippi River, built to transport a thousand passengers in relative luxury while also carrying close to a thousand tons of cargo at the same time. Its massive steam engine turned two thirty-six foot side paddlewheels, and it was known to all as the fastest boat on the Sacramento River. And the ship was no stranger to wagers or races; on New Year's Eve 1861 the Chrysopolis steamed from Sacramento to San Francisco in less than five and a half hours when challenged by slower competitors.

A steward brought the two bundles of papers ashore and set them on the dock. Lester signed for their bundle and handed them to Jack.

"They're all yours," he said. "Just get them to Virginia City before those robber barons do." The two men shook hands and Jack and Ah Moon hurried along the platform to their waiting train.

At 11:15 p.m. the Sacramento Valley Railroad locomotive *C.K. Garrison* left the Freeport station at its usually scheduled time. John Robinson was in the locomotive with the engineer. Jack Norris, Ah Moon and the precious newspapers were in a passenger car behind it along with a fair number of passengers headed east. Following the passenger cars were several railcars full of freight bound for Nevada. With a blast of its horn the train pulled out of the station.

As the locomotive gained speed Jack felt his heart begin to race and his breath grew short with the excitement. This was already his tenth or eleventh trip along the P&SVRR since it reached Folsom, yet the thought of speeding along at almost twenty miles an hour still thrilled him. Watching the hills and fields fly by in a blur he realized that the Next Big Thing that he and Jed had looked for in the Aerial Transport and the Wind Wagon was at last here. Jumping from Sacramento over thirty miles of countryside to Latrobe in less than two hours seemed, as Ulysses Grant put it, "like annihilating space."

"I'm going to go out on the platform to get some air, Ah Moon," Jack said. "Please stay with the newspapers."

The clerk smiled. "We are going to win, Mister Norris! I know it!"

"For Placerville's sake, I certainly hope so, Ah Moon."

Out on the small deck at the back of the car, Jack leaned out to see the locomotive ahead of them and smelled the rich wood smoke bellowing from the stack. Behind he saw the other passenger cars and the freight cars, snaking their way back toward Sacramento around a wide bend in the rails.

At the same time the *C.K. Garrison* was chugging its way across the valley toward Latrobe, the Big Four's bundle of newspapers arrived by horseback at the Central Pacific's dockside station in Sacramento. Their locomotive, the *Atlantic*, was all ready to go. The great black locomotive was twelve feet tall and fifty feet long, with wheels more than four and a half feet across, and topped by a bright brass bell. Bold initials, painted in gold across the side of the tender, read C.P.R.R.. Unlike the *C.K. Garrison*, the *Atlantic* had no cars attached to it, no freight, and no passengers - just the tender, crew and their bundle carrier, Sam Hamilton, who wore chaps, a long black coat and an oversized derby. The unusually light train pulled out of the station the moment the papers were aboard, regardless of schedule, and by just a few minutes after midnight it was speeding east toward the mountains on the Central Pacific tracks.

It took the *C.K. Garrison* just an hour and thirty-seven minutes to arrive at the P&SVRR station near Latrobe, as good if not better than its usual time. The Pioneer Stage was waiting near the platform. The driver, Fargo George, was a veteran of the route they would take and knew every turn and every grade by heart. If anyone could get them the rest of the way to Virginia City in record time, it was George. Jack and Ah Moon tossed the bundle of papers into the stage and Jack signaled to the driver.

"Despite the late hour, I expect there will be a welcoming committee of some sort in Placerville when we pass through," Jack said. "Wave all you like, but don't stop!"

"Got it, Jack!" Fargo George said, and the horses bolted forward up the road toward Shingle Springs and Placerville.

The stripped-down Central Pacific train bearing the Big Four's papers completed the thirty-two miles to the end of their line in just forty-two minutes, almost doubling the speed of the P&SVRR train. Sam Hamilton grabbed his papers and jumped onto the waiting California Stage. A large group of locals, supporting their line's chances in the Great Race, waved from the station as he pulled away and headed east toward Applegate. What the crowd failed to see was when the stage, just a mile out from the station, pulled to a stop. There several men, all in the employ of The Big Four, waited with a horse; a beautiful stallion with sure feet. Sam Hamilton, once one of the best riders for the Pony Express (before that famous institution was rendered moot by the arrival of the telegraph), tied the newspapers to the back of the horse's saddle, leapt up, and rode away with a bold "Ho!" at a speed no stagecoach could ever hope to match.

Bill Cary, Bad Luck Casey, Jed, Lizzie, and a small handful of determined citizens were all that was left (awake and sober, at least) of the revelers by the time the Pioneer Stage arrived in Placerville. Despite Jack's admonition, Fargo George slowed down as they went along Main Street in order to give the few people who had waited up so late a good look. After all was said and done, they deserved at least that much. Jack waved at Jed and Lizzie as the stage rumbled past the bookstore, hoping that this brief sighting was worth their long vigil. The cheers woke up a few of the drunks, who sat up to see what all the noise was about. As quickly as that the stagecoach was gone and climbing up past Smith Flat toward the mountains. The lanterns were the only light they had, illuminating the road just a few dozen feet ahead of the team. Still, the road was sound and wide, and by the time they reached the more dangerous parts of the route the sun would be rising over the crest ahead of them. They stopped briefly at Sportsman's Hall to change horses and then continued east.

Things went well until just before the Pacific Toll House. Fargo George pulled back suddenly on the horses and the stage came to a sudden halt. In front of them, looming large out of the dark, was a lumber wagon on its side. Logs lay scattered helter skelter across the road, from the steep left bank to the cliff at their right, completely blocking any forward progress. Two men were working by a single small lantern, apparently trying to saw one of the logs in half to make it easier to manage. Neither man seemed to be working terribly hard.

"What's going on here?" Jack asked, his head sticking out of the stagecoach window.

"Sorry, folks, we hit a deer and broke an axle," one of the men said. "Our load tipped over."

Fargo George, Jack and Ah Moon surveyed the wreckage and agreed that things did not look promising. It would likely take hours to clear the road enough for the stagecoach to get by.

"We'll have this cleared out by daybreak," the man said, and he returned to his saw.

"This is it," Jack said to his companions. "We'll never make Virginia City in time now."

"Wait, Mister Norris, I have an idea," Ah Moon said examining the wreckage. He pulled a set of ropes from the damaged wagon and hurried over to the furthest log, which rested at the edge of the cliff.

"What are you up to, Chinaman?" one of the men asked.

Ah Moon tied the rope to the cliff-side log at three points, and then wrapped it around the next log, knotting it, then around the next. Soon he had a half dozen of the logs tied securely together. Once done he returned to the cliff and Jack realized what he had in mind.

"George, give us a hand!" he said. "And be careful that you don't get tangled in anything!" Fargo George joined them and all three men pushed with all of their strength. The log rolled once, then twice, and then over the cliff.

"Hey! That's our freight!" one of the men cried out, with less energy than Jack expected. George, Jack and Ah Moon all ran toward their coach as the first log fell. The ropes snapped taught and the next one slid across the road and then down into the abyss after it. One by one the logs that Ah Moon had tied together were dragged across the road, fell into the canyon and vanished into the dark. When they were gone there was a clear path almost exactly as wide as the stagecoach.

"I knew there was a reason I wanted you to come along," Jack told Ah Moon.

"We are going to win, Mister Norris! You see!" the clerk replied.

The trio hopped aboard the coach and Fargo George negotiated the narrow gap between the cliff and the damaged wagon.

"You're going to pay for those!" the man standing in the road called after them, but George ignored them and as soon as the stagecoach was clear he went forward as quickly as he could.

Once they were about a quarter mile further along, Jack was out on the runner keeping an eye out for further obstacles when Fargo George said; "Who moves that sort of heavy freight at three o'clock in the morning, Jack? There's something fishy going on. That fellow back there, I've seen him over in Auburn. I can't say as I'd swear to it, but I'm betting he works for the California Stage."

"Come to think of it, they said they hit a deer, but I didn't see a carcass. Do you think that entire mess back there was set up just to slow us down?" Jack asked, shocked (perhaps naively) that men would go so far just to win a wager.

"I don't say that I do, but I don't say that I don't," George answered, and he concentrated on the road ahead. Jack lowered himself back into the coach.

"Jed was right," he said to Ah Moon. "This has become an adventure."

The mountains were a dark line, silhouetted against the growing light in the eastern sky when Jack awoke. Perhaps 'awoke' is not the correct term, as he was never actually asleep, just dozing off and on when the bouncing coach would let him. He checked his watch, did some quick calculations, and determined that they were still on schedule. The stagecoach was moving at a fair speed, given the steep grade, when suddenly Jack, Ah Moon, and the driver all heard a voice call out; "Help!"

Instinctively, Fargo George pulled back on his team and the coach slowed and came to a stop. Immediately Jack wondered if this was another trick to prevent them from winning the race.

"Help me!" the voice called out again. Out of the trees and bushes at the side of the road came a young woman, pretty if it matters, her hair disheveled and her long dress covered in pine needles. "Please, help me or they'll kill me, I'm sure!"

Ah Moon threw open the coach door and jumped out to take the woman's hand. Jack stood on the runner and looked both ways to see if she was being pursued.

"What are you doing way out here, Miss?" he asked. "Who are you?"

"Oh," she said, "My name is Narcissa, but no one really likes that, do they? So I ask that people call me 'Effie.'"

"Very well, Effie, who is after you?" Jack asked.

"My husband, Pancake Henderson, the scoundrel!" she cried. "With guns and two hired thugs, no less!"

Jack once again checked their surroundings and then motioned for the young woman to climb into the stagecoach. "We can take you to the twenty-two mile house and you can get a coach back to Placerville to seek out the sheriff."

"Oh, I can't go there!" Effie protested. "Herbert is coming for me from Placerville!"

"Who is Herbert?" Jack asked.

"My *other* husband!"

"I think you need to do some explaining," Jack said. "We are in a sort of hurry, though, so please come aboard and tell us on the way."

Ah Moon helped Effie into the coach and sat down next to her. Jack signaled to Fargo George to get them moving again and the horses made the effort to get started on the hillside from a complete standstill.

"You okay lady?" Ah Moon asked the girl. He brought out a handkerchief and, wetting it with cold water, wiped the dirt from her face.

"Yes, thank you, now that you fine gentlemen have rescued me," she said.

The storyteller in Jack was curious now and he said, "Alright, Miss, would you please tell us... why do you have two husbands after you?"

The first of her two husbands, she told them, was Pancake Henderson. Before they met each other he was quite a rogue, or so she had been told, and back in 1859 had nothing to show for all of his hard work mining in California and Nevada, because he never did any hard work. He liked to piggy-back on other people's claims, shovel easy dirt, and placer easy sand. He had been nicknamed "Pancake" because he was so lazy he made flapjacks instead of baking bread. One day, the story went, Pancake saw some miners digging in a remote area and he laid a stake in the ground where they couldn't see him. Then he circled around and walked up, telling them that it was his claim, showing them the stake as proof. Well, the other miners, being honest men, negotiated a deal and Pancake became a partner on a pretty fair strike. He didn't do much of the digging himself, since he believed he was always more effective in a "supervisorial capacity." With his newfound riches he bought a store in Virginia City, ready to live the soft, easy life of an in-town merchant.

It was about this time that a wagon train of Mormons from Utah came through Virginia City, bearing Effie and her husband, Herbert, moving west from Utah to establish themselves in Nevada. They came into Pancake's store and the lazy miner-merchant fell in love with the girl at first sight. "I wasn't that well turned out, dusty from the trail and wearing nothing but calico and the most atrocious poke bonnet. Still, he saw something in me," she smiled, "and I don't know what quite came over me. It was so flattering and all. That very evening he came to our camp while Herbert was out tending to the horses and declared his undying love. Well, what could I say? I ran away with Pancake to Carson City, where we were married the very next morning!"

"But you were already married! What about Herbert?" Jack asked.

"Oh, Herbert was... well... Herbert. A well intentioned man, I suppose, though not the most exciting of men. A good farmer. He rarely made his feelings clear to me, though I daresay he is now!"

Apparently Pancake and Effie were married just two days and still honeymooning in Carson City when Herbert showed up, demanding the return of his wife. Pancake presented the marriage license he and Effie had obtained two days before, providing rock solid evidence that she was, in fact, his wife, and asked Herbert if he had a similar document proving his prior claim. Unfortunately, Herbert did not, and Pancake told him to take a hike. This did not sit well with Herbert and he demanded satisfaction. Pancake offered a horse, sixty dollars and a revolver (unloaded) as means to settle the dispute amicably, but Herbert would have none of that. He said there would be a duel, pistols only, the next morning in front of that very hotel.

"It was most complimentary, I daresay, having two men fight over you, if you have ever had it happen." Jack and Ah Moon both indicated that it had not.

Unfortunately for Effie's honor, Pancake gathered up their things and they left town in the middle of the night, hurrying back to Virginia City. This was most discouraging to Effie.

"It was clear," she said, "that the stories of Pancake's lack of bravado were true. My heart was broken and I resolved to return to Herbert once he found me."

Pancake gathered a few men - and their guns - to set up a guard around his cabin in case Herbert was to show up. The next morning he went down to his store to check on business which, as usual, was very poor because Pancake hadn't the slightest idea how to run a business.

"I sat there in his cabin talking to Charles - he was one of the young men Pancake hired to protect me from Herbert. Charles is such a fine boy, and he told me all about Pancake and how he got rich stealing others' miners' claims and I must say it put me off of Pancake quite a bit. Charles said I likely deserved better than either of these two men, and that I should come with him to San Francisco, a far richer and better situated city than anything in Nevada. Well, how could a girl turn down such a fetching offer?"

"So you ran away with Charles?" Jack asked, not surprised any longer.

"What else was I to do? We made off right away and got to Placerville yesterday morning. We had only just settled in when Herbert showed up. He had arrived at Pancake's cabin and one of the other men told him that Charles was taking me into California. Well, Charles did what Pancake could not do, and defended me, thank you very much. Fisticuffs were the nature of the battle, and they both acquitted themselves nicely. Herbert gave up fighting like a man, for which I shall never forgive him, and shot at us. Charles and I endeavored to escape by hiding in a wagon headed east upon this road."

"Where is Charles now?" Jack asked.

The wagon in which they were concealed stopped at Pacific House and she and Charles disembarked, only to find Pancake and two of his men just arriving from the east, "waving their guns around quite disgracefully! Charles made off into the woods to the north, clearly as a distraction to allow me to make my escape. I have been wandering these woods ever since," she said, glancing back and forth from Jack to Ah Moon, "without any hope of rescue until you fine gentlemen came along."

Jack thought about the situation for a moment. "We can't just leave you at the twenty-two mile house. They'll be checking all the stops along the road. I guess you'll have to stay with us all the way to Virginia City. From there you can get another coach to wherever you like."

"What about Charles?" Effie asked.

Jack suspected that Charles was likely on his way to San Francisco without his troublesome new girlfriend, but he said, "He'll probably make his way back to Placerville and we can contact him then."

The stagecoach rattled along the road as it leveled out along the ridge. Jack was less concerned with Effie and more with the multiple delays they had faced. If their prize bundle of newspapers failed to reach Virginia City before the Central Pacific's did he wasn't sure he would ever be able to face Lester Robinson again.

"So, you are a Celestial?" Effie asked Ah Moon.

"I am Chinese," he said.

"How exotic," she smiled, "to have traveled the world from one hemisphere to the other. I've had such a simple life, stuck on a farm for most of my life, planting wheat, barley, and yams."

"Yams?!" Ah Moon exclaimed. "I, too, farmed yams, in China."

"You did?!" Effie asked. "Shall I tell you more?!"

About this time, near the eastern end of the Donner Lake Wagon Road, Sam Hamilton rode his exhausted horse down a short side trail to a spot where a waiting California Stage had been concealed for the last twelve hours. Hamilton jumped down from his mount and untied his newspaper bundle, transferring it to the stage. Now it was just a matter of riding the coach down the ravine into Nevada and across the desert to Virginia City. Hamilton and his horse had made the trip over the pass in half the time it would have taken the stagecoach.

"Take your time," Hamilton told the driver. "We want to win, but it has to be believable."

The Pioneer Stagecoach carrying Jack and company wound along the road where it hugged the river. Jack leaned out the window in the brisk air and smelled the sweet pines warming in the morning light. "How are we doing for time, George?" he asked. Before the driver could answer the heard a loud crack. Like a dusty gray waterfall, a cascade of rocks showered down the hillside up ahead and blanketed the road. Fargo George stopped the coach and wiped his face with his kerchief.

"Do you suppose it's them again, trying to delay us?" Jack asked.

"Suppose it's possible," George said. "Then again, maybe not."

Ah Moon and Effie got out of the coach and joined the others by the jumble of granite that was blocking the way. Jack surveyed the hillside, looking for any indication of the rockslide's origins. He thought that, for a split second, he could see a human figure hundreds of feet up at the top of the cliff, but when he blinked it was gone. Considering the race and prior events, he thought that he might be seeing things. He looked down and took stock of the road. The pile of rubble wasn't terribly high - just a few inches - but the edges were jagged and it was difficult to see how the stagecoach or horses could safely navigate them.

"Some of these rocks look pretty heavy. I suppose we can clear out a path so the horses don't get cut up. It's going to take a long time, though," he said.

"Wait, Mister Norris, I have an idea," Ah Moon interrupted. He asked Fargo George to bring the coach back around and they rode down to a wide bar in the river about fifty yards west of the slide. Ah Moon took the sacks of mail from the back of the coach and dumped the packages and letters into the storage box.

"What are you doing?!" Fargo George asked. "That's U.S.

Mail!"

Without answering, Ah Moon took the empty sacks down to the bar and started filling them with sand. Jack caught on right away and he and George started to help. After only three trips in the stage they had hauled enough sand up to the rockslide to fill in between the rocks and create a narrow, sandy ramp up and over the slide. The horses carefully picked their way and there was only a single moment when they were afraid a wheel might have gotten stuck. Soon they were on the far side and climbing toward the summit.

"You're amazing, Ah Moon! We've lost no more than a half hour!" Jack beamed.

Jack figured that they were finally in the clear (i.e., safe from further skullduggery) when they reached the bottom of the Carson Canyon. In fact, he was just sitting back and taking a deep breath of relief when suddenly a series of shots echoed off the canyon walls. Bits of the road ahead exploded up and into the air. The horses - either just scared by the shots or hit by flying chips of stone - panicked, and the team careened off into the trees. One of the coach's wheels rolled up and over a huge granite boulder and as it flipped onto its side Jack, Ah Moon and Effie went tumbling in a mass of arms and legs. The stage, sliding along the ground, then crashed into a massive pine tree that had the poor manners to be standing in their way. It took a moment for the dust to settle and for the three passengers to extricate themselves from each other. At last they were all standing on the left door, which now lay on the ground, and Jack popped open the right door (now above them) and climbed out. He insisted that Ah Moon and Effie stay inside the coach for safety's sake while he checked on Fargo George's condition. Crouching low, he worked his way up next to the nervous team. Fargo George was kneeling on the ground next to the lead horses, seemingly none the worse for being thrown from the top of the coach.

"Are you alright?" Jack asked.

"Been better," George replied.

"Did someone take a shot at us?"

"Sure seemed like it," George said just another shot rang out. A puff of granite exploded from the cliff behind them. Halfway up the opposing hillside, from behind some boulders, they saw some movement.

"Listen up!" a voice demanded. "Sorry for spookin' your horses so bad. Didn't mean for it to happen. All I want is my wife, and you can pass! But until I get her, you're going nowhere!"

"Pancake, is that you?" Effie called out from the coach.

"Yes, sugar-dumpling!" Henderson answered. "All is forgiven if you just come back!"

"You wrecked our stagecoach, Henderson!" Jack said. "We don't want any part in this. I can't let you hurt your wife, though. I've sworn to her my protection!"

"I don't want to hurt you, my little peach-pit! I jist want you to come home!" Henderson wailed.

Suddenly Effie came clambering out of the coach and dropped to the road. "I'm here, my lamb! I'm so sorry to have doubted you! Put down your gun and come hold me in your arms!"

Pancake Henderson almost immediately came out from behind the outcrop where he had been hiding and loped down the hill to greet his errant wife. The two embraced in the middle of the road while Jack, Fargo George and Ah Moon stood dumbfounded by their ruined coach. After several minutes the lovers released each other and joined them. Henderson was quite contrite.

"My apologies for your coach, fellas. I figured that turncoat Charles would be lurking around and ready to put up a fight. No hard feelin's?"

"No hard feelings?!" Jack fumed. "We were in the middle of a race, a race that the future of an entire community depends on!"

Henderson pointed to the team, which was still stomping on the ground nervously due to the gunfire. Fargo George was trying to calm them as much as he could. "Why don't you just take one or two of the horses?" Pancake asked.

"Because the rules say it has to come in on the stage," Jack said. "If we come in by horseback, we lose, even if we get there first!"

"Wait, Mister Norris, I have an idea," Ah Moon said, examining the wreckage.

The rebuilt stagecoach had no roof, rode upon a single axle with just two wheels and resembled nothing more exactly than a Roman chariot. It rolled down the grade toward Nevada pulled by just two horses, with Fargo George and Jack at the reins. Pancake Henderson, Effie, and Ah Moon followed them on horseback. Although the stagecoach wasn't quite the same as the one they'd left Latrobe in, Jack felt confident that it still met the rules as agreed upon between the masters of the two railroads. The next afternoon it came rolling into Virginia City. The unusual configuration of the stage caught the attention of a few people as the horses trotted up to the Silver House Hotel. Absent, however, were the crowds that Jack expected would be awaiting their arrival. Jack took a peek inside the lobby and then looked up and down the street.

"Are we in the right place?" he asked Fargo George.

It was exactly at this moment that they heard the distinct sound of a pistol being cocked and a voice said, "Give me my wife!" Everyone turned to see a lanky man in denim overalls holding a revolver.

"Herbert, I presume," Jack said.

"You're darn tootin'," the man said. "And I mean to get satisfaction."

Effie put herself between her ex-(or not-so-ex)-husband's gun and the rest of the party. "Herbert Woodruff, you're going to have to shoot me before I'll let you shoot any of these fine men."

"Don't think I haven't considered it!" Herbert said. "But I'm not here to shoot anyone, I just want some satisfaction!"

"Oh, good," Effie said with a fair measure of relief. "I didn't really want to be shot."

"You fellas gave me quite a chase. Thought I got you when I knocked the rocks down into the road, but by the time I climbed down the cliff you were already over the slide and gone," Herbert said.

"Wait!" Jack said. "That was you?"

"Yup."

"And the best way you could think to stop us was to climb to the top of a cliff and push rocks down in us?"

"Well, I suppose I didn't give it as much thought as I likely should have," Herbert admitted.

"I paid my posse good money to block the road, and they got past that too," Pancake said. "Determined fellas, ain't they?"

"Wait" Jack said again. "Pancake, you were the one who blocked the road? Effie wasn't even with us at that point!"

"Well, my boys wasn't just blockin' you, they was blockin' the whole road! I was trying to make sure that wife of mine didn't get through!" Pancake said.

"You boys did all of that just to get hold of little old me?" Effie asked. "Blocking roads and knocking down rocks? That's just so sweet…"

"I want satisfaction!" Herbert demanded again. Jack looked back and forth between the two men.

"Well, Effie, which one are you going with?" The nubile

young creature looked back and forth between her two husbands, either to trying to make a decision or waiting for lightning to strike and make the decision for her.

"I don't know! They're both so adorable!" Effie declared. Pretty much fed up with the whole thing, Jack reached into his pocket and pulled out a California gold dollar.

"Will you abide by my decision, as a neutral party only interested in ending the dispute?" Jack asked. The two men nodded. "And the winner will pay a reasonable price for the other's losses?" They nodded again. "And, Effie, you'll go with the winner?"

"I love winners," she said.

Jack let the dollar piece rest on his thumb. "Then call it."

"Heads," Pancake said quickly, and Herbert nodded his assent. With that Jack flipped the coin into the air and then let it fall into the dirt at their feet. Everyone's heads craned forward to see what random chance had determined.

It was indeed heads, and Herbert settled with Pancake for seventy dollars and a horse and then went on his way. As you'll see, this turned out to be a fairly steep price.

Pancake and Effie headed off for his store, leaving Jack, Fargo George, and Ah Moon standing in front of the Silver House wondering what they should do next. Ah Moon was about to go to the Alta Telegraph office and send a message to Sacramento when Lester Robinson's assistant Edwards, who had come over on the noon stage the day before, came out of the hotel and discovered them. His expression was dour.

"It's about time!" he said crabbily.

"Where is everyone?" Jack asked.

"Where is everyone?! The California Stage arrived here almost nine hours ago!" Edwards said. "The Central Pacific already has riders headed back to Sacramento with the news so that they can get it into tomorrow's papers."

"Nine hours?!" Jack declared, more than a little shocked. "We were delayed, no doubt! But nine hours? That's impossible! How did they pull it off without cheating?"

"Easy," Edwards said. "They cheated."

"No, they didn't," Jack argued. "Our delays were caused by something else." In an instant the potential future unfolded in his mind; the railroad would be built along the Central Pacific route, Placerville would lose business and shrink, the bookstore would go out of business... and all because a fickle young girl picked that particular day to run away. History sometimes took bizarre turns as it flowed, and often due to very strange and unexpected causes. Jack considered that the future of his community had been decided by nothing better than the flip of a coin. In the twenty-first century we might say something about a butterfly flapping its wings. "We had a load of logs in the road, and a rock slide, but those were all because of... well, it's a long story. But it wasn't the Big Four."

"Really?" Edwards asked. He pulled an envelope out of his pocket and pushed it into Jack's face. "We got this telegram from your partner, Jed Bradford, in Placerville. Read it!" Jack opened the envelope and read the message inside. It said REMEMBER SAM HAMILTON - PONY EXPRESS RIDER - BIG 4 CHEATING - LUCK, JED.

"Hamilton was a Pony Express rider? The rules said the papers had to come by stage! They cheated after all!"

"Even if it's true that Hamilton was an Express rider, we can't prove they cheated," Edwards said. "And Lester approved Hamilton as the carrier. The wager is lost."

"We lose, Mister Norris?!" Ah Moon asked in shock. Jack put his hand on his eager clerk's shoulder.

"I'm afraid so, Ah Moon. We lost."

Okay, I understand that this isn't the sort of happy ending we tend to associate with these stories, but history is history. Jack and Ah Moon returned home on the next stage (their return trip was far less eventful then the first). To their credit, the folks in Placerville didn't hold the loss against them. Everyone knew that the Central Pacific had cheated, although no one could prove it and the newspapers weren't about to speculate in any way that would make the Big Four unhappy. Jed consoled Jack and they tried to put it behind them and get back to work. Jack got back into his habits fairly quickly. It was their new clerk, Ah Moon, who had trouble putting the race behind him. During the day as he moved books and cleaned the stacks Jed and Jack could hear him mumbling to himself about the Big Four and the Central Pacific.

Three weeks later Effie Henderson arrived in town on the noon stage calling herself Narcissa Woodruff ("*No one* really likes 'Effie', do they? Narcissa is a much more proper name, isn't it?") and moved in with Ah Moon. That arrangement did not last for long, however. Just a few weeks after that, Narcissa left Ah Moon and moved in with Almost Bill. This seemed to be, at last, the right relationship for the impulsive girl, and Bill and Narcissa were happy companions for many years after.

Many of the folks in Placerville still had faith in the future of the P&SVRR despite losing the race. Others knew that the writing was on the wall; Henry Hooker gave up and the next year he shut down his store and moved to Arizona (where he eventually became a cattle baron, employed Billy the Kid, and was best pals with Wyatt Earp). Constance Flannery closed her pie shop and moved to Sacramento, where her new bakery flourished.

Lester Robinson kept on fighting for the P&SVRR but

investors were hard to find and progress was very slow. After a while he didn't fight quite as hard and didn't argue quite as long.

Still, of all of the participants, Ah Moon continued to take the loss hardest. Ah Moon was always good at coming up with solutions to problems, and he thought long and hard about how to right the wrong perpetrated upon the people of Placerville. At last he came up with a plan, and after Effie/Narcissa left him he quit his job at the bookstore, left Placerville and became - of all things - a construction worker for the Central Pacific! Being a very bright fellow, he quickly worked his way up until he was the foreman of the Chinese construction teams. Ah Moon estimated that it would take his Chinese teams two years to complete the rail line over the Sierra crest and through to Nevada, so in revenge for the Central Pacific's cheating during the race he made sure that it took almost four. He knew that the railroad would never notice that the Chinese were only working at half their capacity, since even at that speed they were twice as fast as the non-Chinese workers.

In August, 1867, Leland Stanford sent a telegram to Mark Hopkins: "Summit Tunnel broke through at 4 P.M." Six days later the track was completely connected across the mountains. On June 18, 1868, the Central Pacific ran its first passenger train from Sacramento to Reno, a distance of 154 miles. By the end of October the line was open to Winnemucca, Nevada.

Eventually the P&SVRR went bankrupt and its assets were acquired by the Central Pacific. All of the investors, including El Dorado County and the City of Placerville, lost millions. In order to avoid paying on these debts, which they really couldn't afford, the Placerville City Council came up with a unique solution; the entire council resigned and hid for more than a decade.

In the summer of 1869 the cost to take a train from New York to San Francisco was $150 for first class (a cushy Pullman car), and $70 for emigrant (a wood bench). By June 1870, that was down to $136 for first class, $110 for second class, and $65 for third. A permanent bridge across the Missouri River finally opened in March 1872. With the completion of that bridge Ted Judah's dream was at last fulfilled, and there was a continuous ribbon of steel that reached from New York to Sacramento.

And it did not go through Placerville.

Next:
A Dangerous trip through the High Sierra

VII

THE LIBRARY BOOK
or
A HUNDRED MILES IN NORWEGIAN SHOES

*In which a book is respected, it returns the favor, and something
ong overdue turns up*

January, 1856
A Prologue of Sorts

It is popularly believed that the motto of the United States Postal Service is; *Neither snow nor rain nor heat nor gloom of night stays these couriers from the swift completion of their appointed rounds.* Actually, that is not the motto of the United States Postal Service. In fact, the Postal Service has no motto. These famous words are actually chiseled into the granite edifice of a single New York City Post Office, selected by an architect who was a really big fan of Herodotus, the Greek historian who first wrote them around 450 B.C. (long, long before the first letter was lost in the mail by the United States Postal Service.)

In practice the Postal Service is constantly stymied by snow, rain, and heat (and even gloom of night on occasion). During the winter of 1855 the Postal Service felt especially thwarted by the snow bit. The deep snows covering the crest of the Sierra Nevada essentially shut down delivery of mail by land, so during the winter letters and parcels had to be shipped by sea.

In late 1855 (before the notorious fires of 1856 referenced in the prior chapter) Postmaster Thatcher in Placerville advertised for a new mail carrier, someone willing to brave the savage winters of the Sierra Nevada.

People Lost to the World, he wrote. *Uncle Sam Needs a Mail Carrier.*

His plea was answered by a young immigrant from Norway by the name of Jon Torsteinson-Rue (or John Thompson, as he dumbed-down his name in America, since Americans already had the bad habit of being unable to pronounce names with too many vowels or unfamiliar combinations of consonants). Jon (or John) was convinced that he could cross the snowy mountains even in the height of winter and deliver the mail where all others had failed. Early that January he was in the hills near Smith Flat preparing for his first trip over the Sierra Nevada as a mail carrier.

"So, what do you call these things?" Jed Bradford asked as he stood in two feet of cold, wet snow. His shoes were unfortunately not waterproof and he was sure his toes were blue by now. The Norwegian placed his feet onto two nine-foot-long twenty-five-pound slabs of oak which were barely any wider than his boot. The front tips curled up into graceful points. He strapped his boots securely to the top of the contraptions with his heels resting against wood blocks.

"In English I call them snow-skates," Thompson said. "In Norway my father called it a shee. S-K-I, shee. Everybody used them there."

Thompson was quite a sight in the best of times. He wore a red and black Mackinaw jacket and a wide brimmed hat that gave everyone else wearing their standard bowlers a case of brim-envy. Today he added to his ensemble smears of black charcoal across his face, which he said was to prevent snow blindness.

"Just watch," Thompson said. With a kick he started sliding across the surface of the snow on his oak snow-skates, moving faster and faster as the hillside grew steeper. Pretty soon he was moving faster than a horse could gallop, even if it was running away from Two Shovels Mitchell and his unkind whip. Jed quickly surveyed the area ahead of Thompson and saw with alarm that directly in the Norwegian's path there was a sudden drop of about

187

twelve feet before the hill resumed its slope into the ravine. There was no way to go around it and Thompson was moving much too fast to stop before he went over it.

"John!" Jed cried out helplessly.

But Thompson didn't slow down, didn't turn or even attempt to stop. Instead he shot off of the little cliff like a bullet from a gun. His snow skates tipped up and he flew through the air, a Mackinaw-colored bird soaring above the uncontaminated clarity of the virgin snow. Then, like a goose angling in to land on the surface of a still lake, he smoothly touched down on the slope a hundred feet below and continued his race to the bottom.

"I have got to learn how to do that," Jed thought.

Two days later John Thompson stood on standard snowshoes before a crowd in front of the Placerville Post Office. The large pack on his back was filled to its top with mail. The only personal items Thompson carried were some dried meats, a few biscuits, matches and his Bible. His heavy oak snow-skates were slung over his shoulders.

"Them is right fancy snow shoes," No Teeth Tracy commented.

"Don't you even want a blanket? It's freezing!" Jed said.

"That's alright," Thompson said. "I'll just have a fire. If I stop, that is."

"What about a gun?" Jack asked. "There are wolves and grizzlies out there, and at this time of year they are going to be hungry!"

"What I have is heavy enough," Thompson answered. He started walking east down Main Street and a good portion of the crowd followed. "Wish me luck!"

"Good luck, Snowshoe Thompson!" Constance Flannery called out. After that "Snowshoe Thompson" was all that anyone called the young Norwegian.

Well, Snowshoe Thompson hiked eight thousand feet to the top of Carson Pass and then used his snow-skates to ski down to Genoa, Nevada, south of Carson City. He arrived just three days after leaving Placerville and delivered the mail to the postmaster there, just as he would several times a month each winter for the next twenty years. And due to "contract issues" he was never once in those twenty years ever paid a penny by the United States Postal Service.

Thompson did on occasion receive money from individuals to carry items for them over the pass, including medicine, sewing needles, and - in one case - most of a printing press (piece by piece, not all at once). In 1859 gold miners near what would become Virginia City, Nevada, asked him carry a strange bluish rock that was getting in the way of their gold mining to Sacramento for assaying. It turned out to be silver and inaugurated the next great mining rush; The Comstock Lode.

Jed Bradford never forgot Snowshoe Thompson's demonstration of the power of skis that winter day in 1856. When Thompson returned to Placerville from Nevada Jed asked if he would show him how to make a pair of snow-skates. Thompson obliged and together they carved out a set for Jed from an oak tree they cut down by Smith Flat. Jed tried several times to get the hang of the strange Norwegian skates and made some progress. Eventually the spring came, however, the snow melted, and Jed's snow-skates were stored in the shed behind the store. There they would gather cobwebs for the next eleven years.

February, 1867
(Eleven Years Later)
In which this story begins in earnest

Jed and Jack were sitting in front of the fire at Jack's house when Jack brought up the subject of the big fund-raising ball that was being held the next night at the Confidence Engine House. He mentioned that he was disappointed because Lizette really wanted to go, but they had to stay and take care of the kids. Baby Nate had the measles.

"Look, why don't you and Lizzie go to the ball?" Jed suggested. "I'll stay and watch the kids."

"Yes! Come and play games with us all night, Uncle Jed!" Doris said, jumping out from behind the curtains. The Boys hadn't even known she was there.

"Don't you want to go to the ball?" Jack asked.

"Naw, I haven't got anyone to go to the dance with anyway. You should take your wife and have a good time." Jack hurried into the kitchen to tell Lizette. While he was gone Doris climbed up on the chair next to Jed and tried to braid his hair. Lizzie soon came running to give Jed hugs and kisses and tell him in her musical French accent what a good friend he was to her and Jack. "It's no problem," he told her. "I love your kids like they're my own anyway..." - he gave Doris a stern look - "...except when they try to braid my hair."

Shortly thereafter Jed walked home, glad he could help Jack but suddenly depressed about his own life. Placerville seemed abandoned tonight. It was late enough that all the businesses were shuttered and the normal sounds of night were muffled by several inches of snow covering the street. He stopped halfway to the bookstore when he saw the sign hanging in front of the big brick building at Main Street and Buckboard Lane. BAD LUCK

BREWERY it read. With a smile he knocked on the door.

"We're closed!" a voice yelled.

"It's Jed Bradford!" he called back. The latches were quickly undone and the door flew open to reveal Bad Luck Casey.

"Come in, Jed," Casey said happily. "It's good to see you!"

In short order the two old friends were relaxed by the stove and having beers together.

"This is the best ale I've had in a long time," Jed told Casey.

"Thank you," Bad Luck said. "You know, since I got this brewery going things have been better than they ever were before. My whole life I've scraped and dug and washed and dug and had nothing to show for it. Now my brewery is doing big business and for the first time I can think about doing things in the future. Next week I'm going to San Francisco and staying in a proper hotel. A proper hotel, Jed! When I get back I'm setting myself up in a real nice house. Maybe I'll meet a nice lady and settle down like Jack."

"You going to the Fire House Ball tomorrow night?" Jed asked.

"No, me and Two Shovels are going to go hunting up at Sly Park Ranch with Luther Cutler. I like visiting with Two Shovels and you and Jack... any of us who've been around long enough to remember what Placerville used to be like. You remember Hard Head, owned the smithy down by the canal? Dug up the entire street washing the dirt for gold. You couldn't get away with that these days." He shook his head. "Yeah, it will be fun going hunting with Two Shovels. Maybe we can bring home some venison. Then on Monday morning I'm off to see the Golden Gate!"

"I hope you have a good time, my friend," Jed said, giving Bad Luck a soft slap on the back. "Thanks for the beer. I'd best be going. I have to open the store in the morning." He headed for the door.

"Say, Jed..."

"Yeah?"

"I was just wondering, did you ever write a story with that Wheelbarrow fella you were always talking about?" Casey asked.

"No, Bad Luck, I never did," Jed answered.

"I suppose that's how it goes. Life gets busy. Hey, maybe I'll stop by your shop before I leave with a few venison steaks," Casey offered.

"Thanks, that would be nice," Jed said, and he went out into the frigid night air. He grew even more depressed as he walked home.

Unfortunately, Bad Luck Casey never got his chance to see the Golden Gate. He finally lived up to his inauspicious nickname (or "unfortunate moniker" as Fox Reynard put it). The day after he spoke with Jed he headed up to Sly Park Ranch for his hunting trip with Two Shovels Mitchell and was promptly mauled by a grizzly bear. This was not just bad luck, it was famously bad luck. Grizzlies were already fairly rare in California. Even when a man was unfortunate enough to come across one the bears were unlikely to attack unless provoked. In this case Luther Cutler shot at what he thought was a young buck and it turned out to be a grizzly cub. The mother, none too happy, charged Two Shovels and Bad Luck because they were handier than Cutler. Mitchell made it up a tree, but Casey wasn't... well, he wasn't so lucky.

Jed Bradford and Jack Norris stood in the front window of their bookstore appreciating a vision of their town rendered in white; the hillsides painted out and trees weighed heavily down under cold winter coats. The front of the Cary Hotel wore icicle whiskers and the street in front of it, stirred and muddied, was a river of ice. Snow had even settled on the top of the Bell Tower like frosting on a cake.

The Bell Tower was among the newest features in Placerville. After the fires in the mid-1850s the town decided they needed a good way to raise the people in its defense when there was a fire or other natural disaster, and the idea of an alarm bell was quickly settled upon. Unfortunately it took a much longer time than expected to actually acquire and install such a device; First there was the need for an exploratory committee to determine the right sized bell and then a purchasing committee to research the best foundries and get the order placed. A budgeting committee had to assess the costs involved and approve the necessary funds. Finally in 1860, four years after the initial decision was made, the bell was cast - in England. Jed and Jack often ordered books from England to stock in their store, and they were aware that sometimes months could pass waiting for these long distance orders to arrive. Despite this experience, even they were surprised when the bell, cast in 1860, didn't actually arrive in Placerville until 1865. The first support structure, a rickety wooden frame that could barely support the bell, much less any snow, was erected in the center of Placerville, an area which came to be known as the Plaza. Over the years the tower structure would be replaced at least three more times, first in wood and then in all subsequent attempts in hardened steel with cast iron ornaments and a very splendid weather vane. The Plaza stood naked for just one year in the following century when, during 1911, the bell was moved to Cannon Hill, from which it could not be properly seen or heard (making it fairly unsuitable for its purpose.) By 1912 the bell was back where it belonged in the heart of Placerville.

All that, however, is in the future of our tale, for in 1867 the bell was just celebrating its second birthday, and, as you have read, snow covered the top of the tower like frosting on a cake. The whole town was white. Jed and Jack were wearing black, as they had just returned from Bad Luck Casey's funeral services. It was a closed-casket affair considering... well, Bad Luck was mauled by a grizzly bear.

"It isn't right. Bad Luck just got his life in order and was seeing the other side," Jed lamented. "Maybe we should have started calling him 'Good Luck' after he started the brewery. Do you suppose he'd be dead right now if we'd started calling him 'Good Luck'?"

"I don't think a grizzly bear cares what your nickname is," Jack said.

"It just seems like he got cut down right when things were getting better for him. You never know when the reaper is coming, Jack." Suddenly Jack realized the real subject of their conversation.

"So this is about you, not Bad Luck," he said.

"Well, when something like this happens you take stock," Jed said. "We came west to get experience in order to write stories. Yet, here I am, almost forty, and I haven't got more than a handful of short stories published in magazines so far."

"Not even forty! You have plenty of time left!" Jack said with encouragement.

"My father was printed to death at the age of forty-seven."

"Well, don't stick your head in any printing presses and you'll be fine."

The wood stove in the back of the store kept The Boys warm as they sorted through stacks of new and lightly used books which lay helter-skelter along the aisles. Thanks to the inclement weather there would be few customers today, so they decided to use their time organizing several hundred books they just received from Stafford Hickey's Book-O-Wagon (a precursor to the modern Bookmobile). Stafford, a wise business man, appreciated the success The Boys had with their bookstore in Placerville and noticed that many of the other Mother Lode towns lacked such an amenity. In partnership with Jed and Jack he created the Book-O-Wagon, which ran north and south through the gold country selling books to rural customers. Once every three months or so Stafford came through Placerville, trading all of the titles he hadn't been able to sell to Jed and Jack for a wagonful of new books.

"I should probably read this again," Jack said, holding up a copy of *Alice's Adventures in Wonderland*. "Maybe I'll take it home and read it out loud to Lizzie and the kids. I still mean to figure out the answer to that riddle, 'Why is a raven like a writing desk?'"

"Because neither one has ever taken a train to Dorchester with their pet cat Eric," Jed said. Jack frowned.

"That's nonsense," he said.

"So is the riddle," Jed replied. "I think you're missing the point."

"No, I'm not. Just because Lewis Carroll meant for it to be a riddle without an answer doesn't mean you can't supply one. It gets ahead of the book if you can think of one for yourself."

"Poe wrote on both," Jed said, pulling out a copy of *Les Misérables* by Victor Hugo. "Ah, I wish Jean-Claude was still in town. He would have loved this book."

"Look at this," Jack said, pulling another book from the box. It was a slim black leather bound volume with impressed gold lettering on the cover. "I don't remember this one." He handed to it Jed, who gently opened the cover and examined the fly leaf. In beautifully looping cursive the words *Property of the Carson City Public Library* were written in ink. A piece of notepaper was wedged in-between the title and contents pages like a bookmark and it read, in the same flowing script, *October 6th*.

"It's not one of ours," Jed said. "It's a library book from Carson City."

"I wonder how Stafford ended up with that," Jack said,

continuing to sort through the box. "Maybe he got a return or exchange and didn't pay enough attention."

"Today is February 9th. This book is already overdue for return," Jed said. He set the book on the front counter and went back to sorting. Still, the thought that the library book was overdue irked Jed in a way that a thought shouldn't irk someone. It crawled into his brain and sat there repeating itself like a melody that has overstayed its welcome. Every few minutes he glanced up and looked at the offending volume, sitting there on the bookstore counter instead of resting where it belonged, in the stacks of the Carson City Public Library. Finally he stood up and walked over to the counter.

"What's the matter?" Jack asked.

"It's a library book from Carson City. It's *overdue*."

Jack thought for a moment. "Why don't you take it over to the Post Office? Snowshoe Thompson can take it to Carson City when he takes the mail over the pass." Jed shook his head.

"Snowshoe and Agnes are having their first child any day now, over in Diamond Valley. Bootjack Johnston says that Snowshoe may not make another run this month or even next. And with the heavy snows we've gotten over the last few weeks it's not likely anyone else is going to be able to make it through. It might be May or June before a mail team can get through."

"Then let it wait until the weather gets warmer," Jack suggested. "It's late now, it will be late then." He looked over at the library book. "Not as if anyone is dying to read that one, anyway."

Jed tried to put the subject of the library book out of his mind. Yet all day he would find himself coming back to it, pulling its cover open to read the words *Property of the Carson City Public Library*. The delicate hand present in the letters called out to him; "take me home." That night at dinner he kept getting up from the table on some weak pretext - needing more butter, needing more salt - in order to sneak into his room and capture a glance of the book and the declaration of ownership on its first page.

Early the next morning Jack was walking down the hill from his house to Main Street (having dropped off his children at school) when he saw Jed emerge from the shed behind the store. In his hands were two long slender pieces of wood which Jack recognized as the snow-skates Jed made with Snowshoe Thompson more than a decade before. As Jack recalled, despite many lessons from Thompson, Jed was better at falling down on them than he was at going anywhere with them.

"What do you think you're doing?" Jack demanded.

"Just thought I'd give these another try. It's the perfect day for it," Jed said, studiously avoiding eye contact. Jack knew exactly what this meant.

"Listen, Jed, if you're thinking about going to Carson City on those things, then think again! Snowshoe grew up using those skates. You'd be lucky to cross the street on them without breaking a leg!"

What Jack said was partially true, but that didn't matter to Jed. Something had taken hold of him and was guiding him now. Perhaps it was fate, or destiny, the will of God, or the whims of an omniscient narrator. Whichever the case, Jed knew that this was something he had to do.

"Jack, I know this doesn't make sense. Somehow I knew it the minute I saw that library book... I knew that I had to return it. Not later and not through someone else. I have to do it myself, right now. Remember that moment after Rufus Porter's Aerial Transport collapsed in the rain? We knew that we had to go west, right then. Well, I have to do this, right now."

"This is about Bad Luck Casey, isn't it?" Jack declared. "You're feeling mortal and have decided to do something completely crazy!"

"No, Jack, I'm doing this because the book is *overdue!*"

Jack knew that there was no sense in trying to talk Jed out of this crazy notion - once Jed was determined toward a particular course of action there was no way to deter him. Instead he decided to limit the damage as much as he could.

"Let's talk to Bootjack. If Snowshoe isn't hauling the mail then he might be interested in putting together a team to take Snowshoe's place. Maybe we can convince Freddy Big Feet and Point-of-No-Return Willy and a few others to join you. It's safer that way."

But Jack's idea failed to pan out. Freddy claimed he had the gout and Point-of-No-Return Willy left that morning for the toll house at Slippery Ford. Lizzie took a turn trying to convince Jed that the idea of going alone was dangerous and a folly. Reverend Platt even came by the house and explained to Jed that so long as he saw that the library book was returned, God didn't care if it was in February or July.

Throughout all of these attempts to change his mind Jed prepared for the journey. Recalling the provisions that Snowshoe typically packed with him on his trips, Jed wrapped up a quantity of dried biscuits, beef jerky, a sausage, and plenty of matches. He gathered his finest fur-lined coat and oilskin trousers. His boots were a present from Snowshoe Thompson, perfect for wearing with the great snow-skates. Lastly he had a large pair of regular snowshoes which he borrowed from Two Shovels Mitchell.

On his desk, between great stacks of unfinished manuscripts and mostly-completed short stories he laid out the best map he could find of the route he needed to take. The map was the work of Point-of-No-Return Willy and, of course, lead directly to his toll road. During the winter there were very few people using the road (and often none at all) with the exception of Snowshoe

Thompson, and Willy let Snowshoe use the road for free. Still, Jed knew that Willy was going to be in residence when he got there and was prepared to be considered a typical traveler. He had several coins stuffed in his coat pocket in case Willy wanted to charge him.

Early the next morning when Jed brought the pack downstairs to the store he found Jack waiting for him with a new angle of attack.

"What about the grizzly bear? Are you prepared to face the bear?" he asked.

"I'll stay out of his way and he can stay out of mine," Jed declared. He took the library book and the novel by Jules Verne that he was currently reading (*Voyage au centre de la Terre*, which translates as *Journey to the Center of the Earth*) and wrapped them carefully in oilcloth and leather to keep them from getting wet on the trip. He stowed the package in his pack and took it out to strap it to his mule, Longfellow. He would ride Longfellow as far as the Eleven Mile House (also known as Sportsman's Hall) and then proceed on foot and snow-skate from there. The nine-foot-long skates hung on either side of the mule.

"This is madness," Jack said one last time as Jed mounted Longfellow and did a last minute check of his provisions.

"Damn, I left my compass back at the house," he said.

"Let me go back for it," Jack offered. "Without it you'll get lost for sure!"

"That's alright. Snowshoe never carries one. He says that the Sierra aren't all that wide! All a man has to do is keep an eye on the sky to get his bearings and always travel east. How hard can it be?"

"You're doomed," Jack muttered. "All for a library book."

"Jack, I'll be fine. Promise to look after the store while I'm gone," Jed said. Lizzie put her arm around Jack and looked up at his partner.

"You know we will, Jed. I'll have Doris do some alphabetizing. It will help her learn to spell correctly. Our prayers are with you," she said.

"I'll be back next week!" Jed promised and he coaxed Longfellow down Main Street through the muddy snow.

The first part of Jed's trip was deceptively easy, at least when Longfellow was cooperating. He rode up the long slow incline from the Placerville ravine past Smith Flat, then up the ridge toward the Mountain Cottage at Ten Mile Post. As he got higher the view opened up and he could see the imposing summits of the Sierra in the distance - a line of steep, hard granite clad in deep drifts of snow eight thousand feet higher than the bookstore (a fact that they often quoted to travelers passing through). He glanced back toward Placerville just once and by then it was hidden behind the surrounding white hills. Eventually the snow got deeper and more difficult for the mule to manage, so Jed dismounted and donned his regular snowshoes. Luckily the road, even buried in snow, was visible. Other travelers had already tread here and beaten a path.

There were a number of settlers up where the ridge widened. Simon Moon and Jimmy Mulroney were chatting outside of Beck Thomas' cherry orchard and said hello. They asked him where he was headed and when he told them they echoed Jack's sentiments.

"It was nice knowing you, Jed," Jimmy said. "I'm sorry, but you aren't Snowshoe Thompson."

It was getting dark when Jed finally arrived at Sportsman's Hall and unloaded his pack and the snow-skates from poor Longfellow. Johnny Blair, the proprietor, came dashing out of the Hall and took Longfellow's reins, leading him through the deep snow toward the stable. Although the Blair Brothers were used to getting large numbers of visitors at the Hall during the summer and autumn months, travelers were rare during the depth of winter.

"What are you doing here, Jed?" Johnny asked. When Jed told him he said in his light Scots brogue, "It's right noble of ye to try returning that book, Jed, but ye aren't Snowshoe Thompson."

"Why does everyone keep saying that?" Jed said.

Sportsman's Hall was the last roof that he would likely be able to enjoy, so Jed had a hot meal with the Blair Brothers and their family and then settled in early. He rose with the sun and wrapped himself up as warmly as he could. He pulled the snow-skates along behind him on a tether and used his snowshoes along the road. Johnny Blair promised to take good care of Longfellow and return the mule to Jack the next time he made the trip to Placerville.

Later in the day Jed made it to the Pacific Toll House where the county road and the toll road took their separate directions, but Point-of-No-Return Willy wasn't there after all. He decided to spend the night there anyway, even though it was still early. The inn was locked up tight so Jed built a fire just inside the entrance to the barn and wrapped himself up in the hay to sleep. From here until Nevada he would be on his own. At this time of year all the way stations were unmanned, the toll houses empty, and there wouldn't be any other travelers. After this last night of sleep he planned to travel throughout the day and night without stopping unless he was so exhausted he couldn't go any further.

Jed arrived at the river shortly after leaving the Pacific House and crossed using Brockliss' Bridge, the only bridge still standing along this stretch of the South Fork. Most of the bridges were built quickly and cheaply to make money on the tolls, and the first spate of bad weather tended to wash them away.

That night Jed discovered a problem with his plan to use the sun for navigation; it wasn't very practical after the sun set. He knew enough about astronomy that he could use the stars to get his bearings, but dense clouds moved in as the afternoon progressed and kept him from seeing the night sky. Since traveling at night was impossible he gave up and started a fire, curling up on a mattress of pine boughs next to the blaze in order to get a few precious hours of sleep.

The morning after the heavy clouds remained, yet the sky was at least brighter in one direction or the other, and he took this to mean that the sun lay in that direction. For the next two days he did his best to keep his bearings and make as much progress as possible.

The route Jed took was commonly known as "Johnson's Cutoff," and followed the ridge above the American river to Lake Bigler (a body of water which many people had taken to calling Lake Tahoe, a much more pleasant name in Jed's opinion) and then wound down the eastern escarpment into Nevada. The trail was first blazed by explorer John Calhoun Johnson and for those of you who like to refer to maps it eventually became the general route of U.S. Highway 50.

Jed stayed with his regular snowshoes as long as he could and just dragged the oak snow-skates behind, which made climbing through the snowdrifts that much harder. When he came to a long slope that stretched down toward the river he knew he could no longer put off using them. "You can do this," he told himself as he strapped the snow-skates to his boots and glanced with some trepidation at the slopes ahead. "Snowshoe Thompson thought you could."

Bringing up the "balancing pole," as Thompson had called it, Jed kicked off and started sliding across the snowfield. About a hundred feet along he figured he was going too fast and fell over in order to slow down. On his next attempt he made it three hundred feet before he planted his face in the snow. It took a while to get the hang of the things, but when you don't have any alternative you learn quickly.

By the time the sun got low Jed was racing along at speeds he would not have even imagined attaining just hours before. After two hours he finally discovered how to turn one way or another without falling over and this made him feel much better about avoiding the frequent trees and really big rocks. Then, just as he was congratulating himself on a job well done, he saw something in the center of the open slope ahead and went crashing into a good sized sugar pine in a tumbling mass of snow-skates, pole, and pack.

Catching his breath, Jed pulled himself up the side of the pine tree and back to his feet. Once standing he spied carefully around the trunk.

In the opening beyond four or five wolves lay close to the ground, their noses buried in a deer carcass, eating. Abandoning the tree that almost killed him, Jed shuffled on his snow-skates sideways, trying to reach a dense group of firs to his right before any of the canines noticed him. Of course one of his twenty-pound skates came down upon a branch lying on an exposed knot of granite. The heavy oak slab snapped the branch and all of the wolves popped their heads up. Jed froze in his tracks.

"There, there," he said. "You boys wouldn't want to leave that delicious venison to go chasing after me, would you?"

The largest of the wolves sat up and howled at him. Discretion being the better part of valor, as they say, Jed resumed his sideways steps into the trees. On the far side of the firs the ground continued dropping away to the east. He shuffled around until the points of his snow-skates were aimed for the slope and then kicked off. After he was moving quickly down the hillside he took the opportunity to glance back and assure himself that none of the wolves were following. He challenged the trickster gods by saying, "Well, if that's the most dangerous thing that happens on this trip, I'll write a story about it and consider it all good."

It wasn't until the fourth day - just after noon - that he reached the crest. He knew this was the peak of the range because he saw the tip of Lake Tahoe in the valley below, almost hiding behind a massive ridge of granite. By now his feet were heavy and his muscles ached. The sighting of the lake was heartening. With renewed confidence he started skating down into the lake valley.

Dark clouds were moving in from the west and just before dusk a light snow began to fall. The severity of the flurries increased until the driven flakes stung his face like thorns in the wind and he wrapped his kerchief high over his nose and pulled his hat low over his brow. He decided to stop and camp, although the prospect of freezing in his sleep was a worry.

Snowshoe Thompson's *modus operandi*, if you will, was to find a tree, set fire to it, and let it burn through the night. His only caveat regarding this method was that you should always pick a tree that leaned one way or the other and then sleep on the opposing side, for fear the burning tree might fall on you during the night. Jed tried this and found the trees and wood too wet to catch fire. He decided that, if he survived this trip, he would have to ask Thompson exactly how he accomplished it.

Instead Jed found a broad overhanging rock which formed a cave of sorts and he dragged some fir boughs under this to create a sheltered bed to sleep on. After numerous attempts (and most of his matches) he finally got some sticks and needles burning. Although the warmth was mostly in his imagination he huddled next to this meager fire eating jerkied meat and reading Verne's *Journey to the Center of the Earth*.

He was deep into a section of the book where Professor Von Hardwigg and his nephew Harry are being attacked by a sea monster when, it appeared, the world decided to provide sound effects to improve his reading experience. A growl not terribly dissimilar to the sounds one might expect a sea monster to make rumbled threateningly from Jed's left. In fact it took Jed a moment to realize that the low roar had nothing to do with his book. Rather it had something to do with the huge grizzly bear standing at the entrance to his little shelter.

The bear apparently wanted to use the cave him-or-herself and was unwilling to share, so it charged at Jed. With no time to think before he acted, Jed jumped up and ran out into the blizzard. He hoped the grizzly preferred the slightly warm crevice to chasing him down the mountain. At the bottom of the slope he tumbled into a drift. Carefully, he popped his head out of the snow and saw with relief that the bear wasn't following him. Only then did he realize that the snow-skates were still in the cave. Worse, so was the pack containing his food, water and (more importantly) *the library book* and it was probably serving as a pillow for a five-hundred pound bear.

A few feet further down the hillside he found a copse of cedars that worked as a break against the wind and driving snow. He sat there for a while, but the cold soon became unbearable. Snowshoe Thompson had told him that some nights - even with a burning tree as company - he danced old Norwegian jigs to keep warm. Jed didn't know any Norwegian jigs, but he knew a few dance steps and figured that even if he did them badly there was no one out here in the dark to see him (except the bear, perhaps). So for the next two hours he danced and hopped and sashayed between the cedars.

By dawn Jed was freezing and very tired. At least the snow had stopped. In its place were clearing blue skies. As soon as there was enough light he carefully climbed back up to the cave to see if the bear was still in residence. From a distance of about fifty feet he could see clearly enough that the grizzly was gone. That was the good news. The bad news was that his pack was ripped open and the contents were scattered across the open granite. He panicked for a moment, sure that the bear had eaten the library book. The beautifully looping words *Property of the Carson City Public Library* on the frontispiece were gone, digesting at this very moment in the belly of the beast. Then he saw it, still carefully wrapped and framed by a ray of morning sunlight like an angel in a Renaissance painting. He rushed to it and hugged it to his bosom like a lost child found.

The snow-skates were still there too, along with the pole that they were tied to, in perfect repair. Only one thing was missing; everything else. All of his food was gone, consumed by the bear. What was he to do? By now Carson City was likely closer than Placerville, so turning back was not an option. There was no choice but to forge ahead. He packed his books in the shredded remains of his pack, strapped on the snow-skates and kicked off toward the rising sun.

Just before noon he saw the bear for the first time. About twenty minutes later he saw it again, quietly following him up the canyon, always half-visible behind a tree or a boulder. Sometimes, even when he couldn't see it, he could hear it huffing and puffing. At first he thought it was just curious, but after three hours it was clear that it was stalking him. There was no doubt in his mind that once darkness returned it would attack. Jack had been right - this entire journey was a fool's errand and he was going to be mauled by a bear, just like poor Bad Luck Casey. His reflections on life after the demise of his old friend weren't going to lead anywhere but to a shared fate.

Unless… unless he was meant to do this. His jaw dropped as he skated out from underneath the forest shade and into the revealing light of the sun. The dominos of fate fell in front of him and, as you will see, they should have been fairly obvious. "How could I have been so blind?" Jed said aloud. He turned toward the line of trees where he was sure the bear lurked. "I was so busy worrying about my own life I didn't see what was right in front of me!"

Quickly Jed scanned sides of the canyon and identified a ledge halfway up the canyon wall that he was fairly sure was out of the grizzly's reach. He sled over to the granite wall and untied the snow-skates from his boots. Carefully tying the pole and skates together, he dropped them to the snow and took the end of the line. Placing each foot securely in whatever crevices he could find, he climbed up the face until he reached the little ledge twenty-five feet above the canyon floor. If the sanctuary had been any higher he might have run out of rope. He settled here and hauled the skates up, placing them on the shelf beside him. Here, at least, he could relax for a time without worrying about the bear.

With utmost care he removed the package containing the library book from his damaged pack. Each piece of twine, as he untied it, was placed in his pocket. He folded the oilcloth back and then the dry inner lining to reveal the library book inside. Wiping his hands on his coat to make sure they were dry, he pulled open the cover and turned to the beautiful inscription; *Property of the Carson City Public Library.* Then he turned his attention to the title page. It read:

A History of Bear Hunting, Bear Skinning, and Expert Bear Hide Tanning
with several dozen most excellent recipes for bear meat
By The Last of the Great Plains Bear Hunters
Written in vernacular for the casual reader by Keen-Eye Watson
Published by Elway & Sons of Denver, Colorado

Nothing is impossible, Jed thought. You just have to have a book that can tell you how to do it. The sun was setting as he finished the last page. The great beast was snorfeling out in the deepening shadows, waiting for him. "Alright, my great white whale," he called out to it. "I'm educated now. I'm generally not a man of arms, but you have left me no other course of action. This one's for Bad Luck Casey."

The next day a group of trappers out of Genoa, Nevada, were hunting up the Carson River toward Woodford's Canyon. They were following a game trail through the snow when a figure came sailing down from the peaks above, materializing out of the mists. They were startled enough to find anyone out here, but to see this figure gliding down the mountain was extraordinary.
"Is it Snowshoe Thompson?" one of them asked.
"Is it a bear?!" another said with more surprise.
In a shower of snow the skating man plowed into the drift next to them and came to a stop. He smiled at the hunters, happy to see them because it meant that his journey was almost at an end. His belly was full, his cheeks were rosy, and he felt better than he had in many weeks. In particular he was comfortably warm, due to the most incredible bear-hide coat you have ever seen.
"Hello, gentlemen," Jed said to the trappers. "Can you tell me which direction I might go to find Carson City?"

Where the Sierra Nevada end - rather abruptly most people find - the Great Basin begins. Here, in the middle of a broad desert interrupted only by sagebrush and greasewood, was Carson City, a collection of Victorian style houses and hotels packed so closely together that Mark Twain remarked it was "as if room were scarce in that mighty plain." The town had grown quickly when silver was discovered to the north and like the Hangtown of old it was now a booming mining town. Just beyond the Carson Brewery (another reminder of Bad Luck Casey for Jed when he passed it) was a ramshackle building that identified itself as a bath house. At the back, hidden from the street, a shingle hung from the roof with the words *Carson City Public Library* painted in lovely looping script.

Just below this sign a young woman was chopping wood. One at a time she balanced short logs on a flattened rock and brought her axe down to split them. An older woman in wireframe glasses opened the door and peered out from the library.

"Are you going to be long, Butterscotch, dear?" she asked.

"Just a moment, Hannah," the young woman said. "We have to stay warm!"

"You should have a man do that for you. It's what they're good for," the older woman said, and she retreated to the library.

"Well," Butterscotch replied to herself, "there's never a man around when you need one."

She raised her hands to bring the axe down on the next piece of wood and suddenly jumped when she saw - out of the corner of her eye - a large furry shape. This was particularly dangerous for the large furry shape due to the axe. Luckily for Jed she lowered it, took a deep breath, and smiled.

"Hello there," she said. "You startled me. You know, you're quite the sight."

"My pardon," Jed said. "I've had quite the adventure. I'm looking for the librarian."

"That would be me," she told him, holding out her hand. "Butterscotch Williams. What may I do for you?"

"My name is Jedediah Bradford and I'm a bookseller from Placerville in California. I have something that belongs to you." He reached into the folds of his great bearskin coat and brought out the library book. Butterscotch Williams took it and looked first at the book and then at Jed.

"You're overdue," she said.

Over the course of the next several days Jed stayed at a hotel in Carson City and visited Butterscotch in her quaint little library every afternoon. She was very curious about his trek over the mountains and he told her the entire harrowing tale of his wilderness adventure. Even more, she was amazed that he would put himself in mortal danger just to return a library book - the very same library book, as it happens, that saved his life from a grizzly death (please pardon the pun. Or don't.)

The very first morning Jed went to the offices of the Overland Telegraph Company and sent a telegram to Jack in order to let his partner know he was alive and well in Carson City. Every day he visited the office and asked the friendly clerk Hermann if there had been any response from Jack, and the clerk shook his head. In another year the Central Pacific Railroad would be complete between Reno, Nevada and Sacramento, California (although often closed in the depths of winter) and Jed could have taken a train to Sacramento in relative comfort. For now, though, the only way to get over the mountains was to scale them yourself, just as Jed did.

Finally in May the passes thawed and the wagon roads opened. Jed booked passage on the very first stage headed for Placerville. He was sure that by now Jack and Lizette presumed him dead.

"I'll get you there as quick as a wink," Hank Monk, the stagecoach driver, told him. "But you'd best hold onto your hats."

Jack Norris stopped reading when the stagecoach pulled up in front of the bookstore. The stagecoach stopped at the courthouse, at the depot down on Sacramento Street and sometimes at the Cary House, but never in front of *Bradford & Norris: Booksellers to the Savage West,* so it caught his attention. Lizette was arranging stock in the back and joined him at the front door.

Just as they exited the store onto the sidewalk the stagecoach door flew open. Jed Bradford stumbled down out of the coach, his hat askew just as Hank Monk had promised. Instead of reaching out to his partner he turned back to the coach and took a hand from inside. A pretty young woman, as disheveled as Jed, stepped out.

"By my stars, Jed! We thought the mountain got you!" Jack exclaimed.

"No, not the mountain, not the wolves, and not the bear," Jed said. "I'll give you the story and you can read it for yourself. In the meantime, I'd like you to meet Butterscotch or, as I like to call her, Mrs. Bradford."

"Mrs. Bradford?!" Jack said.

"Yes, it was love at first sight," Jed said happily. "We got a quick wedding in Nevada."

"I'm so pleased to meet you," Butterscotch said. She and Lizette embraced, Jed and Jack embraced, and that's about where this story comes to its natural conclusion. A library book was returned, Bad Luck Casey's death was avenged, and many other things long overdue were resolved. Perhaps the person most surprised by the tale, when he heard it, was Snowshoe Thompson.

"You may have some Norwegian in you," he told Jed. "Now that I have a child, I might need help carrying the mail. What have you got planned for next January?"

Next:
A missive from an unlikely source

211

VIII.

AN EPISTLE
or
ADVENTURES WITH TOM AND CORNELIUS

1884

*In which an illiterate attempts literature
and no dinner is obtained*

September 15, 1884

To: Ben Bradford
In Care of the Department of English Literature, North Hall
University of California
Berkeley, California

Dear Ben,

I am betting this here letter is a surprise and a half! I am writing to tell you what I been up to here in Placerville in the year since you been gone. I'm guessing that you are having the devil's time of it in college, reading books and listening to professors and whatnot. Sixteen seems a bit green to have to do all that.

First off, as you can see, I can read and write, maybe not proper like you or your Pa, but good for a Puhzz cause I am the only Puhzz what ever knew how. Your momma Butterscotch is the one that teached me and she said she would fix the spelling in this letter, but not the grammar, because she says a person's letter should sound like their voice, so I guess that means I don't use no grammar when I talk. Your momma also read your Pa's latest story to me. Well, not all of the story. That's a bit of a stretcher. More like just the parts with me in 'em. Truth is it bored me to tears, and don't tell your Pa I said so. I could barely stay awake and I got out my pipe for a smoke to give me something to do and your momma made me put it away as it's such a disgusting habit, or so she says.

What with learning to read and write you would think I was living the high life, and that might be true if it weren't for that no good Tom Blankenship. See, the other day I was working over at Landecker's Provisions hauling hams and sides of bacon up from the cellar and barrels of lard back down. That afternoon Natty Man Prudholm came by with near fifty turkeys, all bled and ready for cutting up, and we put them in the cellar for roasting the next morning. I was powerful tired come suppertime, so I stopped by the Argonaut Saloon to have a sarsaparilla. That's when Tom came by. Tom, of course, was drinking beer. I meant to go up to Confidence Hall, where the ladies from the Presbyterian Church were having a Strawberry Festival, cause I have such a weakness for strawberries and cream. Thanks to Tom Blankenship, I never got to taste them. I told him about all of the turkeys that I put in Landecker's cellar and he said they was for some picnic at Hank's Exchange the next day. He said they was going to roast up all those turkeys and have potatoes and boiled eggs and baked chicken and sliced oranges and then tarts and pies and cakes... Well, all that talk of food got me hungry, and feeling hungry always makes me thirsty, so I joined Tom in a couple of beers... well, maybe more than a couple. Don't it figure that just as we left the Argonaut, Reverend Odom goes walking by and gives me the look like I'm going to hell for sure for drinking with Tom Blankenship!

So, there we were walking down Main Street, near starving, and Tom had a devilish idea. He wanted to know why all them other folks should enjoy all that turkey and we got nothing but beer. I told

213

Tom that when I got paid the first thing I was going to buy was a roast turkey dinner at the Central House, but Tom said why wait? I don't know if it was the beer talking or what but I said sure thing, Tom, what do you have in mind? He says let's go over to Landecker's and go down into that cellar and get us one or two of them turkeys, take 'em over to the Sacramento Street livery and roast them over the yard fire. I didn't care much for the idea, as Mister Landecker give me so much work and all, so I did my darndest to talk Tom out of the fool idea.

Tom's stomach was talking up louder than his brain and he was hell bent to go over there and plunder the cellar. Lucky thing that Mister Landecker had the place padlocked as tight as you please. Tom looked around for a crow bar or something, but I just cleaned up the yard that very afternoon and there was nothing he could use to break the lock. I was just about relieved when Tom came up with another plan; he said we should go up to Natty Man Prudholm's place and grab ourselves some live turkeys. After all, they wouldn't be locked up.

I didn't have much room to argue with Tom about his new idea. I never did much care for Natty Man Prudholm. I remember back when I was in knee britches, the Next Big Thing was skating rinks. As you may remember, there was two rinks what opened on opposite sides of Placerville. Any night you stopped in to skate you would find the whole Board of Supervisors, City Council, Order of Oddfellows, Masons, and even the Clampers barreling along on roller skates in big circles and calling it "the best exercise possible, as testified by doctors back east." I distinctly recall seeing the Natty Man rolling by with Aloysius Culbertson - you know, the undertaker and furniture dealer. By the fall everyone lost their taste for skating and the rink at the east end of town closed and then once the winter passed the rink at the west end of town was turned into a church. So there I am, roller skating down the sidewalk cause I don't have a proper place to do it and ran smack dab into the Natty Man as he came out of Mrs. Thomas' Millinery. He went tumbling over the edge and into the street and got his shirt dirty and he was mighty mighty unpleased. "A silly pastime," he said all stuffy and know-it-all. "Of course, I never did such a childish thing."

What a liar! I done wanted to give him a smack upside the head, but him being an upstanding citizen and me being a Puhzz, well, we know which one of us would end up in the hoosegow! He told my Pappy that I was endangering the life of people with my skates and pappy took 'em away for good. After that I only had the evil eye for Natty Man Prodholm.

So Tom and I made a pact and we climbed up the hill toward the Natty Man's farm in the dark. On the way up the hill we started smelling the most delicious thing you ever used your nose for. It was sweet as a summer day and both me and Tom had to stop and get a good whiff. It only took us a few minutes to realize it was coming from Constance Flannery's place, where she bakes her pies and all. The Larsens been bringin' ripe apples to town the last two weeks and Missus Flannery was busy baking them all into pies as fast as she could. The shack behind her kitchen was just to bursting with cooling pies. So Tom says, hold on! We should grab a pie for dessert! After a nice dinner of roast turkey we will want a proper dessert! I didn't want no part in stealing no pies, as Missus Flannery never got my skates taken away, but I decided to keep an eye out for Tom Blankenship whilst he dashed in and absconded with one.

We sneaked up real quiet and I was waiting by the outhouse when I heard something. I also thought I smelled something, but between the cooling apple pies and the outhouse my nose was more than a bit confused. I looked around to see what made the noise, thinking maybe Missus Flannery or her husband was making a late

215

trip to the outhouse. Instead I saw something scurrying along through the grass. "Tom!" says I. "Tom! Hurry up!" I guess Tom thought the same thing I thought before - that one of the Flannerys was coming out to visit the necessary - and he bolted out of that shack, both hands holding steaming apple pies. Before I could warn him that there was something skulking in the grass, he stepped on it. There was the awfulest shriek you can imagine and Tom went face down into one of the pies and the other went flying into the outhouse door. "What the hell was that?" asks Tom, and directly we knew exactly what it was. I couldn't smell the outhouse no more, and I sure as heck couldn't smell the pies. All I could smell was skunk. I ran as fast as I could back the way we came and Tom was up on his feet running too. It was too late, though. We smelled of skunk from our heads to our toes.

I told Tom we should go back to town and clean ourselves up and he would have none of it. He dropped the pies, but he was still determined to get himself a turkey for roasting. I didn't think we'd have much chance, smelling like we did, since even a turkey has the good sense to run away from a body what stinks as bad as we did. No, he says, we deserve a good turkey dinner, and I allow as we do deserve it, though I'm not sure what we did that particular night to improve our character.

At last and finally we made it to the Natty Man's farm. There was plenty of turkeys up there, just like Tom said, running around the yard. So we climbed the fence and started to chasing them turkeys around in order to try and catch one or two. I'll be a goose's grandma if they didn't just run away and make us look like a couple of idiots, just like I said. I don't know if it was our skunkiness or that we didn't know much about catching turkeys, but they ran so fast we was left falling in the dirt. On top of that, they started up an awful racket that might have raised the dead if we were anywhere near a boneyard. We started worrying that the Natty Man might come out and catch us thieving his turkeys. About this time Tom notices a rifle leaning against the barn.

So Tom grabs that gun and decides the easy thing to do is to shoot one of them turkeys. I'm saying "No, Tom! You'll wake up everybody!" Just as Tom raised that rifle to shoot a particular slow turkey, out from the house comes the Natty Man, waving his arms because he thinks maybe a fox or cat is getting into his turkey pen. What happened next was about a hundred things at once, because Natty Man saw Tom and Tom fired the rifle and I finally grabbed a turkey and then Natty Man fell down and I dropped the turkey and Tom just stared at where the Natty Man had been and I called out "Tom! You shot the Natty Man!"

We ran over to his still body and tried to listen for his breathing or his heart beating or some other tell-tale sign that he was still alive, but my hands was shaken so bad that I don't think I'd have noticed he was alive if he'd jumped up and started singing "Ruler of the Queen's Navee." The Natty Man's missus comes running out of the house yelling "Ronald! Ronald!" (Didn't know his name was Ronald, did you?) Next thing you know the neighbors are all there and someone's gone to town for the Sheriff. Tom took to the hills, but you'd be proud of me, Ben, because I stayed right there to face the righteous hand of the law.

Turns out that rifle had nothing but powder shots in it, because the Natty Man (Ronald) just used it for scaring off the foxes and whatnot. Doctor said he fainted when the rifle went off, but he wasn't shot at all. He said the only doctoring that Natty Man would need was a bath and a change of clothing. The Sheriff rounded up Tom Blankenship and he's going up in front of the judge for trespassing and stealing turkeys and shooting off somebody else's rifle and stealing pies from Missus Flannery. I am getting a better deal, or so the Sheriff says. I was only trespassing, but since I didn't touch the pies or shoot off any guns I get off scot free on all that (I didn't tell them I caught and dropped a turkey). The Sheriff has me on fifty dollars bail or sixty days in the County Jail. As my pappy is in Sacramento (and as I wouldn't want him to know about all this anyway) I am writing to you. If you could part with the fifty dollars and spare me the time in the jail I would be mighty obliged.

        Sincerely and all that,
        Cornelius Puhzz

September 18, 1884

To: Cornelius Puhzz
In Care of the El Dorado County Sheriff
Placerville, California

Dear Cornelius,

I have wired your bail money to the Western Union office. If this should happen again (and I think we both know it will), have the Sheriff go over to the bookstore and ask my father or Jack for the bail. They won't mind loaning it to you, just so long as you share your story with them. All in all your letter was very well written. I'm looking forward to the next one! Say hello to Nate Norris for me when you get out. I'll be home for the Thanksgiving holiday and we can all have a proper - and legal - roast turkey dinner then.

        Your friend,
        Ben Bradford

Next:
Gather around the fire, little children

IX.

THE GHOST TOWN
or
ONE HUNDRED LOST DREAMS IN STORAGE

1898

In which a legacy is rediscovered

The story held them, around the fire, breathless, just as a strange tale told on Christmas Eve in an old house in a ghost town should. The tale, fittingly, was about an apparition in just such an old house in just such a ghost town.

"She was new to Old Hangtown...," the storyteller said.

"Wasn't it already called Placerville then, Mr. Bradford?" one of the children asked.

"Yes, but doesn't Old Hangtown sound better for a scary story?"

"Yes," the child admitted.

"So, as I was saying, she was new to Old Hangtown, and as such she didn't know very many people. When she saw the tall bearded man in the top hat walking with his black dog she thought it might be a neighbor having an evening constitutional. It never occurred to her that what she was seeing was nothing more than a shade... a spectre... an unquiet spirit...." Now he decided to tighten the screws a bit and see if he could elicit a shriek or two. "She was pleasant, as one might expect, and bid the wraith a good evening, but it did not answer. And then as she came closer, suddenly, its black hellhound leapt forward as if it were going to attack! She raised her arms to fend it off, and instead of feeling the impact of its claws and jaws she felt a cold draft as it passed through

219

her body! In shock and horror she spun around, but the dog was not there and, as she soon saw, the bearded man had vanished as well. Both were gone, evaporated or become one with the evening mists."

The children were spellbound now, clay in the hands of the storyteller.

"Thus began the strange events of Miss Eleanor Virginia Pynchon's first night at the Bailey House, in the sorry remains of Potter's Field, even before she arrived at the manor's porch," he said.

Perhaps you, dear reader, having joined our suspenseful tale *in medias res* , may have missed the sequence of events leading up to this otherworldly encounter; I really should go back to the beginning for you and set the stage, as it were, and bring the characters to the gaslights.

The decaying village of Potter's Field was the perfect setting for an unearthly tale, you see, for it begged the imagination to wander. In the 1850s it was a bustling community of miners, some four-hundred or more strong. As the miners moved on to golder pastures the town survived thanks to the dense woods surrounding it, which provided much-needed lumber to shore up the deep mine shafts that were now the preferred over placer mining. A mill was built, taking advantage of the good wagon road that lead from the Field to Placerville. By the 1870s the wood, like the town, began to thin and the mill closed. The hotel shut its doors and the smithy moved to Shingle Springs where the railroad could provide a steady stream of customers. Potter's Field became what was called in these parts a ghost town; a collection of deteriorating, abandoned buildings and empty streets.

A few people still clung to the edges of the Field and rode into Placerville or Diamond Springs every day for commerce' sake.

Most notable was the Bailey family, owners of the defunct Slate Ravine Mine and Potter's Field Mill, who took advantage of the mill to construct what at the time was the largest home in the county. Three stories tall it stood, with a tower at the back that reached up an additional story and was surrounded by a narrow balcony. High up there on the tower balcony old Bly Bailey paced, watching as his family's mine dwindled and failed and as his mill lost money and was finally shuttered.

Regardless of its demise as a functioning community, Potters Field's lovely meadows, colorful wildflowers, and cool forests made it a pleasant enough place to live. These qualities lead Jack and Lizette Norris - and later Jed and Butterscotch Bradford - to build homes at the Field's edge, a half mile down the road toward Placerville from the ghost town. They took their children to school each morning on their way to open the bookstore, and picked them up on the way home.

Growing up in these unfenced forests was far superior to living in the mud and dust of downtown Placerville (at least to Jed and Jack), and their young sons would hardly disagree. On summer days they could be found ranging around the woods and up through the Potter's Field Cemetery, playing *Marshalls and Outlaws* with the Bailey kids in the empty streets of the ghost town. Still, children grow up, and when they were ready to move on to college (as their fathers insisted they must) Nathan Norris and Benjamin Bradford bid Potter's Field goodbye and left for San Francisco to earn their degrees. Upon their departure the already silent streets of the ghost town grew moribund.

There were still Baileys living in Bailey House when Nate and Ben returned from college in 1891. Old Bly Bailey, ground down by life and the failure of his businesses finally "gave up the ghost," as they say, and leapt to his death from that fourth floor balcony. Still, he left more in the way of assets than one might expect, and his daughter Theodora, son Miles and their families all lived under its capacious roof. The men were often absent; Miles, a lawyer, came and went as his needs arose and Theodora's husband, Udolpho, was a surveyor for the state and rarely made it home outside of holidays and special occasions. As a result it fell to Theodora and Miles' wife Florence to keep Bailey House alive with the help of their children and several servants.

It is in this setting that the previously narrated meeting of living and dead took place. Earlier that same evening our young victim - the living one, so new to Hangtown - arrived in Placerville by coach and went directly to a familiar store:

Ben Bradford, one of our principals, was standing at the front counter at *Bradford & Norris - Booksellers to the Savage West* when the thin slip of a girl came in through the front door. A bell hung above the door on a spring, right where Ben's father Jed had placed it, and when she entered it chimed lightly. If this was any normal evening at the bookstore, Ben would have been happily reading *The Invisible Man* by H.G. Wells, his current book. Instead he was pouring over a binder full of columnar paper, checking entries and verifying addition and subtraction.

"Good evening," he said to the girl distractedly. He finished adding the numbers on the page and then looked up at her. She was nineteen, perhaps twenty, with shoulder length curly hair, wearing a high-necked white blouse, long gray skirt and a pert traveling hat.

"My apologies that I must introduce myself," she said to the clerk. "I am Miss Eleanor Virginia Pynchon, children's governess and teacher of reading and arithmetic. I'm lead to understand that the proprietor of this establishment lives in the community of Potter's Field." Every word was spoken very politely and very exactly, the way someone might speak when taking a test in diction.

"I'm not sure 'community' is the right word for it," Ben said. "But, yes, I live there. I'm Ben Bradford." The girl glanced down and Ben wondered if she was referring to notes.

"May I enquire regarding the possibility of transportation from Placerville to Potter's Field and to the Bailey House therein?" she asked. "I'm afraid the gentleman - and I do use the word only through common courtesy -- who was supposed to meet me has failed to do so." Ben smiled and tried to put her at ease.

"I would be happy to take you out there, Miss Pynchon. Someone else will be here shortly to watch the store and I'll gather the buckboard to take you properly."

"I am much obliged," she said, "though I am concerned regarding the propriety of traveling alone in the company of a man with whom I am unfamiliar. My position as a governess requires utmost discretion." The bell on the door rang again as Nate came in.

"That's not a problem," Ben said as he collected up his book and put it in his leather pack. "I'm well acquainted with the Baileys and I assure you they have only the best opinion of me."

"Did you find anything?" Nate asked. Ben glanced back at the ledgers stacked up on the counter.

"No, not so far," he said with little enthusiasm. "I've only gotten through the first three, though. I'm taking this young lady out to the Bailey House. Will you close up?"

"Sure," Nate said. "Miss," he added, nodding toward Eleanor.

"So, you are Misters Bradford and Norris, Booksellers?" the girl asked.

"The Misters Bradford and Norris referred to on the sign are our fathers," Ben told her. "Though I daresay we've sold a few books in our time. Please follow me, Miss Pynchon."

The wagon ride out to Potter's Field was much bumpier and

223

the road much more crooked than Eleanor expected it to be and she did not hesitate to inform Ben of such. He apologized and to his benefit the road leveled out as it came into the little valley below Fort Jim Ridge. He could see the Bradford and Norris homes as they rode by through the apple orchard. The houses were bright and pleasant, even in the dusky light, and inviting smoke issued from both chimneys. A moment later they passed the narrow track that lead up to Old Man Poe's cabin. And then, at last, they turned the corner into Potter's Field. To the right was the cemetery and beyond it the caliginous and uninviting buildings of the ghost town. Straight ahead, silhouetted against the darkening sky, was the imposing bulk of Bailey House. Ben stopped at the manor gate.

"I'm sorry, Miss, the gate seems to be closed," Ben apologized. "Are you quite sure they were expecting you tonight?"

"Quite," Eleanor said succinctly. She lowered herself to the road before Ben could jump down to help her and pulled her valise from the sideboard.

"Let me walk you up to the house," Ben said, "I think that would be appropriate."

"No, that's quite alright, Mr. Bradford," Eleanor told him. "You've been quite kind. There is still enough day left, though waning, and I see it is but a short walk. Thank you very much for your courtesy, I shall not forget it." With a polite nod she picked up her bag and marched around the gate and up the walking path.

Ben allowed his horse to circle the buckboard around so that it was headed back the way it came - even horses preferred not to face the ghost town at this time of night. He paused, still thinking that the most gentlemanly act would be to make sure this young woman, alone at a late hour, made it safely to the House door. But the light was already too dim and he couldn't see her anymore. He waited for a moment and then tapped the horse lightly with the reins and started home.

Eleanor heard the beat of the horse's hooves and the creak of the wagon as it pulled away. Ahead were several buildings aside from the main house; a wagon house, a greenhouse, and a structure that looked like it might be servants' quarters. She didn't think for a moment that she would be lodged there herself; the governess was always kept close to the children. As she passed this building a figure approached along the walk. Drawing closer she saw a tall bearded man in a top hat. At his side, keeping perfect pace, was a moderately sized black dog.

"Good evening," she said, which was, of course, the polite thing to say, and that is when the dog attacked.

Moments later she doubted her own senses, for the man and dog had melted away into the night. Eleanor was not the sort of person who would let these sorts of things color her mood. There were people, especially in the city where it was fashionable, who fancied all things relating to the ethereal. Eleanor was a pragmatic person who had no time for these sorts of frivolous pursuits, and as such she dismissed the event as a result of fatigue due to her long journey. She adjusted her skirt, grasped her valise tightly, and took long, sure steps up the walk to the portico, at which point you have caught up with the tale and you know every bit as much as the children, huddled around the Christmas Eve fire.

"What happened then?" asked Jessica, the storyteller's niece. "Tell us!"

"I can't," he told her, knowing exactly the sort of response this would bring.

"What?!" the children protested. "No, tell us!"

"I'll have to *read* it to you," the storyteller smiled. He walked across the room to the roll-top desk beneath the front window and pulled a small key from his pocket. With every bit of drama the moment demanded he carefully unlocked the desk, pulled out a drawer, and took a hand sewn leather sheaf from inside. "This has been hidden away," he said, "for the contents are far too startling to let just anyone read it."

"Read it to us!" the children demanded. The storyteller pretended to wrestle with the decision and then with a heavy sigh he sat down in front of them by the fire with the book. He opened it and the children could see delicate handwriting in faded ink.

"Alright, I'll read it to you," he said. "You must promise to go to your own beds tonight, though, and not demand to share mine!"

So, he began, Eleanor Pynchon was admitted to Bailey House, where she met the women of the manor, Theodora and Florence, as well as their children; Miles, Jr., Catherine, Ellen, Isabella, Edgar, and little Heathcliff. The Baileys took to Eleanor quickly, appreciating her no-nonsense attitude handling the boys and her ability to instruct the girls in arts more complicated than knitting. With Eleanor's steady hand guiding the children, Theodora was able to return to her study of botany in the greenhouse and Florence retired each day to the upstairs study to play her piano.

The Bailey children - with one exception - were mild compared to the rowdy handful of younger siblings Eleanor grew up herding, and presented little challenge to her firm resolve. Only Edgar, a boy of nine years, required any special care. He always seemed preoccupied and rarely listened to her when she spoke. Even threatening to box his ears - something that always worked with Miles, Jr. - was useless.

"Why aren't you listening to me, Edgar?" Eleanor might say.

"Because I'm listening," he might reply.

"That's what I asked!" she might protest.

"No, no," he might say, "I'm not listening to you because

I'm listening."

On weekdays between the hours of nine and two the children were taken to school by Quint, the groom. These five hours were the center of Eleanor's day. She spent the first two straightening the nursery and the last three helping Mrs. Dean, the housekeeper, prepare for the children's return. Finally, in the evening, once the children had gone to bed and before retiring herself, Eleanor had a small interval alone. This hour was her favorite; it was just the first days of autumn and the day still lingered at this hour. Each night just before sunset she took a stroll about the grounds and along the many paths that wound through the forest. The last calls of the birds sounded from the gloaming and the first cool breezes of the night settled in from the painted sky. In these transitional moments she felt tranquil and whole, a state of mind she never enjoyed in her childhood home. Here she could step forward and be herself, a remarkable young woman capable of forging her own path without the weight of others.

Eventually she came to know the Bailey property quite well and her twilight wanderings took her further afield. On one particular evening she took the main wagon road past the Bailey gates toward the open meadows of Potter's Field. She knew about the ghost town; Miles, Jr., delighted in telling her the family history and planned to take her to the site of the old Slate Ravine Mine some Saturday when the opportunity arose. This evening she ambled along the split-rail fence that separated the road from the cemetery and read inscriptions on the tombstones in the golden light.

"Here lies Bootjack Johnson, who was accidentally killed in his 45th year of age by a falling rock, 1883," one said. Another said, "Died 1853, Tugger Head Phillips, Never Found His Pay Dirt."

"I knew some of these people," a voice said, and Eleanor jumped high enough that both of her feet left the ground. A gray-haired man was sitting in the graveyard by one of the stones eating some buttered bread. She grabbed the top rail of the fence and tried to compose herself. "I'm sorry," the man said, "I didn't mean to startle you. I thought you saw me."

"No, no, that is quite alright, sir. I was in a state of reverie and was not paying due attention," she apologized. The man brushed the crumbs from his legs and stood, using the nearby tombstone for leverage. He teetered for a bit then turned toward Eleanor.

"You're the new governess at the Bailey House, aren't you? I'm Jed Bradford. I believe my son Ben brought you in from town the first night you arrived."

"Oh, yes," Eleanor replied. "You're the bookseller."

"That's right," Jed smiled. "I'm retired now. I come here for supper sometimes and visit my old friends."

"Here? In the cemetery?" Eleanor could hardly think of a less appealing place to eat.

"Here and in the ghost town. It's very peaceful there." Jed slung a pack over his back, picked up a short oak cane, and started walking along the cemetery side of the fence toward the gate ahead. He walked with a slight limp, the result of a bad ankle that plagued him in his later years and let the cane take his weight on occasion. Halfway to the gate he gestured to one of the headstones. "This one is my favorite." Eleanor leaned over the fence to read it. The stone simply said; "Sebastian, 1855, Died of a Broken Heart."

"What a dreadful note to adorn one's resting place for eternity," Eleanor said.

"When I read it I imagine poor Sebastian's story," Jed said. "How did he die of a broken heart? Who broke it? Every time I sit here I imagine a different story. By now I might have an entire volume titled *The Tales of Sebastian and How His Heart Was Broken.*"

"What a joyless tome that would be!" Eleanor declared.

"Tale after tale of anguish. I don't suppose anyone would read it!"

"That's alright," Jed smiled. "I've never written it." Eleanor glanced up and noticed that the sun was already below the horizon. The golden meadow was fading to purple.

"I'm sorry, Mister Bradford, I should be going," she said. "Mister Quint, the groom, will be locking up the house."

"That's quite alright," Jed said. "Perhaps you can visit me here again. I'm always wandering about, and sometimes it's best to have company around here." He gave her a short wave and then limped away through the cemetery toward the dilapidated buildings of the ghost town.

Three days later Eleanor had another opportunity to take a walk down the wagon road. As she strolled along the cemetery fence she kept an eye out for Jed Bradford, but today the boneyard was empty except for the occasional blue jay, grosbeak or evening wren. She continued past the cemetery gate and into the open space of Potter's Field, following what once must have been the main street of a busy community. Each of the buildings, even in states of disrepair, was easy to identify. There was the general store, there was the smithy. To the far end was a small church, maybe a chapel. A larger building was clearly the hotel, with a restaurant or saloon next to it. The stables were in the worst condition; the walls sagged under the weight of the decaying roof, which was caked in moss. The remains of a buckboard, one wheel missing, sat in front of the hotel. When she stopped walking and listened there was merely silence. She imagined what this place must have been like in the midst of the gold rush; the voices, the movement, the scents.

She was about to turn around and start back toward Bailey House when Eleanor saw something out of the corner of her eye. She turned and there, in the middle of the street next to the hotel, was the tall bearded man. The black dog lay in the dust at his feet.

Instead of fear, Eleanor felt relief. Because she did not subscribe to notions of spirits and ephemera, the vanishing man and his invisible dog had vexed her. What were they and where had they gone? Seeing now that they were substantial and corporeal was reassuring.

"Good evening," she said to the man. He did not respond, standing there for a moment, and then, with no indication that he saw or heard her, turned and walked into the crumbling hotel. Eleanor looked back to see if the dog would follow, but the beast was gone. Curious, she moved tentatively toward the hotel. "Hello?" she called out as she stepped onto the rotting floorboards of the hotel porch. The doors were gone, either taken when the building was abandoned or already fallen into ruin. She hesitated at the threshold, peering into the dark lobby. "Hello?" she said more softly.

And then, suddenly, he was there, no more than a foot away. His face was long and thin, worried in the extreme, furrowed and leathered by exposure to the elements. He opened his mouth and a rasping voice issued forth, like the last breath of a dying man. "Book...," it said. "Book..."

Eleanor screamed in surprise and fell backward, crashing through the floorboards and to the ground below. She turned to stand and saw that the doorway was empty once again, though the interior of the building felt dark and deep. Scrambling, she made it to her feet and ran along the road, dashing past the cemetery and not slowing until she was through the gate of the Bailey manor, past the conservatory, and into the House itself.

Late the next day after the children were returned from school, Eleanor was sitting in the nursery mending one of little Heathcliff's shirts. Edgar Bailey came across the room from where he had been playing and sat down at her feet. He stared at her hands as the needle pierced the cloth and she pulled the thread through. "Can I be of service to you, Edgar?" she asked him. "You know, it's almost time for you to turn in. Are you washed?"

"You saw the man with the beard yesterday," Edgar said matter-of-factly. Eleanor practically dropped her sewing when he said it.

"What did you say?" she asked.

"The man with the beard and his black dog. You saw them yesterday, over at the ghost town," Edgar said.

"How did you know that?!"

"I could see it in your eyes," he said. "You have pretty eyes, Miss Pynchon." She set her sewing on the table and picked up the boy.

"Thank you, Edgar. So, this man with the dog… do you know him? Do you know his name?"

"No. He lives in the ghost town," the child told her.

"Is he scary?" she asked Edgar, pulling him close and stroking his hair.

"No," he said after a moment. "He's trying to tell us something. That's why we have to listen." In that moment Eleanor was resolved to her next course of action.

About an hour later - a bit further up the valley - Ben Bradford arrived home from a long day at the bookstore. The weight of the day wore heavily across his shoulders and he walked in stooped like an old man. He dropped his pack on the kitchen table and slumped into one of the chairs. With a deep sigh he stared with fixed intensity at the knotty wallboards.

"Dad, there have been some money problems at the store," he said. "We've gotten deeply in debt and I don't see any way out of it. I think we're going to lose the bookstore. I'm so sorry."

"Don't worry, Ben," Jed said from the opposite side of the

room. He used the kitchen counter for support as he'd left his cane someplace or other. "You know, Jack and I encountered those sorts of problems many times. We always found a solution. In fact, I expect a solution is going to show up at your door any day now."

"I need some sleep," Ben said. "Maybe if I get some sleep…"

"That's a good idea," Jed told him. "Sleep on it until tomorrow. See what the new day brings."

The sun was nearly gone from the flushed sky when Eleanor reached the end of the road and stood facing the ghost town. The forest suddenly lost its voice; birdsong silenced, air went still, and a blanket of dread settled over the dead village. In the street before her were at least a dozen people, although she could not determine where they arrived from. The man with the beard was near the center. Some of the men in the group held picks and shovels over their shoulders. A man in a stovepipe hat removed it in a courteous gesture. A beautiful woman in a cream-colored dress beckoned Eleanor with a wave of her lovely hand.

"I do not believe in phantoms or spooks," Eleanor said bravely. "Still, I accept that the echo of a determined spirit may remain in a place to do good, and if I may aide such a benevolent cause then I am here for you."

The beautiful woman begged her forward again.

"Edgar said you mean me no harm," Eleanor added. "He said I should listen to you. You don't mean to harm me, do you?"

"We mean you no harm," the woman said in a dry rattle that in no way complimented her pleasing form. Still, Eleanor believed her and took tentative steps forward. A man (or shade, she reminded herself - nothing more than a shade) who wore a bulky black duster broke free of the crowd and met Eleanor in front of the stables. The creature's face had the shadow of death upon it.

"Bookstore…," it said in a wretched whisper. *"Bookstore…"*

Ben and Nate were still pouring over their accounts, looking for any bit of information that might give them financial hope, when the bookstore door opened and Jed's little bell rang. Both of them looked up as one - despite their difficulties they were still, first and foremost, booksellers, and service to their customers always came first.

"Good afternoon, Miss Pynchon," Ben said. The young governess surveyed the bookstore and then approached the counter.

"Good afternoon, Mr. Bradford, Mr. Norris," she said. "I'm not quite sure how to explain the nature of my visit…"

"Are you in need of a book, perhaps?" Nate asked with a smile.

"That is one possibility," she said. Eleanor proceeded to tell Ben and Nate about her encounter with the shade and his hellhound the night she arrived at Bailey House, her subsequent second encounter in the ghost town and, in fair detail, her audience with the group of spirits the night before. "They offered no better answer to my inquiries other than the word bookstore. My only conclusion was that they were directing me here, to your establishment."

Now, Ben and Nate, as practical and educated men, might have found the governess's story preposterous if not for two things. First, they had spent their boyhoods playing in the ghost town and over the years seen and heard many things which defied expectation. Second, it was clear to Ben even in the short time he had spent with her, that Eleanor Pynchon was not the sort of foolish young girl who entertained fantasies for common pleasure. Although they reserved giving their entirety of belief over to the notion that phantoms had directed this woman to their store, at the same time they kept open minds.

"What do you suppose we should do?" Nate asked. "This sounds like some sort of prank. Remember the time Old Man Poe dressed up in furs and pretended to be a bear in order to scare away trespassers?

"That's possible," Ben admitted. "Still, I think the most direct response is the best, at least to set Miss Pynchon's mind at ease. We'll go out there and talk to them." He turned the sign in the window to read *CLOSED* and as they exited Nate locked the front door.

They decided to split up in order to cover more ground. Nate rode over to the Cary House past the brand new steel bell tower to pick up his friend Cornelius Puhzz. The two of them intended to ride out to Old Man Poe's and investigate whether the hermit had anything to do with the strange appearances - or at the very least if he had seen any unusual movements in the ghost town below his property. Ben and Miss Pynchon rode out to Potter's Field to see if the spirits would appear during the daylight. Eleanor only had a short time before she had to be back at the Bailey House to meet the children upon their return from school.

Ben and Eleanor arrived at the edge of Potter's Field just after noon. In the midday sunlight, with so few shadows cast and the dark, hidden spaces all bright and exposed, the idea that this was a sinister place haunted by malign phantoms was patently absurd. Even Eleanor began to doubt herself and think the entire episode an attack of the nerves. Ben brought his wagon to a halt just short of the stables and then helped Eleanor down. The meadow was teeming with jubilant birds on their way south for the winter. No one, alive or otherwise, appeared to them, so Ben ventured to the door of the old hotel and peered inside.

"Perhaps it must be night, or very nearly so," Eleanor said.

"Or you have been the victim of a hoax," Ben suggested.

He took her back to the Bailey House and promised that he would return by nightfall. There was always the hope that by then Nate and Cornelius may have found something that would explain the entire affair.

On the way out to Old Man Poe's house, Nate and Cornelius Puhzz had a long talk about *Huckleberry Finn*. This was a discussion they had frequently. Cornelius was not, as they would say today, a bright bulb. Still, he was an honest and well-meaning bulb, so Nate had steadfastly befriended him, through thick and thin, for more than twenty years. Puhzz was not a very good reader, so he avoided books when he could. This, of course, wouldn't do for Nate, so he constantly tried to talk Cornelius into reading something - anything - that would increase his appreciation of the printed word. Finally, just the year previous, Nate had convinced Puhzz that reading Mark Twain's masterwork would be in his best interest, and to Nate's surprise he did. It took Cornelius several months, and he had to ask Nate daily what this or that word meant, but he actually finished it.

"If I ever have a son," Cornelius Puhzz said as they rode out toward Potter's Field, "I think I will name him Huckleberry."

"You should read some Kipling, perhaps *The Jungle Books*," Nate suggested. "I think you'd like it."

"Oh, I've read a book now, and once you've read one book you've read 'em all," Puhzz said. "Besides, isn't *Huckleberry Finn* the best book ever? Why read another after you've read the best?"

"What if you have another son?" Nate asked.

"I'll name him Finn," Cornelius said.

After passing the Bradford and Norris homes they came to the steep and rocky track that led up to Old Man Poe's cabin. They talked loudly all the way up the hill in order to make sure Poe got a fair warning of their arrival. He was known to shoot at trespassers when he was surprised. Nate figured that they would be safe, since he and Ben were two of the only human beings ever allowed as far as Poe's doorstep, and this was because - unbeknownst to anyone else in El Dorado County - Old Man Poe was a reader. Once a month either Nate or Ben made the pilgrimage to his cabin to deliver a box of books.

"What do you want?" Poe called out from behind his door before either of the visitors could dismount.

"Mister Poe, it's me, Nathan Norris, from the bookstore. I'd like to ask you a couple of questions."

"This isn't book week," Old Man Poe declared. "Go away."

"I know it isn't, Mister Poe. We'd just like to ask you a couple of questions about Potter's Field," Nate said. "Some strange things are going on down there and we wondered if you'd seen anything."

There was no immediate reply, which was uncharacteristic. The locks came open one by one and a slim crack appeared between the door and jamb. A long, bent nose split the space and small green eyes peered out from inside the cabin.

"What sort of strange things?" Poe asked.

"People moving about who don't belong. Unnatural things, I suppose," Nate answered. The door opened a little further and a face, folded by time, pushed through.

"It's a ghost town, isn't it? I suppose there are ghosts."

"I'm asking about something more specific," Nate said. The old man sniffed for a moment.

"Been a fellow wandering around down there a lot lately, tall man with a dog. Then I've noticed that things around the town have moved around. Stuff that used to be tucked away in the hotel has been left lying in the street. I thought it was looters at first, but... well, that's all I have to say about that. Now go away."

Nate could sense that Poe's moment of cooperation had passed, and also that the old man had nothing to do with the people

Eleanor Pynchon had encountered. He was ready to thank him and leave when Cornelius decided to enter the conversation;

"Exactly why do you live out here in the boonies all by yourself, Mister Poe?" he suddenly asked. Of course the question had occurred to Nate as well (many times), but it just seemed rude to ask a hermit point blank why he had chosen to separate himself from society. Sort of like asking someone why they spent so much time alone in the bathroom. But Old Man Poe didn't seem to mind the question.

"I went to the woods because I wished to live deliberately, to front only the essential facts of life, and see if I could not learn what it had to teach, and not, when I came to die, discover that I had not lived," he said. There was silence for a moment.

"You don't say?" Puhzz finally said.

"Actually, I was quoting Henry David Thoreau," Old Man Poe added, "but in choosing to live here I was similarly motivated."

"This Thoreau fella a hermit too?" Puhzz asked.

"Come on, Cornelius, I think we're done here," Nate said. "Thank you, Mister Poe." The two younger men mounted their horses and rode off down the hill, while Old Man Poe backed into his cabin like a turtle retreating into its shell, and closed the door behind him.

As the day perished the group of curious citizens gathered at the Bailey House gate; Ben arrived by wagon and Nate and Cornelius arrived on horseback. They pastured the horses in the Bailey corral as they intended to walk to their destination. Cornelius had his rifle with him for protection. Nate pointed out that if the objects of their hunt were truly ghosts then they were already dead and most likely no more substantial than a draft of cold air. A rifle wasn't likely to scare them off. Still, Cornelius felt more secure with his firearm in hand and no amount of logic could deter him. The four of them strolled slowly down the road toward Potter's Field, almost as if they were out enjoying an autumn evening, although their senses were quick and vigilant. Eleanor stopped them when they reached the center of the ghost town and they became still, though hardly tranquil. Each perfectly harmless and common sound that emanated from the darkling wood surrounding the town gave them an attack of the nerves. As they continued waiting there without any odd occurrence they started to relax and just when it seemed the old ghost town would yield up no mysteries Eleanor whispered, *"Look!"*

The tall bearded man and his dog were standing by the hotel next to the man in the bulky black duster. The beautiful woman in the cream colored dress was framed in the hotel doorway. All three specters beckoned to them and then vanished into the bowels of the abandoned and decaying building. The four visitors were rendered immobile and merely stood shoulder to shoulder in the dusty street and stared after the departed spirits.

"Hello, Ben," a voice from behind them said. "What are you looking at?" The quartet practically leapt from their boots and spun around to face Jed Bradford leaning on his cane behind them. Cornelius tripped and went down to his knees.

"Oh, Mr. Bradford! You gave us quite a fright!" Eleanor breathed.

"My apologies, dear, I didn't mean to startle you so," Jed said. Eleanor turned back toward her companions and saw that Nate had joined Cornelius Puhzz on the ground. Ben was motionless still. His jaw drooped to one side and his eyes seemed to be windows to a faraway place. He was so visibly discomfited that Eleanor felt comfortable addressing him by his first name. "What's the matter, Ben?"

"Dad...," Ben said. "Eleanor, do you see my father standing before us?"

"Of course," she replied.

"How is he dressed?"

Eleanor paused at the eccentricity of the question and then answered. "In a pair of denim trousers, a flannel shirt, a nice pair of braces and a short brimmed hat. Oh, and that lovely oak cane."

"Dad, how can you be here?" Ben asked.

"I apologize," Jed said. "I suppose I failed you in lessons of a spiritual nature, so that you are completely unprepared for this visitation. I told you the story of the time your Uncle Jack and I were at Fort Laramie and met Old Man Baker, didn't I?"

"Many times," Ben replied.

"Well, there it is," Jed said. "When you spoke to me the other night in your kitchen I was sure that - at some station of consciousness, at least - you knew I was present. In any case, Jack is waiting for us with the others inside the hotel. We have something to show you." He started limping across the street toward the Potter's Field Hotel, where a crowd of phantoms waited. Cornelius and Nate climbed to their feet, still too dumbfounded to speak.

"I don't understand what is going on," Eleanor said. Ben glanced in her direction and she saw the tears on his face drawing traces through the dust.

"Miss Pynchon," he said, "that man is my father, who died two years ago in his own bed of influenza."

At first sight the lobby of the Potter's Field Hotel was nothing more than a cavernous space filled with rotting timbers. Before their eyes it transformed and was as it might have been when it was new; the polished bar to the right, the mirror lining the back wall, the curtains cascading from the windows on the second floor. The four trespassers from the world of the living stepped into the world of the dead and were quickly surrounded by eager spirits happily welcoming them. Jack Norris hurried over and embraced

Nate and in this strange halfway place between life and afterlife the dead had enough substance that their touch felt real, though fleeting.

"It is highly unusual, I know," Jed told them, "for the dead and the living to mix in this manner. However, we need your help and time has suddenly run short. Jack and I would like to show you something." Nate lit the lantern he had brought and Jed led them behind the hotel counter and down a hall to a small room. They were now so deep in the hotel that not even a glimmer of the red sky was visible anymore. Nate held the lantern high and as he moved it the shadows in the room revolved about them.

"You'll have to move that desk," Jack said. Ben and Nate each took hold of the desk and slid it over to the opposite wall. The space it had occupied was a rectangular clearing in the dust. In the center of this was a hatch in the hardwood floor.

"Go ahead and open it," Jed told them. Nate grabbed the iron ring embedded in the hatch and pulled until years of dust gave way and the door yielded. It swung up to expose a fair opening and a rotten ladder. Ben and Nate looked at each other for just a moment before they both started to clamber down.

"I'll stay up here," Cornelius said. He gave Eleanor a look. "To protect the lady."

At the bottom of the shaft was a brick enclosure. Perhaps it was once a wine cellar, or perhaps it was the remaining walls of the hotel's vault. Plenty of gold came and went through these hills and sometimes miners needed a safe place to store it. Now the space was mostly empty, except on the south side where, along the wall, there were stacks of uniform boxes; three rows deep, a dozen or more long, and four boxes high. Jed and Jack, who had reached the cellar without ever descending the ladder, slowly circled the boxes.

"These will be destroyed soon if we don't take action," Jed

said. "We don't know how or why, but it is an undeniable truth. We have to save them before it's too late."

Nate lifted the top of one box and peered inside. It was filled with paper, some loose and some bound, some still white and many more yellowed with age. "What are these?" he asked.

"Our stories," Jed and Jack said.

And so here is the tale, as succinctly as I can tell it. Throughout all the years that Jed and Jack lived in Placerville and ran their bookstore they wrote; short stories, long stories, short novels, long novels. On occasion they would mail a story off to a publishing house in San Francisco or New York, and on rarer occasion an editor might publish one in a magazine or review. Most of what they committed to paper remained unpublished, however, and was boxed and stored. After their experiences with the Great Fires of 1856 they knew that they couldn't trust their manuscripts to any attic or back room, so in 1860 they hired a space in the brick vault at the Potter's Field Hotel to house their stories. Each time they finished one it was committed to a box and when the box was full it was taken to the hotel. In time the vault was filled with them.

"There are better than a hundred here," Jed said, "a hundred lost dreams waiting to be shared. And if we don't get them out of here soon they will all be destroyed."

Ben reached into the first open box and took hold of the top sheet of paper, a cover sheet with only the title, Jed's name, and the date 1866 written in black ink. "They're all here? All of your stories?" he asked his father. He lifted the sheet out of the box to see it, to appreciate it, to be amazed and delighted by it, and instead it folded up between his fingers and crumbled into dust.

"You see our problem," Jack said. "The boxes themselves are no better."

Nate opened the boxes one by one and examined the brittle

manuscripts inside. Here were reams of paper, some merely stacked and some tied with string, many volumes fat with plot and characters and theme and language. And all of it was ready to disintegrate.

"What are we going to do?" Ben asked.

"Well, we've been thinking about that," Jed said. "If you boys can get us some paper and new quills, a decent amount of ink and a few tables and chairs, our friends here are prepared to help transcribe all of this onto new paper. We can remove these pages, one at a time and with care, and copy them. What you do with the manuscripts once we're done is up to you and Nate."

And that is exactly what they did. Nate and Cornelius picked up the wagon at the Bailey House and rode back to Placerville. They knocked on the doors of their fellow merchants, despite the hour, and by the time that the eastern sky was lightening they had collected every single blank sheet of paper within ten miles. Beneath the wagon's bench they stowed four crates of India ink and more than a hundred quills and fountain pens. Ben and Eleanor went through the wagon house at the Bailey manor and pulled out the summer entertaining furniture - already stowed for the winter - and carried it piece by piece to the Potter's Field Hotel. By the time they made their last trip, bearing lanterns and candles, the ghostly residents of the hotel were already lined up along both sides of the tables. Several spirits, including the ghost of Bad Luck Casey (the man in the oversize duster), formed a bucket brigade line and started passing along the manuscript pages, carefully and respectfully one at a time, from the storage vault below. Nate and Cornelius returned and distributed the paper, pens, and ink. In no time the Great Transcription had begun.

Jed and Jack walked along behind their friends, looking over (or through) their shoulders to make sure that the manuscripts were being copied faithfully. On occasion they even made a slight change or edit to the story.

"We have so little time left," Jed told his son.

"Why, dad?" Ben asked. "What's going to happen?"

"I don't know," Jed replied. "I just know that if we don't get this done soon it will all be lost."

The tall bearded ghost with the dog grunted something in response.

"What's that?" Ben asked.

"Never mind him," Jed said. "He has issues." Before Ben could ask for clarification on this statement they were interrupted by the Bailey governess.

"Excuse me," Eleanor said. "I'm afraid I must return to the House. The children will be awakening any moment and I must be there when they do." Nate volunteered to walk Miss Pynchon back to the Bailey manor.

"Dad?" Ben asked. "I have lots of questions, and this might seem to be a silly one to be asking, but I have to ask it."

"Go ahead," Jed said.

"Is the story of the Wheelbarrow Man here?" Jed smiled at the question, but in a haunted way (which might make sense, as he was a ghost).

"No, I'm afraid not," he said. "During my life I had a dozen or so short stories published in magazines. Besides that I promised myself, over and over again, that Jack and I would finish these novels and forward them with good intention to publishers. Yet every day some small thing distracted me - always just for a moment business moments and family moments and marvelous moments and momentary crises alike. All those moments became years and then the years became a lifetime. Here all of my dreams collected, layering dust and forgotten. Jack and I came to California with a dream of writing its stories, and instead they lay here moldering.

How could I have let my life wander so?"

"Thank God for ghostwriters," Ben said.

Eleanor had no chance to return to Potter's Field for the rest of the day. Once she had the children off to school Mrs. Dean took charge of her to sort the linens and then Mrs. Bailey asked for help moving pottery in the greenhouse. Then, almost before she could take a breath the children had returned. After supper Eleanor collected the children's laundry and did her best to get them undressed, though the fatigue she felt from a night without sleep dulled her. Finally finished with little Heathcliff, she removed Edgar's braces. She desperately wanted the children to tuck in so that she could return to the Hotel and check on the ghosts' progress.

"Where did you go last night?" the boy asked. Eleanor quickly tried to fabricate a lie - she certainly didn't want to tell Edgar the truth - and was saved from this uncomfortable situation by a sudden commotion downstairs. The House was in general so quiet (with the exception of Florence's delightful piano music) that the noise, especially at this hour, was unsettling.

"Just a moment, Edgar," Eleanor said, patting the child on the head, and she went to the top of the stairs. At the bottom, just inside the front doors, stood a tall man with a great handlebar mustache. Theodora embraced him and Florence made a great celebration of his appearance. Edgar joined Eleanor at the banister.

"Who is that man?" she asked the boy.

"Oh, that is Father," Edgar answered with little satisfaction. Intrigued, Eleanor slowly descended the stairs, loathe to interrupt a family reunion but curious to meet her employer. Theodora released her brother as she reached the bottom.

"Oh, excuse me, dear," Florence gushed. "Miles, this is the governess you retained, Miss Pynchon." Eleanor briefly curtsied.

"No need for formalities, my girl," Miles Bailey said in a

booming voice. "I hear very good things about you, very good indeed."

"So what brings you back early?" Florence asked Miles as Mrs. Dean took his coat. "We did not expect you back until Thanksgiving."

"That is the news, I expect," Miles said. "I have, at last, leased the meadow to a farmer who deals in alfalfa for hay. I have men arriving tomorrow to raze the old ghost town. Mister Patterson will be here later in the week to plow the entire field so that he may have it ready for seeding in the spring. That old eyesore of a town will be gone and we shall finally make good income from the land."

"The ghost town will be demolished?!" Eleanor asked. "Tomorrow?!"

"How delightful, Miles!" Florence said and she embraced her husband again.

The entire family stayed up late to welcome Miles Bailey home, much to Eleanor's chagrin. By the time the children were put to bed and she was released from her duties it was already dark.

When Eleanor arrived at the Potter's Field Hotel the lobby was bright with lantern light. Tables were arranged along both sides, crowded with busy ghosts transcribing manuscripts. Jed and Jack sat at the last table in each row, dictating new material to complete the unfinished stories. Ben and Nate, the only living and breathing occupants, provided the spirits with ink and paper, and gathered up the pages when they were done.

"Mister Bradford! Mister Norris!" Eleanor called out. Ben gave the paper he was carrying to the ghost of Bad Luck Casey and hurried over.

"What brings you out so late, Miss Pynchon?" he asked.

"I know what is going to happen that requires such haste!

Mr. Miles Bailey has returned to Bailey House!" She told them everything that had been discussed over the night's dinner; about the leasing of the land and the plans to tear down the ghost town the very next day to allow for plowing of the meadow. Ben thought about the many piles of brittle paper that were still in the cellar downstairs.

"There is no way we can move all of the manuscripts by tomorrow," Nate said. "They would be reduced to dust."

Before Ben could offer anything further the tall bearded spirit who was always accompanied by the black dog held up his hand. "I have an idea," the phantom said in his rasping, gasping voice. "We just a need a bit more time."

Late the next morning two wagons rumbled up the road to Potter's Field, each bearing ten or so men carrying the axes, shovels, and saws they meant to use in tearing down the remains of the town. On the sideboards were the cans of oil they meant to use to light the bon fires that would consume the rotting timbers that they meant to pile high in the old stable yard. If their foreman had his way the job would be finished by nightfall.

The first snag, stumbling block or, if you prefer, fly-in-the-ointment of the foreman's plan was when, just past the Bailey manor and adjacent to the cemetery, one of the wagons took a lurch and fell over on its side. The men riding in it went tumbling out onto the road. One of them, still prone on the ground, looked underneath the wagon to see what had happened.

"The axle is broken!" he said. "There are no rocks... it looks to me as if it was hit with an axe!"

The foreman jumped down from his perch on the other wagon and examined the damage. "Alright, put the oil cans on our wagon, and then you men grab your tools and walk the rest of the way," he ordered. The man behind the foreman hoisted up his shovel and as he did it swung around - for no apparent reason - and clocked the foreman on the top of his head.

"What the hell are you doing?!" the foreman howled, rubbing his throbbing head. The offending man dropped the shovel and held up his hands.

"So sorry, I didn't, I mean...," he protested to no effect.

"Get those tools and get up the road - and watch where you sling them!" the foreman demanded. From the opposite side of the crippled wagon a man screamed in pain and came hobbling out into the road. "What's the matter with you?"

"I think something bit me!" the injured man cried. "I think a dog bit me!"

The foreman grabbed him by the shoulder, thrust an axe and a shovel into his hands, and then pushed him forward along the road. "Quit fooling around and start walking!"

The demolition crew did as it was told and gathered its tools. Soon the second wagon was loaded up with the first's oil cans and the group started down the road to the ghost town. They traveled only fifty feet when a moderately sized cedar on the uphill side of the track suddenly issued a loud crack and fell across the road, landing right across the tongue of the wagon and snapping it. The frightened horses bolted forward, dragging their yokes and the broken wagon tongue behind them. The men who were walking dropped their tools and ran after the horses.

The foreman stood looking at the broken wagon, the tree blocking the road, and back at the first wagon which lay on its side fifty feet behind them. "Dammit! Will one of you losers run back to the House and get Miles Bailey?!"

By the time Miles Bailey arrived it was late afternoon (he had to finish his dinner, and there was no way he was going to allow himself to be at the beck and call of a common laborer). Eleanor

Pynchon insisted on joining him, even going so far as to turn the children over to Mrs. Dean. Bailey might have ordered her to stay, but he found her quite attractive and thought it might be advantageous to have her see him in a position of power, ordering about the menials, so he invited her to accompany him. With his head high and walking slowly to make a point out of it, Bailey arrived at the site of the damaged wagons. The men had been busy in the meanwhile; several had chopped up the tree to make room for the wagon to get through while another group had replaced the broken tongue with the whole one from the other wagon.

"I didn't know I was going to have to replace a wagon on this job, Bailey," the foreman declared. "It's going to cost you more."

"I didn't know you weren't competent enough to navigate a road," Bailey replied, puffing up even more than usual for Eleanor's sake. "I expect this job done quickly for the price originally agreed upon." His reputation as a litigator was well known and the foreman, rather than lose the job or be sued, shut up and helped his men roll the wagon through the gap in the fallen tree.

The group continued forward to the edge of Potter's Field. As they passed the first decaying building the tall bearded man with the black dog came out of the old Hotel. He was joined first by the man in an oversized duster, then a beautiful woman in a quite fetching dress.

"What are you people doing on my property?!" Miles Bailey demanded.

"Go away...," the tall man said in his hideous rasping voice, a sound that froze the demolition crew in place and made the hair on their necks stand to attention. "This is my town..."

"I will not! This is my land and you are trespassing!" Bailey said. He turned to his hired hands. "Run them off and start your work!"

248

Another figure came out of the hotel, one that Bailey thought he recognized.

"That might be a bad idea, Miles," Jed said.

"Jedediah Bradford?" Bailey said, scratching his head. "I thought you were dead."

In that moment the sun, lowering in the sky, blinked behind the trees that circled the meadow. It was by no means sunset quite yet, but the Field plunged into shadow and perhaps that was enough to give the assembled spirits the power of the night. In an instant the demolition crew was surrounded by the shapes and echoes of humans who were not there the minute before. These unquiet dead took hold of their shovels and swung them about, forcing them down on the heads of the neighboring men. The ghost of Bad Luck Casey threw open his great black duster and several of the men screamed and ran, which you likely would do as well if faced by the animated corpse of a man who had been mauled by a bear. The bearded man's black dog ran amongst their legs, biting any piece of man flesh he could reach with his snapping jaws. The ghost of Doc Hollander dashed from one of the workers to the other, feeling their heads, which might not seem as disconcerting in print as it was for the men who felt his eerie touch. One man swung his axe around trying to make contact with any one of the phantoms, and his blade passed through them as if they were nothing, yet when one spook grabbed the very same man's pants and gave them a firm yank the trousers dropped to his ankles, exposing his pale buttocks. In a panic the man pulled his pants high enough that he could move his legs and then he ran down the road as quickly as they could carry him. The rest of the hired hands were gone as fast, running with more vitality than they ever put into any job. The foreman followed them, Jack Norris's spirit kicking him solidly in the rear as he ran.

In a final impertinent act, the beautiful woman wearing the illusory dress appeared directly in front of Miles Bailey, in a translucent fashion so that he could see the entire town through her diaphanous body. She leaned forward and said, very quietly and directly to him, "Boo!" He spun around in terror, prepared to run for his dear life, and came face-to-face with the tall bearded man - and in this immediacy he saw the man's blue eyes, the line of his jaw through the trimmed beard, the peak of his tousled hair, and realized something he hadn't before.

"Father?" he gasped.

"Miles, you little brat," the ghost of Bly Bailey said in his sandpaper voice, *"this is my town and you are the one who is trespassing. Go away and never come back!"*

With a girlish scream, Miles Bailey dashed down the road toward his manor, calling out to the foreman to wait for him. He didn't even bother to determine the fate of his young governess, whom he left standing amidst the spooks as he ran.

"I'm not sure I can continue to work for that man," Eleanor said, "although the children have grown dear to me and I should hate to abandon them on his account." Ben and Nate came out of the hotel to join her.

"This will give us at least the day or two we need to finish copying the manuscripts, I suppose," Jed said. "Do you think we have time to write one additional story?"

"A new one? What story might it be?" Ben asked.

"*The Ghost Town*, of course," Jed said.

Two days later Ben and Nate rode away from Potter's Field, their wagon laden with the last load of manuscripts. They waved at the spirits of their fathers, who stood near the doorway of the hotel, as they departed. Once they turned the corner and the ghost town was out of sight, Ben turned to Nate and they smiled at each other, happy knowing they had saved their fathers' legacy, saddened because they knew, somehow, that with this need fulfilled, there would be no more visitations.

Over the next several weeks in the bookstore they used their Oliver type-writer to type clean, legible copies of some of the stories and then mailed them to a publisher in New York for their editor's review. The editor in charge loved them and offered to buy these tales and any more The Boys could supply. By the spring of 1899 the window at *Bradford & Norris: Booksellers to the Savage West* was piled high with the first volume in the *Tales of Placerville*. When the first royalty check came in that same month Ben and Nate went together to the bank to deposit it, and at the same time paid off the bookstore's debt that had been weighing on them so greatly.

"Our fathers didn't just save their stories," Nate said, "they saved the bookstore!"

"Shall we have a party?" Ben asked.

And that party celebrates this tale's conclusion as well.

You might be surprised that Eleanor wasn't courted by Ben or Nate, as often happens at the end of these sorts of stories. Instead she moved to Sacramento and started a school for girls.

As they expected, The Bookstore Boys (Jr.) were not visited by their fathers again. Apparently Jed and Jack preferred to live on through their books rather than as ghostly apparitions. Ben and Nate continued to run the bookstore. Ben talked to his Dad on occasion, just because that's what sons do, but he never received a reply. In its stead he just read one of his father's books.

"What happened to the ghost town?" one of the children asked the storyteller.

"Well," he told them, "Miles Bailey cancelled his arrangement with the alfalfa farmer. The deteriorating remains of Potter's Field were left untouched until they finally collapsed due to the passage of time. You can still visit the meadow and smell the wildflowers and if you're lucky, just around sundown, you might see a tall bearded man with a black dog taking a walk along the field's edge."

"That wasn't so scary, in the end," the smallest child said.

"I didn't say it was scary. I said it was startling," Ben said. His niece Jessica raised an eyebrow.

"Is any of that story true?" she asked skeptically. Ben smiled wickedly.

"Would you care to take an evening walk down to Potter's Field?" he asked.

Next:
A visitor learns true value of El Dorado

X.

THE GOLD AT THE END OF THE RAINBOW
or
THE SEARCH FOR EL DORADO

1899

In which little people are big, and the only true road to treasure is found

The circus blew into Placerville like a storm. Word of its arrival spread, and the town's previously gray mood became a kaleidoscope of anticipation. The excitement was an infectious convection, sucking in young and old alike. Before the wagons arrived on Main Street a crowd gathered in front of the Placerville Hotel where it was assumed the Circus would stop. But the brightly decorated wagons passed by the cheering throng, the organ playing, horses prancing, and the circus performers waving gaily from the wagon tops where they perched. On a huge red horse at the front of the train rode Tattersall, the owner and Circus master, doffing his top hat at the adoring people lining the street.

The Circus wagons finally stopped at the Cedar Ravine Livery. Apparently advance arrangements had been made with Old Mister for the Livery's services and for the five acres of field at the bottom of the hill. Mister let the wagons pass through his gate, but stopped the children who had been running alongside and told them to get back to school where they belonged. The children ignored his directions and pressed themselves against the fence to watch as the circus wagons were arranged and the circus tents were raised. The resulting tent and wagon community, boasting every hue and tint in the entertainment spectrum, became a virtual town of its own. It also had a most unusual population.

Tattersall himself was a model of masculinity, six and a half feet of charming and robust man, dressed to the nines in his royal purple coat and tails and shiny black boots. The Magnificent Orthelia, on the other hand, was the most beautiful of women - tall, sensually round of body, with wavy blond hair that cascaded to her waist. In her flowing gown she might have captured the hearts of the men of Placerville - had it not been for the equally flowing beard that descended from her shapely chin. Bruno the strong man, who currently weighed in at 500 pounds (all of it muscle) flexed his biceps for the onlookers as he helped raise the final tent. Strangest of all to the children of Placerville were the two tiny people who were working their way down the fence handing out promotional flyers.

Gordon Gale, aged 36, and an ex-farmer, stood just 38 inches tall. His wife, Glenda, aged 32, who was an ex-housewife, stood 39 inches tall. The extra inch she held over her husband was a never-ending source of grief between them. Whenever they weren't working she endeavored to wear sandals or flats - anything that might allow his footwear to heal the difficulties that inch put in their marriage. Today they were working, however. Glenda was dressed in her fairy princess costume. The bright pink cone hat on her head trailed a gauzy pink tail. On her feet were tiny pink high heel shoes which unfortunately added an inch to her diminutive height. Gordon, dressed in his clown costume, had bright blue hair made of yarn (fairly unconvincing as a wig) and sparkling red clown shoes five times bigger than his regular feet. He had learned to walk in them so that he wouldn't trip, but they added nothing to his height. When they stood together his wife now towered over him by a full two inches.

"Tattersall and Murphy, the greatest Circus in the west!" he crowed. "Come to the show! Man-eating lions! Acrobatic feats of wonder! The most incredible sites from the five continents!"

Glenda passed the flyers through the fence to the eager children, who grabbed at them. A few of the kids stayed to watch more, while others ran home with the flyers to elicit promises of attendance from their parents. Gordon and Glenda continued to work the fence until every rubbernecking individual - child or adult - had been served with the advertisement.

"That's all of them. Let's get back to our wagon," Gordon said to Glenda.

"I was going to help Farina with the balloon," she replied, indicating the half-filled hot air balloon that was rising from the middle of the circus grounds. TATTERS- AND MUR- CIR- was visible so far, the rest of the letters invisible in the folds of the balloon. "She's been having a tough time since Merrell left her high and dry in Omaha to join the Miracle Wonderland Circus Company. I mean, she was the brains behind the operation, but it's not easy hauling that balloon around all by herself, and her kids never help..."

"Fat lot of good a midget is going to be hauling around hundreds of pounds of balloon. Tell her to ask Bruno for help. We've got things to do," Gordon snapped.

"There you go again," Glenda clucked, "short-changing what we can do. Just because we're little people doesn't mean we're not just as productive as big people. I can share my burden. That's why the farm failed. Because you decided that you couldn't do it." Gordon stopped and turned to face her, waving his short arms in front of her.

"That's always your answer, Glenda! Do it the hard way! Try to do it on the big folks' terms and accept things the way they are! Well, the answer is out there. The answer that is going to mean an easy life for us and our family. There is a pot of gold at the end of the rainbow. There is a city of gold someplace. And I think this place is it! Why do you think they call it El Dorado?"

With a huff he stomped off in his sparkling oversized clown

255

shoes. Glenda watched him disappear into the maze of the circus and felt tears in her eyes.

"And that's always your answer. The easy money is at the next city on the route. The Fountain of Youth is at our next stop. And meanwhile we're missing Dotty." She fought to keep the tears from overwhelming her and then headed off toward the slowly inflating balloon. Midget or not, she would help Farina.

Leonardo the Incredible, who walked tightropes and trained acrobatic monkeys, quietly watched the exchange between the two small people. He knew it was hard on them, being odd and deformed curiosities in a society that wanted everyone to be exactly the same. Leonardo was a sensitive man - it was what made him so good with animals - and his heart went out to little Glenda, so darling in her pink fairy costume. He wondered if his sympathy was genuine or if some paternal nature in his soul reacted to the miniature adults with the instinctive care an adult felt for children. He promised himself he would make an effort to see what he could do to help the Gales.

Glenda was still upset with Gordon after she finished helping with the balloon, so she took a walk through the tents to where Rutger was feeding the lions. Watching the beasts rip into their big chunks of meat sometimes helped diffuse her frustrations. Today it did not, and afterward she shuffled through the sawdust toward their wagon. She was passing the booth of Donofrio the Fire-Eater when she heard a voice call out her name.

"Dear Glenda! Do you have-a some moments please?" asked friendly Leonardo. She veered over to his wagon, which was parked immediately next to the monkey cages.

"What ho, Leonardo?" Glenda asked.

"I need-a some help. The little vests my monkeys wear when they fly through the air on the trapeze are in such a state. I donna think I can sew them all in time-a for the big show, and my monkeys canna fly through the air nekkid!" Leonardo held up one of the small sequined vests his monkeys wore with their matching bellhop hats. "Do you have some moments to help The Incredible Leonardo, *piacere*?"

Glenda wasn't looking forward to going back to face Gordon at the moment, so she smiled and told Leonardo she would help. They sat in the shade of his wagon on overturned buckets and reattached gold brocade to the hem of the monkeys' vests. At first they worked silently, but then Leonardo spoke up.

"So, Glenda. You and Gordon, you have the disagreement, no? I see you looking sad, crying, and I wonder what The Incredible Leonardo can do to help." Glenda wasn't used to sharing her feelings with people outside the family, but when she looked into the kindly eyes of the Italian trapeze artist she saw only good intentions and her reserve melted away.

"I want to go home," she said. "I want to go home to my daughter."

This was the first Leonardo had heard that the Gales had children. "A *bambina*? Why doesn't she travel with the circus?" Glenda bent low over her sewing, but continued to talk.

"She's normal, my Dotty. A big girl. When we joined the circus Gordon thought she would have a better chance at a regular life if she stayed with his brother Henry. Henry and his wife Emily are big folk too."

Leonardo stopped sewing and leaned over, putting his elbows on his knees, his face inches from the top of Glenda's head.

"So why you join the circus? Why aren't you home with your little *bambina*?" Glenda hunched even lower to hide the fact that she was crying again.

"We used to have a farm," she started. "Gordon inherited it from his father. He worked it with the help of our hand, Zeke, and it made enough that we were happy. But after Dotty was born Gordon became more and more frustrated. He wanted better for his daughter and he thought that he would never be able to offer it to her. He is convinced that the world conspires against little people and makes it impossible for us to compete in business. But there are easy ways to riches, he says, even for us. At first he decided to try farming ostriches for their eggs and then tried raising minks for their coats. But every time he tried a new scheme we went further and further into debt. Eventually we were so indebted that we lost the farm to Elmira Gulch." Glenda looked up, her eyes red and furious. "Oh, that Elmira Gulch! She was the one who drove him to it! She always taunted him, telling him that he might as well give up, that little people were only good for performing in the freak show! She broke him, I tell you. Then she swooped down like a vulture and stole our farm."

"*Strega!*" Leonardo cursed. "I'm so sorry."

"That's alright," Glenda said, wiping the tears from her eyes with the little monkey vest. "Gordon is consumed by this dream of finding the easy road to riches. He used to sit next to Dotty's cradle and tell her stories of the Great Lost City of El Dorado, where the streets are paved with gold and everyone is rich and happy. He told her about the Pot O'Gold at the end of the rainbow, and how the little people of Ireland could find it. At first they were just fairy tales, but after a while he started to believe them himself. The stories of miners getting rich in the California gold rush didn't help. When we lost the farm he said good riddance, and decided we were going to travel west to find our fortune."

"So how did you end up in the circus?" Leonardo asked.

"We had no money. Gordon devised this plan where we would work our way west with Tattersall & Murphy, saving money for mining equipment on the way. When we got to California we would quit the circus, mine all the gold we needed to become rich, and then send for Dotty. But that's never going to happen, Leonardo. The mines are played out, the rush is over. The dream keeps going on, but the gold is gone."

"*Sí*, that is true," Leonardo admitted.

"I'm just afraid that he'll just keep on looking and looking, and then when he wakes up it will be too late - Dotty will be grown and our lives will have passed in a fever for gold." Glenda held up the vest in her hands - the third she had completed. "There, Leonardo, all done. Thank you so much for your sympathetic ear. I really appreciate it." She stood, still no taller than Leonardo was sitting on the bucket.

A cry of "Mail!" suddenly spread through the circus grounds, from one person to another. Farina, the balloonist, came dashing by. "Mail!" she said to Glenda as she passed.

"Murphy must have gone into town and picked up the General Delivery," Glenda said, brightening. "Maybe there's something from Dotty!"

"Maybe," Leonardo said encouragingly. "Just remember this, *Fragolina*. If there is anything you need, you just tell Leonardo. OK?" She smiled back and put her hand to his shoulder.

"Thank you, Leonardo," she said, and she started off across the sawdust to find Murphy.

The sun was low in the sky when she arrived back at their little wagon. She almost expected to find it empty, but Gordon was seated at the table inside, pouring over a stack of documents. He held one up.

"Where have you been, Glenda? Look! Mining maps! I got them from the assay clerk in town. There are still places in these mountains men have not walked, where gold still exists. He was very friendly, this man, and a wiz of a wiz at geology! Look at these markings - you can see where all of the large placer mines have been located. Now the clerk says if you follow the trail of these into the higher mountains, but branch off onto the smaller creeks, you'll find areas that have scarcely been touched. See here? Here?" The map swung crazily over the candle on the table as Gordon pointed to various markings on it. Glenda was afraid it might catch fire.

"There was a letter from Emily in the General Delivery," Glenda said. Gordon didn't even look up.

"Not Dotty?"

"No," Glenda said. She sat down next to him. "Dotty has the measles. Emily has been so kind, sitting at her bedside. That's where I'm supposed to be, Gordon! I'm supposed to be there when she's sick, not wandering around the world chasing phantoms!"

Gordon took a deep breath and continued to scour the maps. He knew how Glenda could get. He didn't want to get into this, he didn't like where it could lead.

"I'm talking to you, Gordon! Our daughter is sick! When are you going to get it through your head? You're never going to find the easy life! Life isn't easy! But it can be good, and this stupid quest for simple riches isn't going to find us the good life!"

Gordon stood up abruptly, the maps flying to the floor. "Right! Just give up! Spend the rest of our lives as freaks, or as fetchit boys for the big folks! Fine, you go home and get a job waiting hand and foot on Elmira Gulch! Maybe I'll send for you when I get my first million. And maybe I won't!" He grabbed his coat from the rack and flung the wagon door open.

"Gordon! Wait!" Glenda said. But her husband, short in temper as well as stature, had vanished into the twilight.

Gordon left the livery grounds and headed back down the ravine toward Placerville, where he had so recently visited the helpful assay clerk. He left the road, traveling through the woods that lined the southern side of the track so that he could be alone with his thoughts. And despite what the big people believed, a man his size had many.

Didn't Glenda see? They could never make it playing by the big folks' rules. But there were ways to make it outside the rules. If a man dared to dream hard enough he could make his dreams come true. Glenda just didn't have the vision he possessed. Someday he would return home in style, in his own train car with servants and assistants. He would go back and look Elmira Gulch in the face and say, "See here, I'm somebody, you old crone. I'm bigger than you are. Much bigger." He would look Dotty in the face and say, "See here, daughter, what a big man your father is. See what I've accomplished." Didn't Glenda have any faith in him?

He stopped, suddenly aware that he hadn't been paying attention to where he was going. The road wasn't visible to his right anymore, and the lights of Placerville that had been visible a few minutes ago were now hidden by trees. Which way was town? Which way was the livery?

He came to a small open grassy glade. During the daytime it was alive in yellow poppies, but now in the purple dusk the flowers had closed. Directly above him, framed by the boughs of the pines, the first star of the evening appeared. Perhaps it was Venus. It didn't matter. Gordon had a ritual he always performed when this happened. It was one he had lovingly taught Dotty when she was just four years old. He dropped the short distance to the ground and, kneeling, focused on the star.

"Star light, star bright, first star I see tonight. I wish I may, I wish I might, have the wish I wish tonight." Then he threw a kiss at the distant point of light and crossed himself. I wished, he thought to himself, I wished and Glenda will see. Tonight I find my El Dorado.

Gordon stood again and started walking in the direction he thought the town probably was. The cliff wall of the ravine rose steeply on his left and he saw the tailings of an old soda works along its base. He remembered that such a wall ran parallel to Main Street in Placerville and he followed it downward. A full moon rose over the trees, so it was easy to clamber over the broken stones and piles of earth, rejected from the soda works and the many mines that had once pockmarked Placerville. Sometimes being close to the ground was an asset.

He almost walked right past the sharp flash of reflected light. But his mind was still on his star-wish and his heart full of hope. His breath caught and hands began to tremble. There it was, glistening and sparkling at him in the night. Pushing aside some small dark tailings, he picked up the bright stone. It was rough, but the many broken faces shone yellow in the moonlight. Gold. Here, on the very edge of a heavily populated town. A gold nugget the size of his tiny fist. My El Dorado, he thought. See, wishes do come true if you believe enough.

"What will you think now, Glenda?" he asked aloud. Shuffling down the other side of the tailing, he saw lights between the trees and hurried toward them. Perhaps he could find the assay clerk or someone else who could tell him just how much this nugget was worth.

The assay office was closed, but a man who was sweeping the walk told Gordon that the clerk, whose name was something-or-other Moore, had gone down the street to the bookstore to meet a friend for dinner. If Gordon hurried he might catch him. Gordon ignored the man's stifled laugh as he made the best time his short legs could manage. He was used to being laughed at by the big people, being the subject of their derision. But that was going to change now.

He caught sight of the sign - *Bradford & Norris, Booksellers to the Savage West* - a block before he arrived. The assay clerk was standing at the door with another man - presumably the bookseller, since the man was engaged in locking up the store.

"...so I'm trying to write it myself," the bookseller was saying. "It's about a man and a wheelbarrow..."

"Mister Moore?" Gordon interrupted them breathlessly. He was forced to bend over, placing his hands on his knees, gulping air.

"Are you alright?" the bookseller asked. The two larger men waited patiently for Gordon to catch his wind.

"Yes, yes," Gordon finally replied, and he held up the shining stone. "This nugget... I found this nugget." He said it proudly, despite the effort. The assay clerk reached out and took the stone, holding it up in the gaslight and turning it.

"Uh huh," the clerk said. "Pyrite."

"What?" Gordon asked. "I don't understand. Can you tell me how much gold there is? How much it might be worth?"

The clerk started to laugh. He almost doubled over in laughter. "I told you, you stupid midget, its pyrite. Fool's gold. Its... its worthless!" He continued to laugh, but the bookseller frowned.

"Terry, you don't have to be insulting to the poor man." This sobered up the assay clerk, who suddenly looked ashamed. The bookseller took the rock from him and looked at it for a moment, then handed it back to Gordon.

"Sorry, Ben," the clerk apologized. "Sorry, Mister...," he trailed off when he realized he didn't know the little man's name.

"I'm afraid he's right," Ben Bradford said. "Pyrite, what's commonly called Fool's Gold. It's a common mistake for novices to make. *Non teneas aurum totum quod splendet ut aurum.*"

"What?"

"It's Latin. As Shakespeare put it, 'All that glisters is not gold.' Or Chaucer, 'Hyt is not al gold that glareth.' Real gold is actually kind of ugly until you clean it up." The bookseller smiled and put his hands up. "I'm sorry."

Gordon felt smaller than he ever had before, so small he felt his tiny body had become a cavern, swallowing him up. "Th-that's okay. I'm sorry to have troubled you." He turned, trying to avoid looking at the two men in order to hide his embarrassment, and started up the street toward the ravine, the livery, and his circus home.

"Not any trouble at all," the bookseller said, and he and the assay clerk headed off the opposite direction. "Poor fellow," Gordon overheard the clerk say. Worse than the embarrassment was the pity.

No El Dorado for Gordon tonight.

Glenda was asleep when he entered their wagon. He sat on the bed next to her, looking at her face, so peaceful in the repose of sleep. It was the face he had fallen so in love with those many years ago in St. Louis. He could remember the first time he saw it, across the park during a picnic with his family. At first he noticed her only because she was small, like him. When he saw her face he knew at once that he loved her. Perhaps this was his El Dorado.

The letter was still on the table, and he lit a single candle and read it.

Dearest Glenda,

I hope this letter finds you well. Dorothy has been in bed these last eight days with an attack of the measles. I have stayed with her throughout. Her spirits seem low, and she keeps to herself most of the time. The only confidant she shares her feelings with is her little dog. With some prying she admitted yesterday that she dreams of you sometimes. In her dreams she said you are always a big person, Glenda, and I asked her why she thought this was. She did not know. I suspect that in the mind of a child a parent is always a giant, at least until they grow to become parents themselves. She misses you both immensely. Henry and I will of course look after Dorothy with all of our affection, but a girl needs her parents. I pray that you see fit to finish your journey and come home to your family. Give our love and best wishes to Gordon.

Your devoted sister-in-law, Emily.

Across from the table Gordon could see his clown suit, draped across his trunk where he had carelessly tossed it. The sparkling red oversized clown shoes tilted across them at an angle. They glittered in the candlelight. Fool's gold. Well, maybe not gold with that color. Maybe fool's rubies. There was no treasure there. But perhaps there was another message.

He slowly stroked his wife's hair, and she sleepily opened her eyes and looked up at him.

"I love you, Glenda."

"I know," she said. "I've never doubted it."

"I've been such an idiot," he said. "I've made myself a small man by not realizing that every man is as big as he makes himself."

"You're not an idiot. And you've never been small to me, either," Glenda whispered.

"There is no Pot of Gold. There is no El Dorado."

"Gordon -"

"No, Glenda, listen to me. We're going home tomorrow. The money we've saved is almost enough to pay the note on the farm. Old Elmira Gulch will be positively livid - she'll turn five shades of red and green - but if we pay the note there's nothing she can do about it. Then I'll work the farm. I can do it, I know I can. The gold of Kansas wheat fields may be all the gold we need. Home is where our family is - where you are, where Dotty is. That's my treasure. That's my dream. Oh, there may be wonderful and fanciful places out there somewhere, but they aren't for me. For me, there's no place like home."

The two small people held each other close for the rest of the night.

EPILOGUE

In the twenty-first century

In which the world has drastically changed

There are many more *Tales of Placerville* where these came from. We never even got around to sharing Ben's version of the Wheelbarrow Man! Storytelling runs in families sometimes, and just as Jed and Jack's joy in turning a phrase and putting color to a character was passed on to their sons, Ben and Nate's love of writing passed on to each new generation of Bradfords and Norrises. The forms of the stories change sometimes and the subject matter varies. The cusp of centuries is overwritten, world wars come and go, and new technologies change our idea of what a book really is. But there are always more stories.

Bradford & Norris: Booksellers to the Savage West is a curiosity these days. The era when a bookstore was the intellectual center of a community is long gone, and even the corporate chain store behemoths are fighting to stave off bankruptcy. Did you order this book on the Internet? Download it as an eBook? It doesn't really matter, since the place you buy a book and the story it tells are two different things. A story is a story, whether it is told aloud around a campfire, performed by actors on a stage, read from the pages of a book, or scanned as high resolution pixels. In fact, if it wasn't for the money from those Internet sales and eBook sales, Bradford & Norris: Booksellers to the Savage West probably wouldn't survive. The latest generation is still in Placerville, mining the stories, long after the gold has vanished.

"We sold a copy of *Tales of McKinleyville* in England today," Rebecca Norris says, flipping her finger across a touch screen tablet.

"Wow!" Alexandria Bradford replies. "That will please Dad. I'll have to mention it on my Facebook page."

Times change, and communities like Placerville have changed with them. For instance, there are no longer Bookstore Boys in Placerville. Now there are Bookstore Girls.

About The Book

There is no bookstore in Placerville called *"Bradford & Norris: Booksellers to the Savage West."* It is completely fictional. The real Misters Bradford-Wilson and Norris did indeed run a bookstore for a number of years, but it was in faraway Humboldt County on California's northern coast (the setting of the earlier volume of stories in this series, *Tales of McKinleyville: Big Doin's At The Chinese Baptist Church*, which - I add in enlightened self-interest - is still available at Amazon.com.) The store described in this book is strictly made up out of my imagination and any similarities to institutions and individuals living or dead is completely coincidental.

It should be mentioned, however, that the *Placerville News Company*, a bookstore and newsstand, has existed in Placerville since 1856 and is, according to their website, now the fifth oldest ongoing business in the state of California. It has been operated by the same family for the past hundred years. You can visit their website at *http://www.pvillenews.com/* . If you are interested in further reading about the California gold country they stock a wonderful array of books on the subject.

The *Mountain Democrat*, currently Placerville's daily

newspaper, began life as the *El Dorado News* in 1851 and has been published uninterrupted since that time. Dan Gelwicks was its editor at the time of the 1856 fire and the quotes attributed to him regarding the battle for the county seat are accurate.

Many of the stranger elements in the book (including Rufus Porter's Aerial Transport, Thomas's Wind Wagon, and the Wheelbarrow Man) are based on real events. The illustrations that accompany the text are in most cases real (see the footnotes with each). Also, many of the characters are historical in nature, including Honest Alex Hunter, Uncle Billy, Irish Dick, Jean-Baptiste Charbonneau, Lizette Charbonneau and Snowshoe Thompson.

Other items are real, but are anachronistically used. For instance, the Stone House brothel on Pacific Street appears in the story circa 1849, but in reality wasn't built until 1865.

The Great Race between the Placerville & Sacramento Valley Railroad and the Central Pacific Railroad, based on historical events, is altered both chronologically and in other ways to best suit the story. (The villainous cheats perpetrated by the Central Pacific are sadly true.)

Pancake Henderson is based on Henry "Pancake" Comstock, who aside from the name change is exactly like his fictional counterpart. Comstock piggybacked on someone else's claim and that silver strike ended up taking Henry's name; the Comstock Lode. Henry did indeed steal another man's wife, lost her again to another man, and then chased after them to Placerville, though all of these events took place prior to 1864.

The entire ghost town community of Potter's Field is fictional, although in the aftermath of the gold rush there were many such abandoned communities, most of which have vanished completely.

270

I enjoyed visiting long lost places and people and using them as a foundation for the stories I wanted to tell. However, despite the fact that the novel is rooted in history, this is a work of fiction, so please take it as such.

In addition to history, many great literary achievements of the era have been used as inspiration, and in some cases direct homage has been paid in the text. In particular I must thank the works of James Fenimore Cooper, Mark Twain, Bret Harte, Edgar Allen Poe, Dashiell Hammett, Raymond Chandler, Mary Shelley, Jack London, Jules Verne, Henry James, Emily Brontë, Shirley Jackson, and L. Frank Baum. In most cases the story inspired by these books takes place at roughly the same time they were published. The exception is Jules Verne's *Around the World in 80 Days,* which is the basis of the railroad race story that takes place in 1864. Verne's novel wasn't published until 1873 (although Verne did publish *Journey to the Center of the Earth* in 1864).

More information about the book can be found at http://www.talesofplacerville.com/.

Perry Bradford-Wilson
Summer, 2011

About The Author

Perry Bradford-Wilson is the author of the humor novel *Tales of McKinleyville: Big Doin's At The Chinese Baptist Church* (which ties into *Tales of Placerville*), co-author of the dark fantasy novel *Midnight In Never Land*, and editor of the World War II autobiography written by his father, *Everyday P.O.W.* He is the former editor and publisher of *Comic Relief Magazine* and lives near Placerville in the Sierra Nevada mountains of California. He is already busy working on his next book.

Acknowledgements

This novel could not have existed (certainly not in its present form) without the inestimable help of Mr. Michael G. Norris, Esq., with whom I previously co-wrote the novel *Midnight in Never Land*. Our friendship, now almost 40 years old, obviously inspired Jed and Jack's. We have memories longer than the road that stretches out ahead.

I also received invaluable support from my wife, Mary, and daughter, Alexandria, who gave me the time to write and listened to the early, rough drafts - read aloud - back when they weren't very good.

Far too many sources were consulted for this book to list here (after all, this is a novel, not a history book). However, below is a list of a few books which offer further reading about the history behind the stories in *Tales of Placerville*. Some are source works from the 1800s, others are more recent academic works. I highly recommend them.

Paolo Sioli, *A Historical Souvenir of El Dorado County, California,* 1883
    (reprinted in 1998 by Cedar Ridge Publishing and available at the El Dorado
    County Library)
J.D. Borthwick, *Three Years In California,* 1857
J.S. Holliday, *The World Rushed In: The California Gold Rush Experience,* 2002
Stephen Ambrose, *Nothing Like It In The World: The Men Who Built The
    Transcontinental Railroad,* 2000
Dee Brown, *The Gentle Tamers,* 1958
Marilyn Parker, *The Pollock Pines Epic,* 1988
    (available in paperback and online at www.thepollockpinesepic.com)

For more information, check www.talesofplacerville.com.

El Dorado County Historical Museum

104 Placerville Drive, Placerville, CA

Adjacent to the county fairgrounds, the county's historical museum includes a fascinating collection of historical artifacts and interpretive displays about the gold rush and its aftermath. An exterior features a variety of wagons, mining equipment, rail equipment and other large items you won't find elsewhere. It is a great starting point for learning about Placerville history.

Fountain Tallman Museum

524 Main Street, Placerville, CA

The Fountain Tallman Museum is located in the former Fountain Tallman Soda Works building (built in 1852) in downtown Placerville. The soda works' brick walls allowed it to survive the fires of 1856 and it is the oldest surviving building in Placerville. The museum is operated by the El Dorado County Historical Society, which was founded in 1939 as a private non-profit group dedicated to preserving the history of El Dorado County.

Hangtown's Gold Bug Park & Mine

2635 Gold Bug Lane, Placerville, CA

At the Gold Bug Mine you can travel almost 400' into the side of the mountain, deep in an actual gold mine, and take a self-guided audio tour. Then visit the Miner's Blacksmith Shop, Hendy Stamp Mill, Hattie's Museum, and the gift shop. This is a great place to see what life was really like in the gold country mines. Gold Bug Park & Mine is a city park, owned by Placerville.

Placerville Soda Works

594 Main Street, Placerville CA

Currently occupied by The Cozmic Café & Pub, the Placerville Soda Works/Pearson Soda Works building in downtown

Placerville was built in 1859. A long mine shaft extends from inside the café into the mountain, and tables and chairs inside the shaft allow you to actually sit and eat very good organic food in the gold mine.

Marshall Gold Discovery State Historic Park
Coloma, CA

Marshall Gold Discovery State Historic Park is the location where, in 1848, James W. Marshall discovered gold in the tailrace of the sawmill he was building for John Sutter. You can tour a replica of the original sawmill and visit over twenty historic buildings including mining, house, school, and store exhibits.

For more information, check www.talesofplacerville.com.

TALES OF McKINLEYVILLE

MIDNIGHT IN NEVER LAND

It is 1805. Captain James Matthew Hauke of the Royal Navy ship *Man of War* has been left by Admiral Horatio Nelson to defend the Caribbean English colony of Dominica from French forces. Father Pádraig Smye, an Irish Missionary has abandoned his duties in the war torn revolutionary nation of Haiti to replenish his faith. On a voyage to the American port of New Orleans (just acquired in the Louisiana Purchase) Hauke and Smye come across an island undiscovered by the British. There they attempt the daring rescue of a young girl; the daughter of a wealthy plantation owner kidnapped by pirates. Their plan goes terribly wrong once the sun sets and the secret denizens of this lost island come out to play. They are very old... and very hungry. The island has no name, and is designated on an ancient map only by a warning: *Never land*. This thrilling dark fantasy novel merges history, mythology, and literature in an unforgettable tale of adventure.

www.ingramcontent.com/pod-product-compliance
Lightning Source LLC
Chambersburg PA
CBHW020602260626
47157CB00003B/826